KISS THE BULLET

KISS THE BULLET

Catherine Deveney

OLD STREET PUBLISHING

First published in 2011 by Old Street Publishing Ltd
Yowlestone House, Puddington, Tiverton, Devon EX16 8LN

www.oldstreetpublishing.co.uk

ISBN: 978-1-906964-63-4

Copyright © Catherine Deveney 2011

10 9 8 7 6 5 4 3 2 1

A CIP catalogue record for this title is available from the British Library.

Typeset by Martin Worthington

Printed and bound in the UK by CPI Mackays, Chatham ME5 8TD

For my family, and all our loved and lost.

THE DOCUMENT

I write this for my daughter Niamh Mary O'Brien, for my grandchildren Johnny and Pat O'Brien, and my grandchildren's children, that future generations may know what has passed, and may understand their place in the long struggle for Ireland. Lodged with William K. Prentice, of Prentice and Turner Solicitors, this 16th day of May 1966, with the instruction that it should be passed to my family after my death.

Mary Seonaid O'Connor

I became a bride as a copper sun set in bands of burnished gold over Kilmainham jail; a widow before it rose again. Every bride tends her groom's body on their wedding night, but in my case it was to gently dab the mud and courtyard dust from the cheek Michael grazed against the flagstones as he fell to his death, to comb the stray strands of hair that flopped soft and spineless against the hard grey pallor of his immobile face. I touched him slowly, tenderly, with all the contained passion of a lifetime never to be lived, while a prison guard watched the corridor furtively and urged speed. I hurried not, my finger lingering on his cheek like a quivering, soft winged butterfly come to rest on sculpted stone. I looked at him, lifeless, and I loved him still. I did not cry.

"Time," the guard said, his voice low and urgent. "Time."

He kept his eyes averted, as though embarrassed by the intimacy he witnessed. He risked much for me. But he had his own reasons. The year was 1916. The guard was married to a cousin of John MacNeill, who was with Michael in the O'Connell Street Post office on Easter Monday, who read the declaration of a free Ireland to his comrades and died days later at the hands of soldiers who squashed him like a moth on a burning light. Michael did not know John MacNeill, but they were brothers in their cause and the guard had some respect for that. Both help and opposition have come from the strangest places.

Michael rose from his sick bed to go to O'Connell Street that day. His face was waxy, the whistle in his chest unabated despite several winter months in the heat of Italy. He would not hear of shirking the task, of leaving it for those who were stronger. There was a greater sickness abroad in Ireland he said, than the sickness in Michael O'Connor's lungs, and a sickness that was in greater need of remedy. I knew, in my heart, that he spoke the truth; that while his body was weak, there was no man stronger than he in honour and conviction.

When he was imprisoned in Kilmainham for the part he played in the rising, there were those who said the sentence of death imposed on him was the second Michael O'Connor had received in his life, one from God and one from man, that he would never, in any case, have lived past another winter. I like to think they were wrong. The greatest medicine a man can receive is a cause to live and Michael had two: Ireland and me.

My brother Padraig introduced us. They taught school

together and were united in a love of Ireland and a loyalty to the Republican cause. Michael had the head of an academic and the soul of a poet. The first time he came to our house he was in a group of teachers Padraig brought home to sample my mother's soda scones and tea. I was darning socks, using an orange stuffed in the toe to keep the shape, the way my mother had showed me. I listened quietly as the talk turned to the freedom of the Irish people, but every so often my eyes were drawn back to Michael.

He was not, in the conventional way of things, a handsome man. He was too pale and slight for that, a thin, almost wolfish face with sharp cheekbones that seemed to push through thin, translucent skin like rocks through paper, and blue eyes that glittered with the intensity of a hunger I could only guess at. I thought later that men who fear their lives will be short live with a ferocity and urgency the healthy have no need of.

"Is it worth it?" cried Joseph Connerty, pouring a spoonful of honey onto a scone that was crammed thick with peel and currants. "We are small and poor and no match for an English army."

"An English army that is already at war elsewhere," Padraig pointed out.

Michael was lifted by soldiers two weeks after Easter Monday. When word came that he had been granted permission to marry before his execution, it was a moment of triumphant sorrow. My wedding dress hung, covered in an old knotted sheet, in my bedroom cupboard. It had hung there three months; our wedding postponed twice through Michael's ill-health. It was a delicate dress of ivory silk and chiffon, and a crown of apricot flowers with a short embroidered veil. There was only one thing I did not have ready.

I hurried along the side of Stephen's Green and down Grafton Street just as the shops were closing. It was a chill evening for the time of year, the cold air sharp in my lungs as I ran. I headed for Connerty's Jewellers, the light from inside the shop a warm, orange glow against a grey, ominous sky. James Connerty stood outside at the windows; I heard the rattle of the shutters as he pulled the grills down over the glass. He glanced up as I hurried past, a nod of recognition. I did not stop to speak, but hurried inside.

The shop was warm, discreet, a soft, thick carpet beneath my feet deadening any noise. My breathing, ragged and uneven, sounded harsh in the stillness and I felt momentarily embarrassed at my inability to speak. I tried to still my gasps with big deep breaths.

"Madam?" said the young woman behind the counter, looking up in surprise.

"A wedding ring," I said, with as much composure as I could muster. "I have come to buy a wedding ring."

She gawped at me but I heard a voice at my back, felt a tiny, comforting touch of a hand on my spine.

"I will deal with this, thank you Mairi."

James Connerty passed round my back and disappeared behind the counter reaching into his waistcoat pocket for a key. He knew, from his brother I suppose, what the situation was with Michael. He unlocked a slim drawer full of gold rings and slipped it out on to the counter top. Then he unrolled a length of red velour, his long slender white fingers spreading it deftly over the glass top before placing a few rings on it.

"You may go home now," he said to his assistant, and she did not wait to be told twice. It struck me, as she moved so swiftly to put on her coat and hat, that this would be a normal evening for her – and oh, how I envied her that.

"Perhaps this?" said James Connerty quietly. "Or this?"

I looked at the rings blankly, unable to truly see them. Should I simply buy the cheapest? It was true the marriage would be short, and after all, a ring was only an earthly symbol. But what it represented, the feeling inside, would last forever. I would wear this ring for the rest of my life. Slowly I picked up a beautiful slim band, engraved with orange blossom and stared at it.

"How much is this one?" I asked.

He did not reply, but merely wrapped the ring in a box and put it inside a bag and handed it to me silently.

"I must pay," I said and he replied that I was paying more than most, which brought tears to my eyes. I thanked him, hurried from the shop and went to prepare. I wish I could tell you more about the ceremony but the chapel of Kilmainham jail has all but faded in my mind, though I do recall how tiny it was. I have only been in it once after all, and that for scarcely half an hour. I do recall, though, kneeling at the arched altar, staring up at the cross on the white washed wall and having a powerful sense that I fully understood the crucifixion, the nature of suffering, for the first time in my life.

Just when it felt that it was more than I could endure, I felt Michael's hand in mine. I looked up at him and he mouthed quietly, "Do not break. For me, do not break." And he smiled and squeezed my fingers. I smiled back, determined that I would seize the joy of these brief moments of union, live them for what they were and not for what they would never become. When we were pronounced man and wife, Michael leant forward to kiss my cheek.

"Mo chuisle mo chroi," he murmured. Pulse of my heart.

Afterwards, we were given just ten minutes before he was taken for execution by firing squad. Ten minutes during which the guards never left our sides. There will come a time, surely, when such barbarity will not be believed. I write this now in truth, in testimony that these events occurred. At first we were so overwhelmed by so many words to speak in such a short time that we fell silent and merely held one another. Then Michael said, "While there is breath left in you, fight for what we believe. For justice and for Ireland." I clung to him and when the guards said time, he repeated quietly in my ear his words from the chapel.

"Do not break. For my sake, do not break." I did not.

I heard the shots from the courtyard, felt them pulse in my own chest. In the morning, I quietly watched the sun rise, the sky pink and streaked, and I felt him then, felt him everywhere around me. It was as if he was beyond the universe, bleeding into the world, into that pink sky, his dripping wounds staining this dawn and every new Irish dawn that was to come.

His words shone for me like stars in a deep, passionate sky. They switched the world on, made me feel I could see the universe better. What he was, guided them, what he felt, breathed power into them. His poetry was everything. Rebellion whispered through it like a breeze rippling gently through long grass. And pride and love and ferocity and hunger and ambition. Ireland, his Ireland. I fell in love with his poems and then I fell in love with him.

I fell for the best of him, I am certain of that. I fell for what was inside him, the thoughts that lined his head. Maybe I saw that his body was disintegrating already, perhaps I looked for the smooth stone of eternity in the physical rubble. I only know that I found it, whatever it was I had been looking for, that the vague feeling of discontent that I had always carried melted magically away. I used to think I had too many questions without knowing the answers. But Michael was the answer to a question I didn't even know I had posed.

I lusted after his mind and he encouraged me to satiate myself with him. And everything else followed. Somehow he knew without being told that the key to my body was my mind. He had both. Forgive my bluntness. When you, my family, read this, I will no longer be able to feel embarrassment. But right now, I must tell you that in any case I feel none. As I came to discover, there were many who wanted me to wear my relationship with Michael like a badge of shame, the mark of the whore. I would not, and will not, do so. All these years later, I carry every part of him with me, including his glorious defiance.

Let me tell also tell you that Michael was a religious man. He attended mass every day he was well enough. When my time comes, I too, will stand before God and answer to him without fear. No, I will not be meek about what happened. I will waste no time on regret or disingenuous remorse. My tribute to Michael is that he liberated my mind, that he freed me from convention. I am an old woman now and I have seen so many changes – my 'revelation' is tame indeed by the standards of many now.

I lay with no man before Michael. My mother was uneasy about the free and easy nature of our time together, the way we roamed the hills all day and talked politics all night. Politics was not for women, my mother said. Dear mother. When I tried once, tentatively, to tell her that I had fallen in love with Michael's poetry and his mind she raised her eyes and muttered, "Oh my God, girl. You'll pay a heavy price for your dreams." I was young; I did not understand her cynicism. Not then. Then she attacked the floor with a scrubbing brush. She could not fathom the equality that Michael and I shared. No man should countenance it, my mother thought; no woman should desire it.

The day we took the picnic to the hills was at the height of summer, a day when the sun beat hot but was rivalled by a stiff warm breeze that cooled the sweat on our brows as we climbed. Michael rolled his sleeves up and I moved more slowly when I heard the soft whistle in his chest. I took off the primrose yellow cardigan mother had knitted to go with my summer dress, felt the rays of sunshine hit the pallor of my bare forearms. There was that special silence up there, the silence that is only broken by the sound of the breeze and the far off bleat of sheep. When we spread the blanket, we felt like we were on the edge of the world looking down.

It was two weeks before the Easter weekend that was to become the Easter rising of 1916. Planning a wedding was unthinkable in those weeks, though we spoke often about our marriage and what it would be. That day we talked of how we longed to reach a time where we would be answerable to no one but ourselves, when we would go home to each other at the end of every day. We looked down over the hillside as if looking over the precipice into another world. Pretend, I said, pretend that the world is ours to own, to hold in our hands and spin. Will it spin into infinity, he asked, spin through darkness and light? Yes, I said, and I lay back on the blanket and let the sun soak into my face, felt the heat on my closed eyelids. I believed in infinity then. I still do. Will you be with me, he whispered, his mouth next to mine, so close I felt the vibration of his speech on my lips.

"Will you be with me for all eternity?

I opened my eyes.

"I will."

He kissed me then, and the breeze carried the smell of burgeoning greenery to me as we lay, and it was translated into a bracken stained kiss, full of sun and promise and summer growth. When his fingers found the buttons of my dress, I did not demur. I knew this was a transition; a transition and a promise and a declaration. For my part, I have kept the vows that I made that day on the hill in the presence of God and Michael. And later, when the fire was still in my cheeks and he held me to him gently and whispered against my hair, "No regrets?" I answered honestly, none.

A month later he was dead and I was pregnant. The knowledge took my breath away, left me gasping like a netted fish. I hugged the secret to me, let it grow inside me with the child in my womb. Then one day I was with my mother, chatting to her in the kitchen while she baked, making her tea. I went to the cupboard to get sugar and I saw her look up casually from putting floured scones onto a baking tray, then her eyes whiplashed back to me. I was standing sideways on to her and her eyes bore into my stomach. I looked at her and she glanced up at me, horrified.

"Sit down mother," I said quietly.

She hesitated wiping a floured hand down her cheek.

"Are you …?" she said, her eyes fearful, willing me to deny it.

I said nothing but nodded.

"Oh mother of God," she said, and sat down suddenly at the kitchen table. "Mother of God," she repeated and she began to rock gently back and forth, wiping her floured hands on her apron.

Her reaction made me fearful but I tried to keep calm.

"Mother," I said, sitting beside her, "I'll have a piece of him, a piece of him left, all of my own. D'you see? He won't have left. It's like he's made sure I won't be alone."

"Ah Mary," she said irritably, despairingly, shaking her head and raising her eyes to the ceiling, "Mary, Mary, Mary, what are ye sayin' girl? Not alone? You're about to find out just how alone alone can be. Have you have any idea … have you any idea … what …?" and then she caught sight of me, the fear rigid in my eyes, my facial muscles turned to stone.

"Come and sit down," she said more gently, pulling out a chair beside her.

"You'll have to go away," she said. "Y'undertsand? Away

from here to have the baby before it's adopted. Folks round here know about Michael, Mary. They know you weren't together after your marriage. There's a convent, takes girls in your position. I'll …"

"I'm keepin' it."

She stopped.

"Mary," she said softly. "You have no idea. No idea."

"He was my husband."

"People are sorry for you right now. But believe me their pity will turn to something else when they hear this. I know. Believe me, I know what they're like."

"I'm not ashamed," I said. My voice trembled.

My mother reached out a hand to my face.

"A high price," she said, running a finger over my cheek. "I always said you'd pay a high price."

The tenderness of her touch cut me in a way her anger never could have.

"I loved him mother. I loved him …" I felt the tears spilling now, my nerve gone.

"I know you did," my mother whispered. She reached out to hold me and I lay my head on her shoulder like a child.

"Don't tell your father," she said, her voice calmer now. "I'll deal with him. Y'hear me, Mary?"

I lifted my head and nodded, reaching out to hold her hand, and the two of us sat in the kitchen that was warmed by the oven, crying silently together, the tears running a salt track through the flour on her cheeks.

My father would not look me in the eye after my mother told him. He would leave the room when I entered and I'd hear the bang of the kitchen door, see his head bobbing past the window on his way to dig the land. I'd look up and mother would pull a wry face at me, as if to say, "Ignore him, silly auld fool that he is."

I wondered had she ever felt about my father as I did about Michael? He was not a poet, my father. Mountainous shoulders, like a range stretching across his upper body. Hand like shovels, calloused, nails ingrained with soil. Mother was his translator. Your father thinks ... she would say, when no one had heard him utter a word. I remember though, the day there was talk between my brothers about a young local woman, and how beautiful she had grown, and my father said gruffly, sure there was never any woman more beautiful round these parts than mother had been. And mother with a sink full of washing had simply smiled quietly and when she looked up at him they exchanged a glance like they had a secret that nobody else knew. So maybe she did. Feel about him the way I did Michael.

He never mentioned the coming baby once. One of my brothers, Seamus, was furious when he heard, told me I was no better than a whore, and my father looked up sharply and said that was enough of that. And the room fell quiet and we said nothing more, though Seamus refused to look at me. Seamus was always a prig. He had notions of the priesthood and it was the best place for him, a place where his principles wouldn't get dirty.

I wanted a boy. I wanted Michael. I was certain the baby I carried was a boy. I even carried him low they way they say male babies are carried. When the pain started I rode it, waves of it, thinking of Michael, and then it intensi-fied, becoming so unthinkingly vicious, so remorseless, that nature felt malevolent, until eventually it clutched at my belly like a screw tightening beyond its own possibilities, and I was frightened then, beyond any fear I'd ever known.

"Sweet Jesus ..." I shouted, clutching the back of a chair.

"Mother ..." and I saw the compassion in her eyes as I looked desperately at her, willing her to help me, to take it away.

She helped me to the bedroom and sent the men folk outside. I heard her speak quietly to my father on their way, telling him to fetch the doctor. Then another wave of pain winded me and I felt the heat flood my cheeks and the sweat break out on my body. The doctor when he came wanted to examine me but I kept panicking at each wave of pain and begged him not to come near me. I sensed his exasperation with a pain he neither empathised with nor approved of (I had made my bed and must, quite literally, lie in it), and he stood stiffly while I groaned. When he leaned over me, I saw the line of dirt round the crisp whiteness of his collar.

When he finally examined me, he turned dismissively to my mother.

"It will be some hours before the child comes. I will look back in the evening."

I whimpered into the pillow in despair.

"No," I said. "No ... mother ..."

She leaned over me and smoothed back my hair.

"Hush, darlin'," she said, and then she looked rather coldly at the doctor and said stiffly, "I will show you out."

The night was dark outside the windows by the time he returned, the stars hammered solidly like nail heads into the inky blackness. I told my mother not to close the curtains because there was no one to see in, and because I wanted to see the world as my baby entered it. I was so frightened, and everything was so out of control, that it felt like the universe was some kind of monster out there and I wanted to keep in touch with the familiar. I wanted to keep in touch with the spirit of Michael that had drifted into it.

By the time the baby was born, the terror was tinged with horror and exhaustion and deep, deep grief, and relief and love and hate, and I was drowning, drowning in an experience that was beyond me, that made me see the world in a new way that could never be rubbed out, however much I tried. I saw for the first time and I wanted to forget what I saw, to be the person I was before, and I cried for the new order of the world and the girl I lost somewhere in the darkness of the old.

The baby was placed, bloodied and blue, on my stomach and I felt the life in it slipping and wriggling like a stranded fish, and in the shock I didn't know how to hold it or what to do. Then I heard my mother say, a beautiful little girl Mary, and I looked at her and whispered, no, in horror. I saw her face freeze in a kind of distress when I said, a boy, it's a boy, mother. She tried to smile at me and she said, a little frantically, no a girl, a beautiful girl, look at her, how perfect she is.

"Take it," I said and my mother lifted her and wrapped her in a sheet, but I turned my face to the wall when she offered her to me. My mother held her close and crooned to her and I stared at the wall until my eyes hurt. I felt the soft, slack belt of skin round my stomach and the trickle of blood and an ache inside that I wasn't sure was physical.

"You'll need to put her to the breast quickly," the doctor advised and my mother nodded.

For the next few days I fed her and handed her back to my mother, refusing to hold her to me. The shock of the birth and the crushing disappointment overwhelmed me. Michael had left me. For good now, he had gone. And the irony was that only my father brought me to my own beautiful daughter, Niamh. He tiptoed in one night and I looked at him, my eyes burning, and he said nothing but laid a hand on my head and pushed the hair back, then peered at the baby as my mother held her. They both smiled.

I watched him from the bed, saying nothing, and I saw the big shovel hands reach out to my mother, and she placed the baby in them lengthways, Niamh's tiny body cupped against his palms, and I felt it, the mountainous tenderness of him, vast as his hulking body, and the dam inside me broke.

My mother was right. There were those who turned against me and my baby. There are none so righteous as the religious self righteous, and none so religiously self-righteous as the Irish. I knew what I had to do the morning I took Niamh to the corner shop and a woman spat at me as I walked past. A middle aged woman with a squashed face like crumpled cushions, and thin lips without a trace of lipstick. And the best of it was that she carried on her way into the church for morning mass without a backward glance.

I looked at the thin circle of foaming spittle on the pavement and knew that I would leave. My mother was heart sore when she heard my decision and my father seemed to shrink a little at the idea of Niamh being taken from him. She was his pride and his joy. I took my daughter to Donegal to remove myself from the tight smiles and the sneering disapproval, and the barely disguised hostility. But as Niamh later came to know, I had other reasons too.

The Easter declaration Michael read in 1916 called for equality between men and women. No matter that De Valera refused, against the orders of Pearse and Connolly, to allow women fighters in the Boland Mill Garrison that day. They fought elsewhere and I came to believe I too should play my part. When Michael gave his life, I wanted to continue his struggle so that he did not die in vain. But by then, of course, I knew what loss was, and I could not impose the possibility of such loss twice on my daughter. I joined the women's league, Cumann na Mban, for a time, but impressed as I was with the fighting spirit of Maragaretta Keogh, who was shot dead outside the south Dublin union,

I knew that as a lone parent with a small baby to care for, my part must be a different one.

I gave in whatever ways I could: allowing the cellar of my house to be used as an arms store, providing a safe house for volunteers of the IRA, taking in the wounded who were brought to me. I could do no less, for my whole life was spent trying to create a reason why I had to lose Michael. I wept the day the Free State Treaty was ratified. It was signed with the blood of the dead, stained with the tears of the bereaved. Michael did not die for half a cause, for half a solution. I knew then that the blood of Ireland would continue to flow, that the children and grandchildren who I hoped would be free, would, by necessity, in their turn be part of the struggle.

My part is nearly over. I have a sense of anticipation, of excitement, that I will see Michael again. He was taken before he had a chance to make his mark in your lives and it is up to me to try to stamp an impression of him on you. Never forget him. Honour his memory. Fight on, that his death might have meaning.

Niamh, these few lines are for you alone. You were my father's pride and joy but you were also mine. If I was too deeply entangled in the fronds of my loss, if my living was badly tainted by your father's dying, forgive me. Never be in any doubt that the reason I put my feet on the floor each morning was for you. And later, when your eldest son was born, when I held Johnny in my arms for the first time, I knew your father had returned in a new generation. I saw him reflected in Johnny's eyes and I wept for the shadow that I saw there. Our fight now is yours.

Eirinn go Brach.

CHAPTER ONE

Belfast, November 2010

The music is thumping loud in her chest like a tribal drum and she looks at the man and thinks there's nothing in the world like a good intro. Those pregnant opening notes when anticipation shimmers out of the sound like a heat haze. The sexy, bluesy, bordello quiver of, 'Honky Tonky Woman', say. Or this, Marvin Gaye's 'Heard it Through the Grapevine'. The beat of the drum is the beat of her heart. She can't tell the rhythms apart. And then the rattle of the tambourine, shimmying out of that ominous pulse like a serpent from a snakecharmer's basket, slithering dangerously across the room towards her. "Oo-ooh, I bet you're wondering how I knew ..."

Danni can feel the heavy, lumpen outline of the gun against her leg. She should be frightened but she isn't. It doesn't matter if there's an accident, if she rains blood into the atmosphere. Her ... or him ... Does it matter which? Inside her pocket, she slides a single finger along the metal in rough caress, her tongue simultaneously running against her lips. She knows nothing about guns. She wonders if she tilts the gun up inside the pocket, if she simply blasts through the material at an upward angle, where it will hit him, and if the release of blood will be violent. Will it seep or cascade?

The music thumps still. The floor vibrates. She feels like she could choke on her own tongue, the way it swells in her throat like a sponge soaking up water. An inner tide of nausea rises in her gut. This is it.

He is looking at her. Looking at her quietly, like he's waiting. As if he's in no hurry. She watches him cross the room, his injured knee crumpling inwards slightly as he walks. He turns the music up, up, up, to full volume and when he turns, he sees that she has taken the gun out. He takes the seat opposite her. She resents his calmness. The fact that he doesn't seem to care. It's like he not only knows about the gun but is deliberately providing her with a mask of music. She could blast him right now and nobody would hear the shot, could distinguish it from the thump of that drum. She could walk right out of here, out of Belfast, and go home. He's making it easy for her. Unless he's taunting her. He sees her hand move but does not flinch. His eyes don't leave her face.

The man is waiting for her verdict. She is still exploring her limits, her possibilities.

"Oh I heard it through the grapevine

I'm just about to lose my mind.

Honey, honey ..."

Black as coaldust, she thinks, watching his hair flop forward so familiarly now, long, fine strands falling into his eyes. Perhaps a stray grey or two. The sleeves of his pale blue shirt are folded back neatly, revealing surprisingly muscular forearms considering his slenderness. Behind his chair, a bookcase stuffed full, piles of books turned on their side and stacked one on top of another. History books. Literary books. Irish writers, mainly: James Joyce, Roddy

Doyle, Yeats. Black folders full of the small, neat, intense writing she has come to recognise at a glance. She sees what he was, and she sees what he is, and she feels confused. She wishes she could classify him simply, like a book. Small beads of sweat prickle on her back.

Fear makes her angry. She despises her own hesitation. In the last few weeks her hatred, her determination, have rushed together like a river in spate at times, then at others dwindled to a pathetic trickle. It's time for the indecision to end. Her finger curls round the trigger. Someone in the flat below is thumping on the ceiling with a broom handle.

He looks down at the vibrating floor but he does not move. He does not turn the music down. He looks at her and then he leans his head back against the curve of his chair, closes his eyes and waits. There's nothing like a good intro, it's true. But it's not where you begin that matters most. It's where you end up.

CHAPTER TWO

Glasgow, 1992

Danni sees her husband and her son always in the same way, trapped in the bubble of a December Saturday in 1992, a bubble that she can neither reach into, nor pull them from. They are standing outside a shop in Glasgow in the grey light of a winter afternoon, a light that is slowly being nibbled at the edges by darkness. They are Christmas shopping and later, they plan to take Angelo to see the lights of George Square. Danni is at the bottom of the street, walking to meet them. Garlands of multicoloured lights hang above them outside the shop, tapping their own rhythm as they beat on and off. Even from her place at the bottom of the street, Angelo's face seems illuminated by them, as if the lights shine through the translucent pink apple of his cheeks that the cold has breathed into the milky whiteness of his skin.

For Danni, Angelo is forever dressed now in a navy jacket with a bear on the breast, a red woollen hat, and a red woollen scarf wrapped tight around his neck. Afterwards, it became impossible to think of him in anything else. At the bottom of the road, she waves up to them but they do not see her, caught as they are in their own private moment. Marco is crouched on his hunkers beside Angelo, on the balls of his feet, resting on his heels. Angelo pulls something from a brown paper bag, but at this distance it too far to see what it is. But she sees Angelo drum his feet in excitement, a little dance of ecstasy at the contents of the bag. She feels a pang of exclusion from the moment, hurries towards it to be part of it, to enter the bubble.

She never reaches it. In her imagination she tries to change history, to actually reach Marco and Angelo and pull them from that bubble into safety. Such a small change that would be needed to make things normal, to rub out what really happened. If she had not been five minutes late in meeting them, they would not still have been standing there. They would be safely in a café, Angelo pushing his nose to the glass of the cake cabinet to choose. She sees the next moment in slow motion, a longer, more painful version of real time. The noise of the explosion fills everything, reverberates through her, as her world is blown upwards, cascading into raining fragments.

Later, Danni realises she does not see Marco again after that moment he knelt in front of Angelo. But she sees her boy, lifted like jetsam, blown upwards in a tornado of energy as easily as gathered leaves in an autumn wind. She sees the flash of red woollen scarf, the brown paper bag arcing into oblivion, and then all is lost in a mist of smoke and stour and falling debris. She would like to say she runs instantly but human nature makes her stop instinctively, turn her head, raise her arms to protect herself. There is a moment when her entire emotional system stalls, when the enormity of what is happening makes her incapable of feeling anything other than a bewildered blankness. Later, that hesitation seems perilously close to a glimmer of betrayal.

When the terrible primal screams fill the space around

her, it jolts her into action and she moves instinctively towards them, running into the sound, running towards the space occupied by Marco and Angelo.

As she moves further up the street, she becomes aware of water from a burst mains spraying into the air, running down the road towards her.

Ahead of her, several cars are on fire, the flames licking into the jet of water, element against element. Danni's feet crunch now on broken glass and she turns her head as a woman is carried past her by a wailing man, his face contorted in a frozen grimace of horror and fear. The woman's clothes are torn, jagged fragments of glass embedded like miniature axes in her skull. If there is anything recognisable that breaks through the terrible blankness of her expression, Danni thinks, it is the reproach of the innocent.

At first, she does not notice the water. It cascades and froths round her feet and eventually, she looks down and sees that her feet are soaking. Her eyes register what the rest of her cannot; she does not feel the wetness. Then she sees that the water is pink, that the bottom of her cream jeans are stained raspberry with diluted blood. It's like a river now, gushing down the gutters at the side of the road, sweeping debris with it. Later, in her one and only therapy session, she tells the counsellor what she told no one else: that what haunted her most from that day was the sight of a severed hand rushing towards her, spinning in a swirl of bloodied water, as disposable as the discarded crisp packet that followed it.

At the top of the street, where Marco and Angelo were standing, the windows have been blown out of the shop. A mannequin hangs grotesquely across shattered glass, as though impaled across the stomach. Next to it, a real person, though Danni is uncertain whether it is a man or a woman, blown against the shop frontage, human flesh discarded as disdainfully as plastic. From somewhere deep in the debris, a scream pierces everything, the thin wail of a child in pain.

"Mummy, mummy, mummy," the child screams and Danni know that it is not Angelo, and the knowledge is the trigger of a pain that will never leave her.

"Angelooooo …" She wails, her head tipping back. The water has reached her ankles; she stands helplessly as it rises against her like a tide.

"Angelooooo!" And then she runs again, heart hammering, into the water and the blood and the screams, into the oblivion of a tomorrow she could never have imagined.

CHAPTER THREE

Danni closes her eyes and leans back on the sofa, trying to blot out the shrillness of the sound. The phone rings so consistently that she has begun to hear it inside her head even when it isn't ringing. Roberto, Marco's brother, has come round to man it, to answer the door and open post, to make her food. He never questions her, never asks what she wants, which is a relief.

"Eat," he says simply, handing her a plate.

She can't deal with the stilted expressions of sympathy, the condolence cards with their angels and crosses and doves. Their talk of peace angers her. She opened a card one morning and felt such a surge of rage at its benign message that she picked up a jar of jam and hurled it against the kitchen door. The glass shattered, and she watched in shock as the clumps of red fruit slithered slowly down the wooden door towards the floor. Did she do that?

She felt ashamed, then, her cheeks flushing as she crossed slowly to the sink for a cloth. The water trickled warm on her fingers. Such a confusion of emotion, the anger and the fear and the horror of this growing black hole at her heart. She crossed back to the card, raised it with wet fingers. "May the joy of happy memories bring you peace in your heart." How can she find peace when her child has been violently plucked from the vine and thrown back into the earth to rot? When Marco's vitality has been snuffed out so prematurely, a firework only half lit, fizzling before it had a chance to soar?

After he died, the press made much of the fact that he was one of their own, an investigative journalist, that he specialised in the Northern Ireland troubles. They liked that irony. The press always liked irony, Danni thought, heating coincidence in a crucible of such intense emotion that it liquefied into something of almost supernatural significance.

There were headlines about the fact that Marco had travelled into the heart of the Belfast troubles, met top level terrorists on both sides of the divide, and yet was killed in his own safe back-yard in Scotland's only ever Irish terrorist attack. Why, the headlines demanded, had the Irish republican fight moved its focus from London, and included Scotland in its campaign, when some were pressing so hard for peace?

It distressed Danni to see Marco's picture alongside those stories, marking him out as victim. Marco was the story teller, not the story. Seeing his picture in the paper he once wrote for castrated him somehow, stripped him of that visceral energy that had always attracted her. A power all the more vigorous because it was casually wielded. Marco was not a victim. He simply was not. The IRA might have taken his future but she refused to let them have his past.

Strangely, she had not worried for his safety. She had scoffed at his supposed invincibility but secretly relied on it. When he travelled to Belfast, he kissed her as casually as if he'd been going to the corner shop and she felt him in no greater danger than that. Marco was lucky. He felt it. She felt it. She simply could not imagine him not being there

25

and later she realised it was simply her way of rationalising the sense of loss that had run like a wood grain through her life. The only way she could contemplate his loss back then was to mark it as something inconceivable.

The doorbell again. Danni closes her eyes. She hears Roberto open the door, the low murmur of male voices in the hall. Perhaps whoever it is will go away without speaking to her. The sitting room door opens cautiously with a creak.

"Traynor!" she says, getting up out of the chair and smiling genuinely.

They hold one another for so long that they begin to rock gently together, Traynor whispering quietly in her ear.

"I'm so sorry Danni. I can't believe it. I don't know what any of us will do. I'm so sorry."

Roberto stands awkwardly behind them, arms folded, eyes to the floor.

Marco had not travelled alone to Belfast in recent times. He had been teamed with Eddie Traynor to work on a major investigation, researching links between the funding of terrorism and Irish crime rings. Both Marco and Traynor had a maverick streak, an independence, that singled them out as good journalists. They weren't pack hunters. So there was some resistance when their editor first instructed them to pool resources and work together on the investigation, and they had sniffed round one another like two mongrels, marking out their territory with ill disguised animosity.

In fact, they worked well together. Each brought good contacts that the other respected. Marco had been working for years on stories about weapons acquisition within the provisional IRA, investigating links with America, Libya and the KGB. Traynor had scoops on IRA links to a number of bank and warehouse robberies. They had, at first, tentatively shared contacts and resources but each came to admit that they achieved more together than either would have done alone. They were close: less than brothers; more than friends.

Danni found her own niche in their camaraderie. She lost track of the times she would put Angelo to bed, fall asleep on the couch waiting for Marco to come home, and then hear two voices when the front door opened.

"Traynor, do you not have a bloody home to go to?" she'd shout sleepily. Marco would come in and kiss the top of her head where she lay and when she prised her eyes apart, Traynor would be standing sheepishly waving a carrier bag of Chinese food.

"I come bearing gifts."

"Any spring roll gifts?"

"Yep."

"You can stay then."

It was their little comic ritual that they repeated often, but almost immediately after Marco's death, Danni feels there has been some subtle shift in their old, easy rapport. It doesn't work now that Marco has gone. He was the silent element facilitating it. He didn't need to say anything; he just needed to be there. They used to sit, the three of them together, talking politics, arguing over Irish Republicanism. Marco, with his Catholic background, had been more instinctively supportive than Danni and Traynor. Yah dirty Prods, Marco had joked if things looked like getting heated, but that was Glasgow for you, a city that always wanted to know if you were a Billy or a Tim. The three of them had shared the Chinese food by passing it round in the tin trays without bothering about plates and talked and bickered companionably. But their roles were clear in those days. She was indisputably Marco's and she and Traynor could chat, argue and flirt mildly in the security of that knowledge. Now, almost immediately, she finds herself calling him Eddie. It seems less intimate than Traynor.

"I've asked around, Danni," Traynor is saying, and she suddenly comes to, her interest quickening, "and as far as I can tell, it's some kind of mistake or maybe an internal battle that's going on. There was certainly clearance given pretty high up in the organisation for a bomb in Glasgow but not on this scale. I think it was meant to be a shock, a warning that if there's no agreement, there's going to be an escalation."

A mistake.

Danni is staring at him, trying to make sense of his words.

"How can you know what … how can you know …?" she stutters.

"There's a contact I made not long before this happened," Traynor continues. "He's a major figure in the Belfast criminal world but also a senior IRA member. Part of the nutting squad."

"The what?"

"Internal IRA discipline. Anyone guilty of betrayal or indiscipline in the IRA is dealt with by an internal court. They're the ones who deal with knee cappings and executions and stuff. You have to be trusted to be part of it. This guy is part of the nutting squad so he's a senior source. He also undertakes jobs to fund IRA activity, though as much goes into his back pocket as it does into the IRA. He's part of the active unit that I think is connected to the Glasgow bomb and …"

"Hold on Eddie … wait, wait, wait …" Her heart is thumping. "Part of the active unit connected to Glasgow?"

"Yes." He's not following her.

"You *know* who's responsible for Glasgow?"

"Well … not definitely … but I have a pretty good idea."

"Have you told the police?"

Eddie frowns.

"What? No, of course I haven't."

"Why not? Danni's eyes are boring into him. "Why the hell not?"

"Danni, I'm asking questions for a story," he says gently. "I've been asked to investigate the bombing for the paper."

The pain inside her feels boundless, engulfing, like a wave. Marco reduced to a few lines in a story that if there was any justice, he should have been writing. Not Traynor. Not bloody Traynor.

"So?" she says belligerently. "So what? Is that all Marco is to you all at that paper now. Another story?"

Traynor looks winded.

"No, of course not."

"Prove it. Tell the police what you know. Or give me the names and I'll tell them."

"But Danni, a journalist can't ask questions and then reveal their sources to the police. That's not the way it works." Traynor's voice is gentle. He looks at her with a furrowed brow, appealing for reason. "You know that. You know that."

"I know that I want Marco and Angelo's murderers behind bars." Actually, she thinks, I want them dead.

Traynor watches as she gets up out of her chair and walks to the window. Roberto has sat silently throughout the whole exchange but moves to put one arm round Danni's shoulder.

"Christ, Danni, if I passed on information to the police, I'd be a dead man," Traynor says quietly, at her back. "A dead man walking."

Danni has begun to tremble. She bites her lip, trying not to say the words aloud. "I don't care," the voice inside her head is saying. "I DON'T FUCKING CARE." And then, with the speed of an echo, a more dispassionate voice whispers, "Grief is making you a monster."

The silence says everything that needs to be said. Roberto is motionless beside her. She doesn't turn round but a moment later, she hears the click of the door and sees Traynor disappearing down the path. There is something in the crumpled walk that prompts a stab of guilt. Poor Traynor. He cannot help it. He is simply not who she needs him to be.

The phone rings in the night. Does it ring in reality? Does she pick it up from beside the bed? She is sure she does. She hears it rock in its cradle when she reaches for it in the dark, banging against the wooden bedside table. She feels the coolness of it against her face as she holds it to her ear. Silence. She is not frightened. She knows. "Marco," she says. Does she say his name aloud?

She can hear a voice stutter in the distance, a victim of a faulty connection. The line hisses like a wind blows through it. If she is honest, the voice is indistinguishable but she knows. This is no stranger. She knows. "Try again," she urges. "I can't hear you. Try again. Speak to me." A wave of muffled sound. She presses the receiver hard against her ear. "Love?" she says. "Did you say love?"

An electrical storm of sound blows up on the line, so loud she drops the receiver onto the cover. She snatches at it instantly, half sitting up, leaning on her elbow. Her eyes are open now and she is fully awake but when she puts the receiver to her ear it is as though no one was ever there. The dialling tone buzzes steadily. She falls back into the pillow without replacing the receiver. It sits hopelessly in her hand. Her eyes strain against the darkness and then she hears a voice, clear and crisp. Please hang up and try again. Please hang up and try again. Please hang ...

CHAPTER FOUR

Their bodies are shrouded in muslin, a soft-focus lens through which to view the enormity of their injuries. Danni stands rigid at the door, until the seeping cold of the room reaches out to meet her, making her shiver involuntarily. It creeps insidiously round her, inside her. Preservation, she thinks. But still ... her child ... she wishes it was warm. Her instinct screams to turn the heating up, fetch a blanket.

A box of tissues catches her eye, placed discreetly on a corner table just inside the room. It frightens her somehow, that anticipation of her grief, the certain knowledge by those who run this place of what she is going to feel when she passes through this door. Emotionally, everything is mapped out. She hovers still, not passing through the threshold. The stillness, she thinks fearfully, looking at the rock solid immobility of the shapes beneath the muslin shroud. Dead stillness.

"You can change your mind, Danni. You don't need to go in." The police liaison officer at her back touches her shoulder as she steels herself.

"I do," she says, turning briefly to look at him. "I need to." Her expression softens as she takes in his bear-like solidity, the ever present dark shadow of stubble round his chin. She thought him gruff when he was first introduced as 'her' assigned officer, surly even. Now, he is a reassuring presence.

"Let me come in with you, then."

She shakes her head. "I want to go alone."

"Please Danni. Take my advice on this at least. I won't say anything or intrude. I'll just be there."

She hesitates.

"Please."

Danni shrugs. The emotional effort of facing the room is too great to be sidetracked into some other tussle.

It has been this way for days. The police just want to protect her, she understands that. But instinctively, she also understands that knowledge is less dangerous than imagination. A few days ago she had sat in the office of the Chief Constable's office, her eyes drawn to the folder on the table in front of him.

"Danni," he had said gently, "We will support any decision you take but please take my advice seriously. I strongly advise you not to view the bodies."

"I have to."

"Take some time. I know you have come to see the photographs today but my advice there is the same. There's nothing you can gain from looking at them."

"I have to," she repeats.

"You are certain?"

She nodded.

He opened the folder.

"As I've already warned you, Danni, some of these are very difficult to view. If you want me to stop at any time, just say."

"I will."

She had reached down then, to her feet, feeling for her handbag. The Chief Constable hesitated as she took out her wallet, removed a photograph of Marco and Angelo together, and placed it carefully on the table in front of her. It is the last image she will look at, one of the two of them together, whole not broken.

She said nothing as the Chief Constable handed her the photographs silently, one by one. She looked at each, refusing to flinch from a single one. She wanted to know everything. Everything. She would have no uncertainty haunt her in the coming years. She would never say inside her own heart, "I wonder if ..."

Marco. His body twisted awkwardly beneath him. She tried to view the images clinically, recognise why each one had been taken. This one to show the exact position of the body in relation to the explosion. This close up of his face for identification purposes. The left eye socket and cheek were a bloodied mass and she trailed a pinkie gently down the photograph, as if the blood flowed still and she could stem it. This ... and whoosh, the air was sucked from her lungs making her gasp ... this one was ... She closed her eyes momentarily. Angelo. Her eyelids fluttered. To show, she said carefully inside her head, to show the separation of the right arm and shoulder caused by the blast. She placed the photograph with deliberation on the table.

After three or four more, she had picked up her own photograph and willed the image of their smiles into her consciousness. Then she carried on relentlessly, taking each photograph, examining it, handing it back silently. She had gone home exhausted, beyond tears, unplugging the phone and lying open eyed and unmoving on the sofa.

Now, stepping through the funeral parlour room where Marco and Angelo lie, she feels the same unflinching determination that her love has to be strong enough to face what they faced, that she will share it in the only way she can. This is her time.

She inhales sharply, a gasp that can not be contained, as she moves closer to the muslin shapes. She feels Pete's presence behind her and moves forward to the coffins lying side by side. It is Angelo's hands, his tiny, shrivelled little hands that shock her. She had always loved the dimpled fatness of those hands, the warm, soft, newness of them as they explored the world and patted her face and stroked her hair. Why are they shrivelled? Shapeless. Useless. His body is like some badly constructed doll, the life, the blood, sucked out into grotesque, plastic facsimile.

Pete's hands reach out to steady her.

"Can I touch his hand?" she whispers, gazing into the coffin. Her hand hovers over the muslin curtain. She turns round briefly. "Can I touch his hand?"

"Best not, Danni."

The bodies are pieced together. Pete's hands remains on her shoulder and the warmth of his touch, the pressure of it, the energy, make her realise that Marco will never touch her ever again in her life and the simple truth winds her, drains the power from her legs. She looks at Marco, looks for him, and cannot find him. She has the sudden feeling that his absence here, from this room, means she will spend a lifetime looking for him.

"My love ..." she murmurs, surprised to hear her own voice.

She crosses to him but does not touch him.

"Could they be in the same coffin?" she asks suddenly. She looks up at Pete and catches the jolt that crosses his face. "Could they ... maybe?"

"I don't think ... I think probably ... it's maybe best this way, Danni." He exerts a little pressure on her shoulder, guiding her towards the door.

Danni looks back, frowning.

"I wish they were together," she says.

Touching, she thinks.

Pete looks at her awkwardly.

"I understand," he says.

But he doesn't.

At the door, she looks back, She has come to say goodbye but they have already gone. They have left without her, and for a moment, it feels like betrayal.

She dreams of him often in those early months of searching. Sometimes, he is behind glass, a floor to ceiling barrier. There is no way round it, no way through it. She catches her breath each time he appears, holds it, scared to breathe out in case the tiniest of movements will make him disappear. Only when he holds out his hand, palm towards her, does she risk reaching out tentatively. She tries to lay her hand against his, feel the warmth of his skin, but the glass barrier lies between. She sees his lips move but can hear no sound.

"Marco," she whispers. "Marco ..."

She knows it is not just a dream. He comes while she sleeps but she woke once, she knows she woke, her eyes screwed tight to keep him there inside her head, a whispering apparition she strained to listen to. It was important, what he came to say. She watched his lips carefully, wanting to reach out and run her finger across them as he spoke. He nodded as if she could hear, pleaded with his eyes, then suddenly fell silent, watching her. "Don't go ..." she whispered. "Marco, please don't go ..."

Both his hands came to the glass then, and he bowed his head, his hair falling forward. He was no apparition, she thought. No ghost. If only she could reach beyond the glass, she would feel real hair, thick and wiry in her hands. She could remember the exact feel of it; her fingers running gently down the nape of his neck as he kissed her, the little

35

involuntary shiver that ran through him, the pause as he looked at her. That night by the lakeside, she remembers suddenly, in a silvery June darkness that never quite blackened, her fingers knotted in his hair. The slow heat of the memory washes over her now, the warmth of summer, of longing ...

He is going. The pressure of his fingers on the glass is ebbing and she feels a jolt of panic. He lifts his head and his eyes wash over her, pleading. His mouth moves.

"I can't hear you," she whispers frantically. "I can't hear you."

He shakes his head.

"What are you trying to tell me?" She presses her hands more firmly on the glass, as if that will make his hands remain on the other side. But his fingers are melting away.

"NO," she screams. "MARCO ..." His body is shimmering, as if in a heat haze, but still he continues to talk silently. "I can't hear you ..." She slaps her hands on the glass, feels the cold hardness of it. "I can't hear you." She is crying now, banging her hands over and over against the window, ignoring the sharp bursts of pain against her palms. "I CAN'T HEAR YOU!"

He has gone. She does not want to open her eyes but she does. Outside, the dawn chorus has begun, stray, plaintive chirrups filtering through the open window. The room is bathed in half light. Her pillow is damp and streaked with the remnants of black mascara, an ominous, spidery dark trail across white linen.

CHAPTER FIVE

Sable, the eyeshadow pot said. Danni looked at it doubt-fully. A creamy brown, the colour of wet sand but with a grainy sparkle in its darkness. She tucked her short hair behind her ears, then smoothed it on, a light, shimmering slick over her eyelids. What was she doing this for? She didn't want to go out. It was her best friend Katy who wanted her to go out.

"It's only a party, Danni," Katy has said. "You said yourself you haven't been out in a year. You might meet someone."

"I don't want to meet someone."

"For God's sake! I'm not asking you to jump on the near-est man. Just be … be open to possibilities."

Possibilities.

Danni looked critically at her reflection, fingering the dark circled area under her eyes. She sank her head for-ward onto her arms on the dressing table. How long was it acceptable to feel this way? There were social boundaries to grief, she realised now. It was expected – demanded even – that the young widow be heartbroken … and then, sud-denly, time up. Other people were made uncomfortable by a grief that was too long, too intense, too unyielding. But where was it supposed to go, all that emotion?

The day of Marco's funeral, one of his oldest friends had taken her hand with tears in his eyes. "Don't worry, Danni," he'd said. "We'll all be here for you. Always." He phoned three times after that, but she never saw him again.

Life moved on, she knew that. But other people's expectations were always a shock. A year after Marco died she met a friend she hadn't seen for six months. She greeted Danni with a wave and a smile and then followed up with a frown. "Oh you look tired," she said. "Everything all right?" All right? Danni thought. All right? Oh, Danni had replied vaguely. She wasn't sleeping that well. "You're not still …?" said her friend, then halted abruptly "Well, of course," she said, eyes softening. "It takes a while doesn't it?"

Danni took her dress down from where it hung from the old picture rail, slipping into the smooth, fitted silk, an abstract print of purple and pinks with soft storm clouds of charcoal black. She had loved it in the shop but now looked critically at it in the mirror. Why had she bought this, for God's sake? She was far too short to carry it off. She hauled a pair of higher shoes from the back of the wardrobe, cursing.

The radio is on as she gets ready. She pauses, one foot unshod, as some pop princess is interviewed. "Anyone special in your life?" the interviewer asks. "I don't have time for relationships," says the princess. "I just have …" and she pauses, giggling lightly. "… liaisons!" Yeah, Danni thought, slipping her other foot into the shoe. Dead right, whoever you are. She couldn't cope with relationships any more. Liaisons. That's what she'd have.

"Drink?"

It is his hand on her back that makes her panic momentarily. A light gesture but there is something proprietorial about it. She is not ready to be owned Where the hell is

Katy? Why has she left her with this guy … Raymond did he say?

"Wait here," he says. "What would you like?"

"Anything."

He laughs.

"Gin? White wine? Anti-freeze?"

"What year's the anti-freeze?"

"The wine's better."

"Okay."

For a moment after he leaves, she stands against the wall but it feels too exposed. The music thumps in her head.

"Excuse me."

She pushes out past the group standing at the door, and heads to the stairs, sitting on the second step from the bottom, half sheltered by a pile of coats draped over the banister. She leans her head against them, the music distant now. Her coat might be under here, she thinks hopefully. Perhaps she could just go.

"Are you hiding?"

Raymond's head appears over the banister.

"No … sorry … it got … I needed to sit down."

He says nothing but swings round and sits on the step beside her, handing her a drink. She steals a sideways look. He is sort of handsome, she decides, but in an insignificant way. Dirty blond hair that is cut a little too neatly to be stylish. Blue eyes – or are they grey? – that have too little vivacity to be interesting. He wears jeans and a black shirt and the jeans are fractionally too short. Marco always … well he is not Marco. He is too neat. Too polite. Too, too, too …

"I haven't been out in a year …" she blurts out.

"Goodness!"

"I had a husband." A bicycle. A cuckoo clock. A husband. She could be saying anything.

"Oh."

His response is so neutral; she glances up curiously.

"Didn't work out?" he says solicitously.

"It did," she says. "It did work out. Except it didn't." For a moment, she thinks she might lay her head down on the stairs and howl because it's just too much effort not to.

She takes a gulp of white wine, feels the chill of it hitting her empty stomach.

"His name was Marco," she says.

He nods politely.

"Did he leave?"

"Yes. Yes he left." She wipes her cheek roughly, quickly, with the heel of her hand.

"His loss."

"He died."

She hears a scream of laughter as the door opposite them opens wide.

"Fuckin' idiot ..." says a man in a striped shirt, walking to the door. A girl with waist length hair follows him, tottering on silver, platformed stilettos.

"Oh, get a sense of humour, Gerry."

"You've had too much to drink."

Danni watches as he opens the front doors and slams it behind him. The girl stares at the closed door, hesitating. The world is bedlam, Danni thinks. All this emotion whirling and colliding ... The man in the striped shirt's anger. Her grief. The drunk girl's bewilderment. And Raymond, she thinks, glancing up at him. What's he feeling?

"I'm really sorry," Raymond says. His eyes have flicked down to her legs. "About your husband."

She catches the glance. Desire, she thinks dispassionately. He feels desire. She wishes she could be pleased but it makes her feel lonelier than ever.

There is no normality. There will never be normality.

"It was a mistake for me to come out," she says, half to herself.

"I don't think so."

When she looks at him, he smiles.

"How long ago?" he asks.

"A year."

When she talks, he appears to listen so acutely she wonders if he listens at all. Sometimes, too much 'interest' is a giveaway that you have none at all. But the need to speak about Marco is overpowering. She cannot help herself.

"He was a journalist."

"Interesting job."

Still she ploughs on

"He wrote about terrorism." She sniffs. "He was ... he was ..."

She has to stop this and yet she can't. She looks at him bleakly and there is something about his politeness that tips her over the edge. Politeness is unemotional. Controlled. Everything she feels is the opposite. She doesn't blame him for not caring. How can he care? And how can she not? But it's so alienating. She's in a small, select group that no one wants to be part of, no one wants to join.

"I miss him," she says.

Her voice cracks and she buries her face in her knees.

She feels his hand on her shoulder.

"It's okay," he says.

"I'm sorry."

"There's nothing to be sorry for."

She lifts her head.

"It's just ... it was a big deal you know ... coming out ..."

"You don't need to explain."

He has not asked how Marco died, she thinks. She sniffs again.

"I'm sorry. Do you have a tissue?"

He fishes in his pocket.

"Napkin from earlier. Can't certify it's 100% un-used."

He talks oddly, she thinks, as she quickly swallows down the last of her wine. As if making a selection from a phrase book.

"It'll do. I'm not the fussy type."

"You look very ... particular ... to me," he says.

Particular, she thinks. What a strange word.

"That's ... well ..." she says. The chilled wine bites.

"I like your dress."

"Oh," she says looking down at it. "It's new."

"Fits like a glove."

Danni drains her glass, though she knows it's empty.

"You're blushing."

"I'm not the blushing type either."

"Must be the light."

"Must be."

She pulls at the coats beside her, trying to find hers.

"Look," she says, "You've been kind. But I need to go. She pulls her coat from the pile and the others topple. She picks them up quickly, arranging them haphazardly in her confusion.

"Here, let me."

He takes her coat and helps her on with it. It makes her feel awkward. Her dress sleeves ride up inside the coat in her haste but she keeps stuffing her arms in, longing to be out.

"Thanks," she says. "And thanks for the chat. I'm sorry I got upset. Marco was ... well, he was everything to me. I miss him. I never stop missing him. He was ... you know ... we were married and ... and I know it's a year but maybe it's too soon ... too soon for me ... maybe it's always going to be too soon ..."

She stops suddenly.

"Anyway … nice to meet you."

"Listen …" says Raymond.

Someone bumps into Danni from behind and she turn to see the girl with the silver shoes.

"Oh sorry," the girl says, holding onto Danni for support. "I'm really sorry …"

"No worries," says Danni.

"Sorry," repeats the girl. "Just looking for the wee girls' room."

"Shirley!" shouts a voice behind them. "This way!"

"Comin'!" She turn to Danni again. "Sorry."

"Anyway …" says Danni, lunging for the door "Nice to meet you, Raymond, and thanks again."

"Listen …" says Raymond.

Danni turns from the door.

"Can I take your number?"

"Sorry?"

"Your number."

"Oh."

And then she laughs. He doesn't mean anything by it, she thinks. It's just that he's alive and therefore open to possibilities. And she isn't.

She saw him for a few months. There never seemed to be a particular reason not to. And maybe some of it was okay but it was all that effort. The feigned politeness. The dressing up. There wasn't enough excitement in it to give her the impetus to keep trying. Her relationship with Marco had moved into that comfort zone where they knew one another too intimately to have to pretend. A laugh was all it took. A look. A flicker that licked into a flame without a word being spoken Things didn't need to be spelled out. The truth was Danni wanted to be there again without the effort of all those early stages. She had forgotten what hard work it was.

And then one night Raymond came round to her house. He had never mentioned the pictures before but she saw him silently looking at the framed photographs of Marco, the baby shots of Angelo. She wished suddenly she hadn't invited him here. She didn't want him in her space.

"Drink?" she said.

"Lovely," he replied.

"Do you think," he said, when she came back into the room, "that perhaps it would help you to take these pictures down?"

She scarcely missed a beat as she handed him a glass.

"No," she said. "I don't."

"But you've moved on from Marco. If you have photographs of him everywhere, he's always going to be around."

"He died, Raymond! It's not like we divorced!"

Raymond put his hands up in a 'don't shoot me' gesture.

"Just saying," he said. "Just trying to help." He took his drink and looked up at her. "Don't go all huffy on me."

"I'm not," she said, trying to keep the tightness from her voice.

"Good." He patted the seat beside him.

She tried desperately to smile as he kissed the top of her head.

"Maybe," he murmured against her hair, in that ever reasonable tone that was really beginning to grate on her, "you should talk to someone … you know, a counsellor or a psychiatrist or something."

No more parties, Danni told Katy. No more men. No more.

CHAPTER SIX

Glasgow, 2010

She wants to reach inside the television. She wants to smash the glass with her fist and pull those figures out of the safety of that square screen. And when the glass breaks and cuts her skin, she wants to pull their stupid fucking balaclavas off their heads and smear her blood all over their faces. Stain them with it. Standing there in their black uniforms, waving their guns like a badge of honour. Their props give them an identity they could never achieve unaided. An identity, a purpose, a power, a perversion. Danni's hand shakes as she picks up the remote control to increase the volume.

A documentary. The young dissidents of the Republican cause in Northern Ireland being filmed on a training mission in a wood. She has caught it only by chance. There is, Danni was to think later, a mere heartbeat separating one path in life from another. Between triumph and disaster, joy and tragedy. It was the lesson of her life.

Eighteen years ago, had she not been five minutes late, her husband and son might still be alive. Tonight, had she stopped off at the supermarket as she intended, had she not had that sudden overwhelming desire to get out of the world and back into her own self-contained space, then she would have missed the television programme that changed her life. Tonight, when she flicked channels impatiently, with the same restlessness she had felt all day, she did not even look at which button she pressed. Life was a series of whims. Was it chance that she saw this documentary today, of all days? Or was it meant to be? Today should have been Angelo's 21st birthday. The phone has not rung once. The morning brought no triumphant rattle of the letter box, no heavy thump onto the mat. There has been no torn wrapping paper, or curled ribbon, or half open boxes, littering the neatness of Danni's sitting room. There has been silence, order, emptiness.

Today, she has been haunted by the feeling that Angelo has died all over again. Not Angelo the child, but Angelo the man. She has only ever experienced him running to her, a child lifting his arms up to her for comfort. All day, she has tried to imagine the reverse, the comforted becoming the comforter, the strangeness of lifting her arms up to a grown son to hug and be hugged. Her lost, unknown, man-child.

She is not, normally, an anniversary kind of person. It isn't the missed today that matters so much, but all the thousands of missed yesterdays leading up to it. So she tells herself, and yet ... in the early hours of this morning, she had stood in the kitchen, unable to sleep, watching the new pink dawn creep stealthily across the old night sky, remembering the morning light rising all those years ago, just after Angelo was born. A new beginning.

On the screen, a masked youth aims at a target and fires. In a disguised voiceover, he explains his rejection of the peace process, the justification for violence in his search for national identity. Identity, Danni thinks bitterly. Where was Angelo's right to identity? Today, he should have come of age but he has no face, no shape, no substance. No story. The speaker's anonymity enrages her, the camera close-up lingering on thin lips that speak through the slit of the balaclava, on eyes that can only seem unyielding when surrounded by the aggression of the black woollen mask. "Who the fuck are you?" she yells suddenly at the screen.

God knows the peace process had been hard enough. In 1994, two years after Marco and Angelo died, news of an IRA temporary ceasefire was announced and she would never forget the feeling that swept through her. It was good news, she insisted to herself. Good news. But really it felt like watching someone you loved die painfully from cancer, only to be told the next day that a cure had finally been found. The ceasefire hadn't lasted.

When it broke down in 1996, and she watched coverage of bombings in Manchester and the London docklands, she felt secretly ashamed of that earlier moment of ambivalence. She hadn't wanted this.

So when the 1998 peace process moved to a positive conclusion, she tried desperately to be glad. But it was hard. Too late, she thought, watching the politicians gather on the steps of Stormont, the Northern Ireland parliament, after the Good Friday agreement. Too bloody late. The prisoners could be released, and the parliament could be constituted, and the talk could be of optimism and peace and moving on, but she didn't want to move on, only back. Where was *her* new dawn?

Marco and Angelo were the sacrificial lambs to peace. The people who had to die to make it possible. Well, if you offered Danni a choice – peace or her husband and son back – she'd choose her family, and both sides could get on with blowing each other to bits as far as she was concerned.

She had balked at the proliferation of programmes on "reconciliation". It was a word that meant nothing to her, prompted only a vague feeling of disdain. Religious words had that effect on her.

She resented the psychological tyranny of people who had only ever paddled around in the shallow waters of forgiveness trying to tell her how important the concept was. Let them swim out to the deep waters, feel the currents of her experience, the power of it, and *then* let them try and tell her. Why should the people who murdered her husband and her son be forgiven? Terrorists stole her life. The emotional terrorists who told her how she should feel about it could go to hell.

She had forced herself one night to watch one of these programmes. "A series that brings together people from different parts of the world who have reason to hate each other," she had read in the paper. "A fascinating investigation into the depths of human hatred and the capacity for redemption. Is reconciliation possible for a Rwandan Hutu and the Tutsi whose entire family he butchered to death? Or a black South African and the white policeman who "legitimately" shot his brother dead? Mark Henderson brings another high concept series to our screens with the help of psychologist Ray Brandon and grief counsellor Derek Turner. Tonight's programme shows an IRA man confronted by the widow of one of his victims. Unmissable."

I can miss it, Danni told herself. But she couldn't. She had been simultaneously repulsed and mesmerised. She looked at the ex-terrorist, his pasty, white faced flabbiness filling the screen and her consciousness, a man in a cardigan with thinning hair and a belly that hung over the waistband of his trousers. Guilt and grief didn't take away his appetite then, she thought sourly. What you were. What you are. Can there ever really be a difference? Can you really stop being capable of an action once you have done it? There was a tear forming in the pouch beneath the man's eye. "I never meant …" he said. His voice dropped to a whisper. "I never meant him to die …"

The camera had cut to the victim's widow. Danni watched her immobile face, set like stone and blanched with tension. The crows feet around her eyes were covered in face powder as if the lines have been hewn from dusty rock, but then two muddy black lines formed tracks down her cheeks, tears and mascara running in rivulets down the grooves. She was looking at the man intently and it was clear that there was some inward implosion going on.

"Oh don't," Danni muttered in exasperation under her breath. "Don't …"

But suddenly the woman on screen held out a hand to the man and he grasped it like a lifeline and began to sob.

"Oh fuck off," Danni had thought, snapping the remote control at the screen before throwing it onto the sofa, unable to torment herself any more with feelings that she couldn't pretend to have.

Anger is familiar to her, an old companion. People say you'll feel better, be less bitter, if you let go, but she'd rather carry the burden inside her. Sometimes the only thing left to hold onto is pain. The only thing left to remind you that you are alive. After eighteen years, she's used to bitterness being part of her. Maybe the rawness of the hatred is gone but not the hatred itself. It holds her life up, supports the structure of who she is, like the girders supporting the span of a bridge.

What did he look like now, she wondered, the man who killed Marco and Angelo? How old would he be? She looks at the screen and sees the evidence of his replacements: a row of balaclava clad youths, a new generation of an old problem that, unlike Marco and Angelo, simply won't die.

Just as the Provisionals had been born from the old IRA, so now the dissidents were rising from the ashes of the Provisionals' hard-fought peace.

"In every month of 2010," the presenter is saying, "there have been terrorist explosions in Northern Ireland that have failed to get much attention on mainland Britain. Young republicans are becoming frustrated. In recent weeks, the government has announced that the threat level from an Irish-related terrorist attack has now been officially raised from 'moderate' to 'substantial'. Indeed, the head of MI5 has warned the public not to assume that the only terrorist threat comes from Al Qaeda, and that a dissident Republican attack on mainland Britain is becoming increasingly likely."

Where was reconciliation now? Danni thought. When it all kicked off again? She ran her finger down the remote control, picking at the plastic. There's no way she would sit in a room with the man who killed Marco and Angelo. Then suddenly, in the midst of her anger, she realises that is exactly what she would like to do. Sit in a room with him. Just the two of them. Take away his props, his black uniform, his balaclava. Strip him of his anonymity and look into his eyes. Was he still active? And if he was? What would she do? *What would she do?* She shivers slightly. She would want to kill him.

She snaps the 'off' button on the remote control, the black balaclava face on the screen disappearing into a dot. If only it were as simple to make people disappear. Suddenly she has a thought. If a murderer can supposedly repent and become somebody else, somebody new, could she, Danni, who has never harmed anyone in her life, become somebody new too? Could she kill a man?

CHAPTER SEVEN

She goes to her desk as usual to work, sitting frowning in front of her computer screen but feeling no inspiration. Her research notebooks are spread in front of her but she can't translate any of it into real thought. She is writing a biography of a famous English writer who now lives in Hollywood and Danni has only recently returned from America. Her brain should be overflowing. But she finds her pen hovering over the spaces in her notebook, doodling.

She needs to talk to Traynor. And she knows with the cool, almost brittle perspicacity that had always amused Marco (you'd have it too if you hadn't been spoon-fed all your life, she'd goad him) that Traynor's unease over his old pal's widow, and the way he maybe hadn't quite seen her as right as he might have, would come in handy now she needed a favour. She could utilise his guilt.

The rain is slashing against her window, low grey cloud closing down like a helmet over the house. The world seems smaller, darker, with little horizon to see beyond the straggling plastic bag that has been blown into the hedge at the bottom of the garden, and flutters pitifully against the driving wind wrapping it tight around the centre branches. She might as well be that bag, she thinks, impaled on a force she has no control over and trapped into moving in one direction only.

When Marco and Angelo died, there was a sense of needing to survive, of making it through just *this* bit, and now this, and this, and this. And each survival was a kind of relief until she realised that there was nothing else ahead but a series of hurdles to jump. When she was through one, another would leap up ahead of her. There was no free run, no sense of having made it. She was trapped in the constant effort. And maybe she had stopped resisting the fact that there was nothing more, had simply put her head down against the rain and battled ahead. Until now. Something has changed. She turns from the rain spattered window to pick up the phone. It is not possible to simply continue life as it is.

Her doctor thinks she's depressed. He's one to talk, she thinks. Morose old codger with an undertaker's lugubriousness and fern green cord trousers that are permanently covered in dog hair. Last time she was there, for something completely unconnected, he insisted on running a variation of Goldberg's standard depression test on her. Now, he'd said, could she just answer yes or no to the following statements.

"My future seems hopeless," he said, and then looked up at her expectantly, above his glasses.

"Yes" she said, and he nodded.

"I feel trapped."

"True."

She doesn't want to hear her own answer to these questions, resents him for asking them.

"My sleeping pattern has been interrupted."

"No," she replied, defiantly.

He looked up again over his glasses, a vague disapproval present in the slight arch of eyebrows.

"My sleeping pattern has been interrupted," he repeated mildly, like he's giving her another chance to think.

"Only a little."

He ticks the 'true' box.

"I find it hard to make decisions," he continued, and she felt a lump forming, hard and bitter, in her throat. She looked at his hand hovering over the yes box. Yes or no, she thought, fighting unwelcome tears that were gathering like storm clouds inside her.

"Oh, I can't decide," she said wryly, and instinctively. He smiled and put down his pen. Listen, he said, his professional manner slipping into a comforting outpouring of fellow feeling, when his wife died he thought he'd die too with the loneliness. Has she ever thought about a pet ... a pooch maybe? She had looked down at the film of hair over his trousers and then up into his hang dog face.

"Not since I last watched Greyfriar's Bobby."

But he is right. Something has to change. In the first weeks after the bomb she used to think, if she could just get through the identification of the bodies. If she could just get through the funerals. Then, if she could just get through the first month, the first year, the first Christmas, the first anniversary. And now eighteen years have gone. She's been too busy surviving, making it from one obstacle to the next, to realise she hasn't been living. She's pushing forty and there is nothing behind her, and nothing ahead of her, but that empty space she ran into on the day of the bomb.

She picks up her phone book, running a finger down the letter T to find Eddie's number, telling herself she has nothing to lose. Here it is. He moved to the London office a few years ago, a move that was always coming. In that first week after Marco died, Traynor called in on her every day. In the first month, every week. In the first year, every month. After that it dropped to every few months until, by the time of the fifth anniversary, they were exchanging annual Christmas cards. Danni didn't resent it. It was just the way life was. It was almost a relief in the end. At first Traynor was a comforting link to her dead husband but in the end he became just a painful reminder of what she had lost. Traynor's life went on as before, and hers didn't.

The number rings out.

"Eddie?"

"Yeah?"

"It's Danni."

"Sorry?"

She half smiles into the receiver.

"Danni Piacentini."

"Danni! God, sorry. How are you Dan?"

"Yeah fine thanks, Eddie."

"Sorry it's been so long." he says awkwardly. "I've been meaning to phone ... you know how it is ..." His voice drifts off.

"No worries," she says. "I'm the same. Time just ..."

"Yeah."

"Still working hard?"

"Big time. Crazy hours."

"You always were an ambitious bastard. Marco always said so."

He laughs. Their conversation always seemed to lapse into more comfortable territory with insults.

"Saw your last biography of whassisname ... the politician."

"Unforgettable was it?"

He laughs again.

"Joe Brennan."

"So you were the other person who bought it. I wondered how come there were two."

"Who was the first?"

"Mrs Joe Brennan."

She laughs herself now, feeling inside her a tiny spark of something warm and nostalgic, like a nip of alcohol that burns comfortingly all the way down.

"Eddie, I want to ask a favour."

"Of course. How can I help?"

"I want you to help me with some Irish contacts."

Danni looks out into the garden, watching a small flock of sparrows swoop down into a deep puddle on the path.

"Contacts?" Traynor asks non-committally.

Danni half perches on the window sill. The birds are using the puddle as a bath, wings quivering, hovering over the water, pushing playfully against each other.

"I want to go to Ireland to find the men who killed Marco."

Silence.

At the bottom of the path, she sees the postman turning in from behind the tall hedge, walking up towards her door. The birds in the puddle fly upwards, wings beating furiously. Except there's one, one last one, who plays on obliviously, who seems to look up and see suddenly that it is alone, and then darts after the others. Wait for me! She smiles at the comedy of it, her eye following the trailing bird until it catches the others.

"Danni ... I ..."

"I know it sounds odd," she says, trying to sound as nonchalantly normal as possible. "I watched this programme the other night about the peace process and the emergence of young IRA dissidents." Her mind is ticking over, working overtime, thinking, thinking ... how would Marco have presented this to newspaper people when he wanted them to buy it? "Did you see it?" she asks.

"Yeah. It was interesting. What ...?"

"Well, it got me thinking. What's possible ... what's not ...? What would I feel if I went to Ireland now and I met Marco's killer? What does he feel about a new generation entering the fight? Is he still active? Of course, it's eighteen years now so I've had a chance to think more objectively about it all, and yet I have a personal connection that would make an interesting piece."

The thump of the letterbox sounds in the hall. The postman crosses by her window and waves to her. She smiles back through the glass.

"And I wondered," she continues, "if you could persuade your editor to commission a piece from me where I go to Ireland and write about my journey. You know, even if I didn't meet Marco's killer, just confronting IRA men about everything that has happened." Damn it, she shouldn't have said that. She's not interested in meeting IRA chiefs. Just the killer. She needs Eddie to track the killer for her.

"It is a really interesting idea," Traynor admits.

He's seeing the possibilities. She can hear it in his voice.

But what if there isn't only one killer, she asks herself. What if it can't be attributed more to one person than another ...?

"Danni, are you sure you could handle it ...? I mean ... my God ..."

"Don't worry about that. I can handle it," she says, looking out as the breeze whips up, sending a shiver through the hedge. She knows Traynor's concern will recede in a minute. He's a journalist. He lives on emotional possibilities.

"And of course," she continues, "with the terror threat being raised recently, the time is right to look again at the peace process and exactly what it has achieved and whether it can hold. There's the national peace process, alongside the personal peace process for me, laying ghosts to rest ... all that. And with all your experience, Eddie, you could do a piece alongside it about the years since Marco died, whether real resolution is possible … your personal connection with Marco."

"Actually, Danni," he says quietly, "that sounds really, really good."

Doesn't it? she thinks.

"We might not track down the people who killed Marco, though," he continues cautiously. 'It might have to be more symbolic than that."

"Yeah, but you never know. It would be great to get that personal connection – really powerful. And I wouldn't be looking to name the person. Not even to know his name. I just need to meet him. C'mon Eddie. You know people at the absolute heart of the IRA. You've dealt with them for years. It's worth asking isn't it?"

"Yeah, it's worth asking."

"You always said you had your suspicions about who was involved anyway."

"I did, yeah."

There is an awkward silence, a sudden memory of Traynor's crumpled walk down the path after Marco died, when she wanted him to tell the police who had been responsible for the bombing.

"Could you do a bit of digging for me?"

"Maybe. Look leave it with me. I'll talk to the editor about it."

"Great."

"Not sure how much money there'll be for commissioning the piece though, Dan," he says, sounding apologetic. "But I'll do the best I can."

"Don't worry about that. Just get the contacts and that will be worth everything. I might be able to sell something on to an American magazine as well."

"Good idea. I'll get back to you in a week or two when I've had time to look into it."

A week or two! An eternity.

"Thanks Eddie," she says.

When she puts the phone down, she sees the tremor in her own hand and tries to still it, walking briskly to the front door to pick up the letters from the mat.

CHAPTER EIGHT

Days later she has her head in her hands. What madness is this? What was she thinking of? Perhaps it would be better if Traynor simply doesn't get back to her. If he just melts away as he has done so often in the past. But when Traynor phones a couple of weeks later and says his contacts are not that keen to speak to her, instead of being relieved, the sense of disappointment is overwhelming. "Keep trying," she urges him. "Persuade them."

Her anger is like an infection. When she is in the throes of it, when she indulges in thoughts of the past, or watches the latest political manoeuvrings in Ireland, it rages through her body like a virus, poisoning her bloodstream. She is lost somewhere inside her own dark fury. She could kill with her bare hands.

When the anger begins to abate, she is left with a vague sense of shame. But the strange thing is she knows it can rage through her again at any time. No matter how much she resolves never to let it take hold, it flares up like an old recurring injury that is never far from the surface. There is a sickness inside her. There will always be a sickness.

Today she was in the home section of a department store and she found herself looking at kitchen knives, glinting coldly in the artificial light of the shop, an array of precision. She suddenly imagined them, steel tips streaked with blood. The thought unnerved her, sickened her. Too physical, she decided immediately. But the point is she *thought* about it. She considered it. And her own capacity to consider it unnerved her, and she had walked quickly out of the shop and into the crowds of Argyle Street, letting herself be swept along in the tide.

It is one thing to realise you want somebody dead. Another to be willing to be the instrument of their death. But another again to be able to turn that into a practical physical action. How does a person like her kill another human being?

A gun, she thinks, a gun would be cleaner. Curl a finger. Pull a trigger. It gets messy then, of course, but she doesn't have to touch him directly. But she could never get a gun. Where would she get a gun? Someone normal like her. Is she normal? Do normal people think this way?

Mowing him down in a car. Is that possible? Letting her anger control the accelerator pedal, letting it force her foot down to the floor. Or poison perhaps. Weedkiller. Paraquat. Crushed paracetamol? She feels despair gnawing her. How much would you need? You might have the determination, but how do you get the knowledge? One thing she does know. You have to get close to a person to kill them.

It's a full two months later that her mobile rings in the middle of the supermarket. She looks at the number. Traynor. Her stomach lurches. His contact is promising nothing, but he has finally agreed to meet Danni to decide if he wants to help her.

"He's not a nice man, Danni, but he's powerful," Traynor warns. "Are you sure you're up for this?

Danni grasps the shelf in front of her, finds herself gazing into row after row of breakfast cereal.

"Yes, Eddie" she says, as calmly as she can. "I'm up for it."

* * *

She phoned Katy late that night when she was calmer.

"I need to go back to America for a bit."

"Hollywood?"

"Yes. I need to do some more interviews for the book. Sometimes, it's only when you start that you realise the things you don't have."

Katy yawned.

"How long will you be away this time?"

Danni hesitated.

"Not sure. Will you keep an eye on the house again?"

"Yeah, yeah. When do you go?"

"Monday."

"Tough job you've got there, honey. Guess someone's got to do it."

"Yeah," said Danni. "That's exactly the way I look at it. Someone's got to do it."

CHAPTER NINE

Belfast, October 2010

The man they call The Wasp has a first floor office in a dingy sidestreet of Belfast. When Danni gets in a taxi and gives the driver the address, she is aware of his eyes flicking upwards to look at her curiously in his mirror. He says nothing; simply signals and moves out seamlessly into the flow of traffic. When he drops her under a streetlight, the only words he has spoken are to tell her the fare. She hands him a note and he takes it silently. Only when she gets out onto the street and looks around does he speak.

"You a visitor?" he asks, fumbling for change.

"Yeah," She squints into the darkness at a side alley trying to see the name. "Is that it?"

The driver nods.

"Wouldn't hang about here if I were you. Meetin' somebody?"

She is aware of his eyes travelling down her, assessing her, of that male capacity for simultaneous disapproval and desire. On the corner of the street, a moving shape catches her eyes. A woman in a thigh high skirt, heels and a short, flimsy, fake leather jacket. The woman is stick thin and shivering. She wraps the jacket tighter round herself. The taxi driver looks over.

"Rattlin'," he says.

"What?"

"She's shakin'. Needs her next hit."

Danni moves away from the lit street into the alley, walking past metal bins that spew garbage from half open mouths. She jumps at a movement behind her, realises a silver Vauxhall is crawling slowly at her back. The driver looks intently as she moves to the side. Instinctively, she avoids his gaze. The paper with the address is scrunched into her palm. Number 42. She peers into the darkness. Odd numbers on the left, even on the right.

When Traynor had called back with an address where she was to meet Sean Pearson, he said he wanted to come with her. She put her foot down. Not that it wouldn't be brilliant to have him with her, she lied, but it was a journey that for the sake of the piece she should do alone. For the sake of the piece. That was Traynor's kind of talk. He would understand that. It would make it too emotionally safe with him there, too comfortable, she said. It had to have an edge to be interesting.

Reluctantly, Traynor had finally agreed but said he wanted her to keep in close contact with him. He had told Pearson her name was Danni Cameron, he said.

"And listen," he had told her, "pander to his vanity. Call him the Wasp."

"What?" she'd said incredulously.

"Oh don't ask. He's a psycho so be careful. But he's connected and he can help you. He knows everyone."

"Was he ... was he responsible ...?"

"In the planning, I think, but not on the day."

"Got a light?"

The young woman on the street corner is calling down the alleyway to her.

"No sorry … oh no, wait a minute."

Danni remembers one of those books of pub matches she picked up somewhere and which has been lying discarded at the bottom of her bag since.

"Here …"

"Thanks."

The woman walks towards her, tottering in her heels on the rough stony ground of the alley. She walks like a wee girl in her mother's shoes, like they're too big for her, forcing her bare knees to turn in towards each other in the cold. Her arms are round herself still, holding her jacket closed over a black, boned, corset top. Her fingers shake as she lets go and she grasps the matches, flaring one against the side of the pack immediately.

"Ta."

Up close, Danni sees she is not as young as she first thought.

"Ah'm Myra," she says. "You a Scot too? I heard you talkin' tae the driver. Glasgow, aye?"

She takes a puff of the cigarette, hands trembling.

Danni nods. It's intrusive looking at her shake like that, she thinks, like being unable to avoid looking at something that should really be too private to view. Myra's eyes seem vague, as if they don't quite focus on what she sees.

"I need a hit," she says, drawing deeply on her cigarette.

The driver who had circuited earlier in the silver Vauxhall drives back round into the alley and they move to the side of the road.

"Wanker," Myra mutters as he crawls by, staring out the window.

She looks at Danni.

"Sorry. But he's been doing that for the last half an hour. He won't pay for business, he'll just get off on touring round in his bloody family Vauxhall peering out at us. Middle-class ponce who thinks he's living on the dark side."

She draws in on her cigarette then laughs, choking on the smoke.

"Tell you how much he knows ... he thinks you're one too."

She looks at Danni through eyes narrowed with smoke to see if she's affronted at the idea.

"Did you see the baby seat in the back of his car?" she continues.

"No ... no I ... didn't notice."

"You get loads like that."

Danni nods, unsure what to say and starts to move off, turning round to look for number 42.

"Here," says the girl, calling after her. "Do you want your matches back?"

"No, it's okay. Keep them."

The girl slips them into her pocket.

"Who you looking for round here?" she asks, suddenly curious.

Danni hesitates.

"A guy who calls himself the Wasp."

She sees the girl's face harden, the blue eyes focus more clearly on her.

"You a friend of his?"

"Never met him. You know him?"

"Oh yeah."

"What's he like?"

"Complete bastard."

Danni nods. Well he would be wouldn't he, she thinks. That's what these people are. She shrugs and moves off.

The girls watches her go, then suddenly shouts,

"You're going the wrong way."

Danni turns.

"That way," says the girl pointing back.

She watches Danni walk for a minute then suddenly darts forward, closing her jacket over again, trying to run in her heels, the click clack ringing out in the alley.

"Here, I'll show you. I need to see him myself."

"How do you know him?"

"We're in the same line of business."

Danni wants to go alone. She doesn't want to negotiate a first meeting with someone else beside her. But it doesn't look like she has any choice. Myra leads the way up stairs and pushes on an intercom. There is a buzz.

"Yeah?"

"Myra."

The door pushes open.

The stairway is clean enough but dark and dingy, lit by a muted wall light that can barely summon the energy to light past the first half dozen steps that curl upwards in a semi spiral. Myra pushes forward up the stair, still shaking, still grasping her jacket over her chest.

The Wasp's office is small and bare, the wooden desk decorated only with a telephone, an opened packet of chewing gum, and a glass of whisky. The windows block out the outside world with closed Venetian blinds. They are covered with dust, as if never opened. The one luxurious item in the room is an expensive looking leather chair, which the Wasp has sunk into, at the desk. He wears black trousers and a thin, black cashmere polo that would make him blend into the chair except for his startlingly white shaved head. Bizarre, Danni thinks immediately, looking at the unusual shape of his skull, the lumpy, ridge like effect in the baldness that moves underneath the surface. He sits forward in the desk when the two women enter, clunking a heavy gold bracelet against the desk. Then he very exaggeratedly lifts his arm and looks at his wrist watch.

"Myra ..." he says and the voice is quiet and pleasant enough but manages to convey a sense of threat.

"Yeah, I know, I'm early," she says. "It's bloody freezing out there."

"You're not dressed for the weather, Myra," says a sarcastic voice behind them.

Danni turns. She hadn't realised there was another person in the room. Behind the door there is a small area with soft chairs and a low, square, coffee table. A man – a boy, thinks Danni – lounges in the chair, feet up on the table. His thin, striking face is slashed by elegant cheekbones.

"And you're going to attract the wrong kind of man in that stuff," he continues. "Didn't your mama ever tell you?"

"Fuck off, Coyle," says Myra sourly.

Coyle grins, raising his hand innocently, as if backing off. Slim, white, long fingered piano player hands, Danni thinks. He looks lazily at Myra. His eyes are beautifully shaped, like dark, glistening almonds, but hard and malicious. She wonders how he manages to combine effete boyishness with such a suppressed sense of viciousness. The Wasp is watching her.

"Who's your playmate, Myra?" he asks, still watching Danni's face.

"We met on the way in," says Myra.

"Danni Cameron." Danni keeps her voice and her gaze steady but a growing unease emerges inside her like a butterfly struggling from a chrysalis and fluttering its tentative wings. There's something surreal about this room, its blinded windows acting like a closed eye to the world. It's like being in a dimly lit ball suspended above the universe. She thinks the Wasp is like an alien. Her eyes are drawn repeatedly to the ridges in his bald head that ripple and crease as he talks and moves.

"Oh yeah," he says, with a momentary note of interest. "Eddie Traynor's wee friend. The writer lady."

His eyes flick back to Myra who has become lost inside herself, eyes closed, shaking.

"Myra, why are you here?" he asks impatiently.

Myra opens her eyes. She looks completely grey, Danni thinks, save for the small, angry red crop of spots on her forehead and at the side of her mouth

"C'mon Pearson," she wheedles.

The Wasp says nothing but holds out a hand to her. She unzips an inside pocket in her jacket and hands him a small pile of ten pound notes. He doesn't even count it but simply keeps his hand held out towards her and beckons with an imperious finger. Myra opens her mouth as if to speak but closes it again silently. She fumbles in a small outer pocket, pulling out a couple of crumpled notes.

He counts it out, hands her some back, and in one seamless movement folds the rest in two and slips it in a pocket.

"Please, Pearson."

"Where's Stella?" the Wasp asks, ignoring her pleas.

Myra's face crumples into agonised petulance.

"She's up the other end of the drag. Near the pub."

Her arms are wrapped right round herself, like she's trying to still her body.

"Please Pearson."

The Wasp's mouth twists in disgust as he looks at her.

"You're becoming a liability, Myra," he says, opening a drawer beside him. He throws a small sealed plastic bag onto the desk. Myra's whole body changes in an instant. It's no longer bent in supplication, but greedy, atavistic. She swoops on the bag and heads for the door, saying nothing.

"Myra."

"Yeah."

"Another hour."

"But …"

"Another hour."

Myra closes the door forcefully.

"Take a seat," says the Wasp, as if the interlude with Myra had never happened and he and Danni had only just met. In the corner, Coyle yawns lazily and slides further into his seat.

"I had a message about you," says the Wasp. "You're writing about our Troubles."

There's an edge of sarcasm to his voice that Danni doesn't know how to respond to.

"Yes."

"And what makes you think you know enough about it?"

"I'm a writer. It's my job to find out."

"A journalist?"

"Not exactly. Though I am writing this for a newspaper."

"And you want to talk to someone who was an active member in the 1980s."

"Someone who was involved in the Glasgow bomb."

"Why so specific?"

She shrugs but her heart thumps.

"Because I'm a Scottish writer. And it's embedded in the experience of the people who'll read what I write."

"Don't your Scottish audience care about the poor bastards further south in London and Manchester and Birmingham – Warrington even?"

He smiles suddenly, the ripples running up under his scalp like ripples of sand marked by the flow of the tide. He's playing with her. She can feel Coyle's presence at her back. She want to turn round but keeps her head fixed on Pearson. Her back prickles.

"Of course they care," she says. "but they know about the Glasgow bomb because many of them were around then."

Pearson stares at her, then laughs lightly.

"I tell you something," he says. "I don't know about your readers but I think *you* care about the Glasgow bomb." He turns to Coyle.

"I think we can help the lady, don't you Coyle?" he says. Danni feels intimidated by the words. She half turns to Coyle, who is sprawled in the seat but opens one eye lazily.

"The Fox," says the Wasp. "Johnny. He's your man. He's very interested in the Glasgow bomb too." He looks at Danni appraisingly but without interest. "She's just Johnny's type, I'd say," he tells Coyle, like she isn't there.

By the time Danni turns back, the Wasp is writing an address on a piece of paper.

"Who is he?"

"Like you said. It's your job to find out. Ask him lots of questions, Danni. He'll enjoy that. "He's proud of his work, is Johnny."

"He was definitely involved in the Glasgow bomb?"

"The key man on the day."

The fabric of her top is actually pulsating slightly with the thump of her heart now.

"The one who planted it?"

He glances up, alerted by something in her voice.

"Yeah."

She lets her eyes drop.

"The thing is," he says, sitting back. "What do I get in return for helping you Danni?"

She looks at him uncertainly.

"The Fox has only been back in Ireland a few months. I'd like you to take him a wee message. Do you think you can do that, Danni? Tell him that I'd like to see him, that I'd like him to call by some time. I was going to drop by but maybe it will be better if you give him some warning. Let him know that we know where he is, and that all his many friends are thinking of him."

Jesus. What is she getting mixed up in? Danni takes the scrap of paper, realising with relief that she is being dismissed. She nods curtly.

One landing down, she stops long enough to call a taxi on her mobile, fingers trembling. Outside, Myra is sitting on the bottom step. She has stopped shaking. Danni sees something in her hand, and as she draw level, realises it's a chocolate bar. Myra half turns, leaning herself against the railing next to the step.

"He's a bastard, him," she says, taking a bite out of the bar.

"How long have you worked for him?"

"A year."

"Know anything about him?"

Myra shrugs. He keeps things pretty tight."

Her eyes are flickering.

"Is he married?"

"Yeah, married to …"

She stops talking. The light from a streetlamp is casting a half glow over her face. Danni peers into the semi darkness at her. Her hand is half way to her face and a thin, fragile ribbon of toffee stretches precariously from mouth to hand.

"Myra?"

Myra's eyes open and she looks vacantly at Danni.

"Myra?"

"Sorry," she mumbles. She begins to chew the bite in her mouth but her eyes droop again and she drifts towards sleep.

"I need to go," says Danni gently, bending towards her and touching her arm.

"The Lady Margaret," says Myra.

"What?"

71

"His wife," she says, jerking her head backwards towards the building. "The lady Margaret we call her. None of us have ever met her. He keeps all that well separate. We don't know where he lives or anything. He's dead private."

"Have you ever heard of a guy called the Fox?"

Myra shakes her head.

Danni moves from the steps onto the street and pushes her bag onto her shoulder.

"Nice to meet you, Myra."

Myra watches her through half closed eyes, then seems suddenly alert, jerking into life.

"I'll walk you to the corner," she says.

"Are you going home?"

"You heard the bastard. I'm not allowed."

"What would he do if you didn't do what he said?"

"Break me in fucking bits. But I'm going to get away from him soon."

Danni's taxi is waiting on the corner. She turns back before getting in.

"Myra, who is that guy Coyle?"

"Number one boy. They're always together. He's ehm … …" she leans against a lamppost and her eyes are drifting again, struggling to meet Danni's. In a moment, she looks up. "What …?" she says.

"What were we …?"

"Coyle …" Danni prods.

"Yeah, Coyle. Pretty boy. He's supposed to be part of Pearson's security team. She fishes for her cigarette pack in her pocket. "I don't care how macho Pearson is, I'm waiting for him to climb out of the closet." She laughs and flicks another of Danni's book of matches. "But Coyle's waiting harder."

Danni climbs into the taxi and as it takes off, sees Myra standing smoking under the street light, her eyes half closed. The Vauxhall car has returned, crawls slowly by her. As the taxi turns a corner, Danni is thrown sideways, and she turns her head forwards again, back into the darkness of the cab.

CHAPTER TEN

The outer door of the flat is flaked with peeling blue paint, the colour like cheap, chipped nail polish on a dirty nail beneath. A dingy white net curtain hangs over the glass. She's feeling sick looking at that door, at the ordinariness of it. Because this isn't ordinary. It's ... it's volcanic ... and it feels like nothing should be ordinary ever again. The floor of the close is unswept, dirty, the windows looking out from the stair landing smeared with grime. The walls are painted the same sickly green as the walls in the hospital where her mother died.

There is a bell to the right of the door. She can hardly breathe as she lifts her finger towards it. The main man, the Wasp had said. The one who planted it. Press the button. Press the button. But still her finger hovers. Something tells her if she does, nothing will ever be the same again. If she doesn't press the button, she can walk away, go back home, pretend she was never here. But if she does, that's it. Forever.

Her hand is shaking. She presses the button. Nothing happens. Damn it. Is the bell working? Did it ring inside the flat? She waits, then lifts her finger again, listening intently for any sound. She hears nothing and in frustration, stabs her finger on the button and keeps it pressed.

She sees a shadow in the hall, the slight movement of the net curtain but somehow she cannot lift her finger from that bell. It screams in her name. The door opens cautiously. She sees the eyes first, piercing blue eyes in a pale, angular face. Inside their blueness, she sees Angelo reflected and the hatred that twists in her is like the sharp, raw pain of salt on a mouth ulcer. The man's hair is long and dark, curling below his collar, sweeping back from his face in a way that creates a kind of drama, like opening curtains on a stage. He is not a handsome man, exactly, but he has an elongated elegance; high cheek bones, broad, lean shoulders, long tapering fingers.

"I heard you the first time," he says quietly.

His eyes are intent, unblinking.

"Did you?"

She cannot keep the animosity out of her voice. That makes him curious, she can see.

He leans one hand on the door frame.

"What do you want?"

"The Wasp gave me your name."

She watches his eyes flicker shut momentarily.

"Sweet Jesus," he mutters in exasperation, his jaw clenched tight. "Whatever it is, I can't help you."

"My name is …" She begins, but he cuts her off.

"I don't want to know your name," he says dismissively, and he begins to close the door. "I'm sorry, I can't help …"

But she sees it coming, her dismissal, jams her foot in the door, startling him. He looks down at her foot and then up at her face.

"I just want to talk to you," she says.

"If Pearson sent you, I don't want to talk to you …"

"Just for a few minutes."

"Take your foot out of the doorway," he says. It is not menace in his voice exactly, but she senses his force. She hesitates but draws back.

"What are you here for?" He looks at her coldly.

"I just want a word. I'm a writer and I …"

"No," he says, shaking his head quickly, and this time he moves so fast the door slams in her face.

She feels anger shooting up inside her, spraying like a fountain. How dare he dismiss her! He's taken everything from her this man, everything. She's the one who will do the dismissing here. When she's finished and not before. She bangs her closed fist on the dingy pane above the door and rattles the letterbox.

"I want to talk to you!" she yells.

She puts her finger back on the bell and keeps pressing. In a minute, she hears the sound of music thumping back at her through the door, the raucous beat of the Rolling Stones and she knows, however much noise she makes, he isn't coming back.

She comes back in the morning, early. She can't sleep anyway. There's nowhere that feels safe. An hour later, he opens the door, steps over her and leaves. He carries books and folders; looks like he won't be back for some time she thinks, dispirited. She is determined to be here when he returns.

Early evening. Outside, the light is fading. Danni sits, her back to the wall, arms folded, feet stretched out across his mat. Tiny flakes of blue paint from the door have rained onto her legs. Footsteps. Light, steady. Her heart thumps. He rounds the corner from the stairs, stopping short when he sees her. He has a newspaper, tightly rolled in his hand as well as his books. She looks up at him, her eyes questioning.

He has black jeans on and a grey sweater that hangs long and loose on his angular frame. A black scarf is tied round his neck. She looks at his feet. Black boots. A cheap version of the Italian leather boots Marco used to wear. He steps over her and puts his key in the lock, pushes the door open and closes it without turning back to her. She doesn't move. Marco wore clothes well, she thought. Didn't he? Didn't he just. Her bones are aching from sitting and she feels stiff with cold now.

Three hours later, the door opens.

"Have you been there all day?"

She's been there so long she can't be bothered answering, does not look up. He leans against the doorframe, his head resting on his arm. He is beginning to feel uneasy. She can tell she troubles him.

"You can't sit there all night."

She's almost lost the sense of why she's there. Her eyes stray down to his feet. Those boots. So strange. So inconsequential. Yet they've conjured up Marco in a way he hasn't been conjured for … oh, at least a couple of years. She used to think about him all the time. She was frightened to let go of him because memory was all there was. The last connection. But in the end, loss becomes a burden you scarcely even notice any more. You absorb it until it's no longer an appendage but simply part of you. Part of your weight. A second skin.

"You can't sit there all night."

"You said that."

He looks at her with serious blue eyes. They don't dart over her; they simply look and absorb. She has the feeling that she will come to know that look. There is something almost familiar about it already.

"Go home."

"I'm a long way from home."

She leans her head back against the wall.

"What do you want?" he asks curiously. His brown hair is beginning to fall forward onto his forehead.

"To talk to you."

"Why me?"

"The Wasp sent me."

"Is he still using that fucking stupid name?"

His voice is a whiplash of irritation and she glances up in surprise.

He leans on the door.

"How do you know him? Are you one of his girls?"

"One of his girls?"

He shakes his head.

"No, of course not. No matter. I'd like you to go now."

"He says you are called the Fox."

"Playground names. He needs to grow up."

"Is the Fox an operational name?"

Her voice is tight with the effort of trying to keep the hatred out of it. He senses it, she can tell. Maybe not the hatred but the effort, the importance of this to her. He stares at her and for the first time she notices one left eye has a small tiger stain in the blueness. Once it's noticed, she can't *not* see it, can't imagine how it took so long to strike her.

"Well?" she says. "Is it an operational name."

"My name is Johnny," he says quietly, and he closes the door softly.

She continues sitting, staring into the stairwell. She hears voices outside, kids voices. A banged door, running feet, laughter. Footsteps on the stair and three children come running round the corner, almost falling slap bang into her outstretched legs. They stop, stare, go into single file to pass, and then she sees them look at one another and burst into fits of giggles. The feet run again up to the next landing, whispered voices. A banged door above, and then silence.

An hour later, his door opens again.

"Go home."

"I can't."

"I'm not talking to a newspaper."

"I'm not a newspaper."

"What do you want to talk about?"

"Not here."

He hesitates but then stands back, opening his door wider. It takes her a moment to realise he's letting her in. She tries to move but her legs have seized and she moves awkwardly.

"You've got five minutes," he says.

He holds out a hand to help her up, a thin, almost skeletal white hand that shows his veins like a network of arteries on a thin, autumn leaf. The hand of a murderer she thinks, with a mixture of fascination and revulsion. She does not take it. She cannot bear the intimacy of touching him. His hand drops back to his side.

Inside, the flat is clean but sparse and dreary. A dark carpet and black leather sofa and chair, light woodchip walls and a couple of nondescript cream cushions. In the corner, a small television set that is still switched on. The news. The biggest thing in the room is a bookcase spread along one wall, crammed floor to ceiling with books and files and papers. There is not an inch to spare but she gets the feeling everything is in its place. Murderous order.

He says nothing but holds out a hand to the sofa to indicate she should sit. But she doesn't want to touch anything in here. She doesn't want to sit in his seat, or have her shoes tread his carpet. She doesn't want to know where that landscape on his wall is. She doesn't want to know the name of the novel that is spread open on the arm of his chair. She wants to see him but she doesn't want to know him.

He shrugs, sits down in the chair, and watches her. She sees now, much more clearly than when he was standing, that he is tall. There is so much of him to settle into the chair. He unfolds himself into it, long, lean lines.

She thinks that in her case, 'why' is the most redundant, useless word in the world. What does it matter, 'why'? There is no 'why' that makes sense. No explanation that ameliorates what happened. It's not like he can explain and then she'll say, "Oh right. Okay then. That's fine. I'll be off home." But when she asks herself why she is sitting here in his sitting room, instead of in a police cell for throwing acid in his face when he opened the door, she cannot explain it in any terms other than the curiosity of why. Why this man was involved. Why he is what he is. Why he did what he did.

Besides, she has to make sure he is who she thinks he is. She has to be sure. And there is something about cold, not hot, revenge that seems right. She wants him to suffer. To rot. She doesn't want it all over in a few minutes. She wants to take her time and see him sweat. She has the feeling that she is like a bomb herself. She wants to plant herself firmly in his life and explode in his face when he least expects it, like his bomb exploded in hers.

He is looking at her calmly but expectantly. He tilts his head to one side.

"You said you wanted to talk to me."

"Yes."

"You haven't said anything."

"I told you I'm a writer."

"And? What's that to me? What do you want to write about?"

"I want to write about terrorism."

"Terrorism is your word, not mine."

"I want to write about what has happened to the aspirations of those involved in the IRA bombing campaigns of the seventies and eighties in the light of the 1998 peace agreement. And what they feels now about the continuation of violence by the dissidents ..." A hot dryness in the back of her throat catches her, makes her voice stumble as if she's nervous. She *is* nervous. "Whether they feel," she repeats, "that they have achieved what they set out to achieve."

Johnny catches the hair that is tumbling onto his forehead with one hand and sweeps it back.

"I don't want to be interviewed."

"Let's just talk then. And I don't need to use your name."

"You don't know my name."

"Johnny."

He half smiles, grimly. "There are a lot of Johnnys in Ireland."

"So it wouldn't matter."

"You want me to tell you about myself?"

"Yes."

He shakes his head. "I can't do that."

"Why not?"

"I just ... just ... can't. I'm a private person."

"You could help others understand what's going on here."

"I doubt it."

"Nobody will know it's you."

"You will."

"Does that matter?"

"Yes."

"Why?"

"Because," he says, and the tiger spot in his eye glows warm and brown in the slant of light thrown from a standing lamp, "I would have to trust you."

Johnny watches her go from behind the curtain, sees her pass through the pool of light of the street lamp. He feels confused. He does not know why he let her in. There was

81

something about her, sitting with her legs stretched out like the picture of Polly Flinders in his childhood nursery rhyme book. The taxi she called is waiting across the street. She does not look up to the window as she gets in. Even from up here, he can hear the bang of the taxi door. The trundle of the taxi as it shoogles away.

Something about her. Such a tiny figure, like a child almost, yet very feminine. The short, elfin hair and pale, porcelain skin. The enormous clarity of her light brown eyes under the precise, elegant arch of dark brows. She drew him in, he can see that now she's gone. Maybe it was because he sensed something missing in her, a kind of handicap that was more subtle than his own slight limp but just as real. It moved something in him. He recognised it, reached out to it.

And if he's honest there was a curiosity about her connection with Sean Pearson. The Wasp, he thinks disdainfully. Pearson was always in his own ridiculous underworld. Whatever the rest of them were fighting for, Pearson was fighting for something else. Himself mainly. There is no surprise that Pearson knows he's back in Belfast, that he knows where to find him; he has always made it his business to know those things. He has been half expecting him to get in touch, knew he would still want to pull his strings …

Danni, she said her name was. But then, maybe you couldn't believe everything she said. He tries to remember the last time someone had been in this room, a woman anyway. When he had to be with people, when he wanted to be with a woman, he made sure he went out into their world. He didn't bring them into his. Anyway, it was a long time since … a long time. Women changed things. Wanted to see inside you. Eventually they needed a bit of you he couldn't give. It was simpler not to go there.

He adjusts the curtains back into place. She's gone now

but he thinks he can still smell her perfume in the room. Perhaps he imagines it, is simply conjuring up the memory of it. He sniffs tentatively at the air, looks around as if there will be some concrete difference to spot.

He has agreed to meet her again.

He needs to know what she wants, he explains to himself. He needs to know what Pearson wants. But that is not all of it. He looks down into the street, into the empty pool of light where she had so recently stood.

CHAPTER ELEVEN

Danni lies on the hotel bed, trembling still though she is not cold. It is strange, the effect of being with that man, that stranger. The way he made Marco more real than he had been for years, when she hadn't even been aware of him becoming *un*real. Strange how Marco has come to life, how he walks and talks inside her consciousness. Ironic that meeting the man who took Marco's life resurrects him, breathes him into being again.

She was inside Marco's murderer's house. Actually inside his house. She starts suddenly, sitting up. Did she lock the hotel room door when she came back? She did. She knows she did but she gets up anyway. Locked. She unlocks it, then locks it again to make sure it is properly done. There is nowhere safe.

She longs for safety, she thinks, lying back down on the bed. The feeling Marco used to provoke inside her. Almost from the first moment. Her eyes close, thoughts drifting. Marco and Roberto, two brothers in black shirts, serving in the deli owned by their parents. The hiss of frothing milk, and the sound of shoes on a polished wooden floor, and the gleam of glass cabinets stuffed with foods she never sees except in here: dark black olives floating in brine like polished gemstones, the ruby red of plum tomatoes flown in from the Naples market, their shiny skin dulled with a thin veneer of dust. The room is scent rich, a cacophony of smells, of rich dark coffee, and fresh, garlic stuffed mortadella, and hand baked crisp almond biscuits.

She's sixteen. Saturday afternoon and the brothers are sparring verbally when she comes in, the Glaswegian accents at odds with their dark Italian looks.

"On yer bike, Roberto," the younger one is saying. "Ahm no daein' it again for you. It was the same last Saturday 'n all."

They turn and see Danni and the way Roberto looks at her makes her turn her eyes to the glass cabinet. When she looks up again they are both watching her.

"Piece of strawberry cheesecake please," she says.

"Bet it's not for you with a figure like that," grins Roberto, leaning on the glass counter.

"Aw, away and don't embarrass yourself Roberto," Marco says impatiently, pushing him out the way. "Your chat up lines are just pish." He holds a hand up to Danni. "Sorry for the language," he says, and she tries not to laugh.

He reaches into the cabinet, lifts out a plate of thick creamy cheesecake and takes a knife from a plastic ice cream carton of water. The cake is for her mother's birthday. She can't afford a whole fancy cake but cheesecake's her mother's favourite anyway. Marco cuts enough for two slices and puts it into a box, ties it with curling ribbon and charges her for one. She smiles.

"Thanks," she says, and she walks to the door, aware of Marco's eyes on her back. Through the shop window she sees Roberto flicking him with a tea towel.

Two weeks later at a party she's pinned against a wall by a wolfish looking boy who's had too many beers. She's desperate to escape. The boy is talking drunkenly and moving ever closer and then she sees the boy from the deli, Marco, and a minute later his arm is round her waist, guiding her gently away like she's little Red Riding Hood, and he's saying to the wolf, you don't mind me stealing my girlfriend away for a dance do you? I've been neglecting her.

The boy is looking confused but is too befuddled with drink to work it out. And she's saying, girlfriend? What was that about? He says, you're not going to make me a liar are you? I'm a good Catholic boy. She'd laughed then, and all these years later she can feel the ghost of that smile on her lips while this man Johnny's voice is ringing somewhere in the distance.

They were so young. She remembers Marco one Friday night, fuelled by a few illicit beers. They had been for a day out, were walking back for the last train when he jumped up on the narrow edge of a high bridge that crossed fast flowing water, swollen with heavy rain, beneath. The edges of it had crumbled away and there could only have been a solid width of about two inches on which to stand.

"Get down," she'd said at first, not believing he would really walk the span of the bridge with a drink in him, but he kept going, laughing and singing at the top of his voice.

"I love Danni," he shouted into a velvet night sky.

"Marco don't be an idiot," she had hissed, walking on the road side, but he laughed still and when he reached the middle she didn't dare distract him by saying anything at all but stood rooted to the spot watching him wobble. Oh my God, she whispered to herself, hands flying to her mouth. His hands were outstretched and in the semi darkness she saw the white froth of the water, and saw his hands wave wildly, and his body bend towards the water side before rectifying his balance and continuing with a suppressed giggle.

He jumped off at the other end, laughing and hooting triumphantly. He had grabbed a lamp post then and whirled round with his head bent back to the sky shouting, "I AM INNNNN … VINCCCC … IBLLLLLLE," exultantly and deafeningly. And she had run to him then, bashing her handbag off his body as he spun, and shouting, "You bloody idiot, Marco! You could have drowned!"

Marco had caught her hands then and laughed, and he said,

"Rubbish Dan! Can't you feel it? Tonight I feel like I am going to live forever." Then he'd pulled her to him and kissed her under the light, surprised to find the salty tracks of tears on her face.

Sleep evades her. She has gone beyond tiredness into a contradictory state where exhaustion and agitation co-exist. Being here in Ireland has given her a sense of purpose, of being alive again after years of simply existing. It feels like waking up and realising that you have no memory of ever having gone to sleep in the first place, that you simply slipped out of consciousness without agreeing to.

She turns over in bed, tries to pull Marco's face out of the darkness, then Angelo's. Keep them in mind, she thinks. Remember what it's about. Focus. She has found herself standing almost outside herself and asking what she's doing here, if she's really here to kill or just to explore the parameters of her unresolved grief. But there is no doubt that since she determined to come to Ireland she has felt Marco around her like a real physical presence. Something tangible, she thinks, not mystical not spiritual. None of that stuff. She has turned sometimes, thinking there is someone behind her, only to find an empty space.

CHAPTER TWELVE

His flat is filled with the smell of strong black coffee. For the first time in years Johnny is aware of breakfasting alone. His tastes are simple, meagre even. Coffee, a single slice of toast scraped with butter. Perhaps, he thinks this morning – and it is a surprise to him that he is even noticing – his tastes have become too Spartan. Why does he never, just for a change, replace the toast with, say, a croissant, flaking buttery pastry with seeded raspberry jam? A pain au raisin at the weekend? But he does not like indulgence.

A thin October sunshine trickles through a browning canopy of trees as he walks for the bus. Sitting on the upper deck he does a double take when a petite figure with short dark hair emerges from a baker's shop near the university. For a moment he thinks it's her, Danni. He sees her face several times that day, suddenly whirling out of the pages of a textbook towards him when he thinks about her in the library. Coming into focus out of a crowd of students at lunchtime.

He tells himself that of course he understands why this is. When you regulate a life as much as he has regulated his, anything that impinges on your world, on your reality, will take on a greater significance for you than for the ordinary person. A woman who turns up unexpectedly at his door, for reasons he does not understand, and who is attached in some way to the bloody entrails of his past ... well it is not surprising that she should unsettle him. As he gets older, he tries to understand: himself, other people, the world ... Understanding takes away fear. When he decided to study properly for the first time in his life, it was natural for him to choose psychology and literature.

The air is cold outside but the sun surprisingly hot through the glass. Today he is reading about the role of the id, the ego and the superego in Freudian theories of personality. 'The id,' he writes in his notebook, 'is contained almost wholly within the unconscious mind. It consists of man's instinctive drives and natural tendencies. It is amoral, infantile, non-rational and demanding immediate satisfaction ... ' His pen drifts to the margin, draws an outline of a watching eye. He lifts his head, glancing through the library window to a world that today, seems somehow to be in sharper definition.

He agreed to meet her but not here. The room has become his own again after her intrusion, self-contained, a world apart. It smells of old wood and withering apples, warmed in a glass bowl by shafts of trapped, afternoon sunlight. If it feels emptier than last night, it also feels calmer. He wears the silence like a comforting garment, wriggling into its protectiveness with a measure of relief.

He would come to her, he had said. At the bar of her hotel. Her hesitation was only momentary. She had taken an envelope from her bag, torn a ragged piece from the flap and written the address. When she handed it to him, their fingers touched and instinctively she snatched her hand back quickly. He noticed that moment and tried to make sense of it, but could not. 8 p.m., she said.

He switches the television on while he makes some beans on toast. Local news. "The body of a brutally murdered prostitute has been found dumped in a metal bin and covered with rubbish in the city's red light district. The woman, who was strangled and had serious burns, is believed to have been dead for up to thirty-six hours. Police have not named the victim and are trying to trace relatives ..."

Johnny takes a block of cheese from the fridge and grates it on top of the beans. The newscaster has moved on. "A three week amnesty has been launched by police," he hears, "in a bid to reduce knife crime in the city ..." He takes his plate to the table, shifts the bowl of apples from his line of vision so that he can see the television, and eats slowly, staring at a screen that he is no longer watching.

He chews slowly, thoughtfully. She wanted to understand what had taken young men into the Republican movement, she had said. He wonders if he should take the copy he has of his grandmother's testimony. Mary Seonaid's words could say everything more eloquently than he ever could. But would Danni understand the threads of history that ran through those words, the threads that tied him to Michael Connerty and the legacy of Kilmainham? Would she understand that Republicanism was not just his choice but his heritage?

CHAPTER THIRTEEN

The hotel bar is empty save for an elderly couple who sit with drinks in silence. The man's blue shirt collar peeps out from a round necked patterned jumper, an assortment of swirling navy and blues. He has the silver shadow of evening growth on his face and he folds his arms over a domed stomach, gazing into the middle distance as if actually alone. The woman has a woollen dress, and neat, stubby heels, and a cherub's bow of pink lipstick, like pressed sweetpeas, painted on her mouth.

As she waits in a private booth against the wall of the bar, Danni eyes are drawn repeatedly back to them in a mixture of pity and horror. Perhaps after so many years together you simply run out of conversation. Is it that you know every thought, every opinion, before it's spoken? Or just that you are too bored to care any more? Sometimes she looks at the elderly and tries to imagine her and Marco if they had been allowed to grow old together. But she never can. It's like trying to imagine purple grass or red sky; it is simply not part of the natural order. Like trying to imagine Marilyn Monroe with a pension book.

He may not come, she thinks. Perhaps it would be a relief. She hears the music from a function suite drifting into the bar, zooming in and out of focus as the doors swing open and closed, the faraway jollity of other people's happiness. Then suddenly he's there, standing in the bar, hair slicked back with rain, lost somehow, looking for her in the empty space. And she sees in that moment that he could put himself in the centre of a crowd and be alone, that he does not belong here, that perhaps there is nowhere in the world that he does belong. Despite everything, for a fleeting moment she feels strangely moved by the thought.

"I thought you might not come," she says awkwardly.

"Why would you think that?" He frowns. "I said ..."

"Yes, yes I know, but ..."

Their silence is different from the old couple's. Taut, rather than slack, full of too much to say rather than too little.

"You're wet," she says.

He shrugs, lifts a hand up tentatively to his hair, running the water off the ends of damp curls with his fingers. She feels twisted inside watching him, warped with hatred, convulsed with the effort of concealing it. She keeps focused on his eyes, thinks the tiger skin patch that gnaws the edge of his pupil has grown bigger. She imagines it taking over the eye completely, a canker, a sign of his internal sickness seeking physical manifestation.

She cannot any longer think where to begin.

"What do you want to know?" he asks quietly.

"Who you are."

"I told you my name's Johnny."

"The Fox?"

"That's Pearson's name," he says impatiently.

"Are you from Belfast?"

"My family is originally from Dublin but my grandmother moved ... well she moved out to the country ..." He pauses. "And then my mother came here when she married."

"Why?"

"Why did my mother …?"

"No, your grandmother."

"She was on her own with her child. Her husband was … well it's a long story but … her husband was dead and she needed to get away from Dublin."

"Needed to?"

"Needed … wanted …"

Perhaps he should give her Mary Seonaid's pages now.

A waiter appears at their side.

"Guinness, please," says Johnny. "Pint." He looks questioningly at her.

She looks up at the young waiter, addresses him directly rather than Johnny. He will never speak for her. He will buy her nothing.

"Ginger beer and lime, please."

"I don't know the best way to explain," he says, "the best way to help you …"

He looks at her for a clarification that does not come.

"You said you wanted to know," he continues slowly. "What motivated the IRA cell I was part of."

She merely waits.

"You'll have heard of the Easter Rising in 1916?" he asks.

"Yeah."

She digs her nails into the palm of her hands. She simply cannot bear it if he launches into some bloody history lesson. Angelo, Marco … they weren't a history lesson. They were hers. They were the first things in her life that felt like hers. Apart from her mother, of course.

"My grandfather was shot in Kilmainham jail for his part in it," Johnny is saying, and finally she flicks her eyes up to his face.

"Kilmainham?"

"In Dublin."

She knows nothing of any shootings in Dublin jails. She suspects he is lying.

"That's why my grandmother left Dublin."

"And that's why you joined the IRA," she says, with such unguarded sarcasm that he must surely hear it. Internally, she tries to pull back. She has promised herself discipline.

"There were a lot of reasons for that," he says, "and yeah, maybe that was one of them."

Maybe? There is no maybe about it.

"We know their dream; enough to know they dreamed and are dead," he says softly.

"What?"

"Yeats."

The waiter who returns with their drinks seems conscious of the strain, disappears quickly when he puts the glasses down. Johnny takes a sip, shuts down part of his brain. Simply barricades it. He sees her resistance, is in no hurry to continue. After all, he gave up long ago trying to explain his views. Why is he even thinking about trying with a stranger?

Sometimes it is impossible to rationalise even to himself the simmering stew inside him. How can he describe the mysterious combination of dreamy aspiration and calculating cruelty, the tumbling, conflicting shadows of pain and guilt and determination, and sadness and pride, and principle and amoral obsession, and clarity and confusion, and terrible, terrible black regret. What explanation is there?

He has come here for the wrong reasons, he sees that. Fool that he is. She has drawn him in a way that for so many years he had left behind. A purely feminine way, though God knows he gave up on women – on people really – a long time ago. Still, those instincts, they can catch you up, take you by surprise. Her eyes have the amber tones of malt whisky, he thinks, swirling amber in a sea of peaty brown. But whatever in those eyes pulled him here was an illusion. There can be no resolution to this conversation, no clarity of understanding between them. Already he is contemplating leaving.

He senses her hostility and feels his own.

"It's hard to understand the history of another people when you're not part of it," he continues, his voice tipped with steel, "what they think and what they feel and what they aspire to. You can't know."

"And what did *you* aspire to?"

"What everyone else did who joined." Not everyone, he thinks. Not Pearson. "A free and united Ireland. An Ireland that belonged to its own people and was at ease with itself, and lived in peace."

"Peace!"

Her voice is loud, ricocheting round the room like a bullet. The silent, elderly couple look over. Danni sees the man finally speak, saying something to the woman and glancing over.

"What would you know about peace?" she says, and while she has lowered her voice, the heat is pouring out of her like sweat.

Johnny puts down his glass and pushes back his chair as if about to leave.

"Sometimes, Danni," he says quietly, "you have to fight for peace. That's the irony of life and of human nature. But I don't really think there's any point to this. You're not here to find out anything." He stands up. "You've made up your mind already – so write what you like."

CHAPTER FOURTEEN

Damn it. She's thrown it already. Discipline. Discipline.

"Okay, okay, okay," she says, holding up her hands.

She tries to force her lips into a smile.

"Sorry ... I'm just trying to understand ... Stay for a bit. It's like you say ... it's hard when you're not from here."

He hesitates and he doesn't know why.

"Please," she says, "sit down."

Her eyes are so familiar.

They sit in silence. Danni runs her finger up the side of her glass, catching a drip, licks her finger.

"How did you meet Pearson?" she asks.

"We grew up together, went to school together."

"Why is it that whenever you talk about him you do that?

"Do what?

"Clench the muscles in your cheek."

He shrugs.

"Are you friends?"

"No. I don't think you could call us friends."

"But you were?"

"A long time ago. But Pearson ..."

"What?"

"Nothing."

Across the room, the older couple are leaving, the man walking ahead, the woman following with her brown, gold clasped handbag hanging over her arm. Danni's eyes are drawn to her, watching her strange, companionable isolation. Johnny follows her eyes.

"We had this group at school," he says. "Pearson was in charge." A whisper of a smile flits across his mouth, rippling across his cheek and blowing instantly away into solemnity. "We called it Rebel Sons of Ireland, because we were a bit grand, like." He looks at her and she forces her mouth to twist into a semblance of a smile but her eyes are cold.

"Sounds a bit unlikely. I can't imagine being that politically aware at school."

"You didn't grow up in Belfast."

He says it mildly enough but she takes it as another rebuke that she doesn't know what she's talking about.

"And you didn't go to school with Pearson," he continues. "You know, most kids threw stones at the army. That was as far as their politics went. But Pearson saw politics as ... well as an opportunity I suppose."

"An opportunity for what?"

"To make money. And to legitimise what he was."

She waits for him to explain but he doesn't.

"And that was?" she prompts. Why is he making her dig for everything?

"A cruel, ruthless bastard."

He looks her straight in the eye and she blinks, unnerved.

"He was bright, you know?" he continues. "He would gather us all together and talk about how we needed to fight for Ireland, fight till we bled and give till we dropped. It was a lot of shite but he had a way with words. It took us years to understand he didn't mean a word of it."

"He's not to be trusted?"

He laughs.

"Pearson? I wouldn't advise it, no." He looks at her curiously.

"What's your connection with him?"

"Don't have one. A journalist friend put me in touch with him."

"So you *are* a journalist."

"No, I write books mainly. I am writing this for a newspaper but maybe it will become a book." She won't be writing any more books if she kills him, she thinks. Or maybe that's all she'd do if she ended up in prison? God, no. She'd rather kill herself too.

"Anyway, you were saying … Rebel Boys of Ireland or whatever it was you were called …"

"Half the time we didn't know what Pearson was talking about but he stirred you sometimes you know? … The sound of the words, the feeling in the room. One time he read this extract from Yeats' poem, Easter Rising 1916." He takes a sip from his glass.

"Everyone heard about it. Next time, there were twice as many at the meeting. Most of those who crammed through the door didn't have a clue what it was all about but they all knew something was going off with Pearson and they didn't want to miss it. Pearson talked a lot about blood and guts and that appealed to teenage boys as well. Who doesn't want to be a rebel son when they're sixteen?"

She watches him, his face like a movie screen, emotions dancing across and evaporating into nothing.

"It was Pearson's way of making money, of course. Everyone had to give him money every week and Pearson said it was for the armed struggle of Ireland. Was it hell. But those who paid were offered protection and those who didn't, weren't. And that, of course, was the whole point. It was a racket that he has continued ever since."

"What if you couldn't afford to pay him?"

"Then you were in trouble, so you were. Not me, so much. I was part of his inner group. But there was this kid … Joseph. His dad was dead, his mum was on her own. He never had any money. He was terrified of Pearson and my God Pearson loved it, the power of that. He always sniffed weakness. He went looking for Joseph one Friday afternoon, took three of us with him. I tried to tell him …" He shakes his head. "Joseph was round the back of the school, hiding, praying for the bell to go, poor bastard … The look on his face when he saw us … Jesus."

"What happened?"

"He told Joseph he had to meet us after school. There was an area of woodland that bordered on the cemetery near the school and he told him he had better be there or he'd get hold of him and rip him apart. Then he passed the word round the boys that everyone was to be there."

"Did he go, this kid?"

"He knew it would be worse if he didn't."

"What did Pearson do?"

Johnny exhales, raising his eyes to the ceiling.

"Ritual humiliation. Pearson's speciality. Asked the kid for his money in front of everyone and of course he didn't have any. Pearson said he didn't think he was committed to the struggle for Ireland and he would have to pay some other way. He got hold of this huge branch thing and said maybe he should lash him and then he made him take his shirt and jumper off. He was skinny, Joseph, and just white as a sheet by this point. He stood there shivering while Pearson toyed with him."

And what did you do? She thinks. But she is frustrated. She does not want to talk about this. She wants to talk about Glasgow and does not know how to.

"Then Pearson told him he'd better take his trousers off," Johnny continues. "The whole place was in uproar when he got down to his underpants, all this whistling and laughing and cheering. And then Pearson says, 'take them off', pointing to the underpants. A couple of us tried to tell him he was going too far but he wouldn't listen. So Joseph ends up naked." He shakes his head. "Shivering and crying he was, with Pearson watching."

"You all just watched?" she says. "You didn't stop him?"

His eyes catch hers and challenge them.

"We were just kids. Don't you remember what it was like to try and go against the group? You didn't. Part of you was ashamed, but the biggest part of you was just glad it wasn't you at the centre of it. And if you spoke out, you knew it would be you next."

She wants to dismiss him as a coward but she's knows it's true.

"I told Pearson afterwards, though, that if he ever stripped anyone again, I would tell the others it was because he was a bent bastard and he got his kicks from it."

"And did he?"

He looks shrewdly at her.

"Yeah, I think he did. Pearson mixes everything up with the kick of violence. But that day was the first time he saw me as a threat. He was furious, went for me physically when I said it, but he was smaller than me. That's why he developed other techniques over the years. Anyway, he didn't strip anyone again."

"You know Coyle?"

His eyebrows raise in question and he shakes his head.

"Young guy … thin … pretty … but vicious-looking somehow …"

Johnny's snort of laughter is short and unamused.

"Sounds like Pearson's type."

"You know what business he's in now?"

He nods. "Oh I know all right. Yes. I know."

She senses a bitterness in his knowledge that she doesn't yet understand.

"He said to tell you he wanted to see you."

"Yes. You said last night."

"And …?"

"And what?"

The pause that follows grows into uneasy silence.

"When did you last see him?" she says eventually.

"Years ago."

"Is he still active?"

"I have no idea. Maybe. The IRA was a way of making money for Pearson and for indulging the sick violence that was inside him. He can do both inside his own empire now … prostitution … protection … But he'll still have his contacts and if there's money to be made, he'll take it." Johnny's tone is clipped. He taps impatiently on the table with the fingers of one hand. "He's using you as a connection to get back to me."

"Why does he need a connection?"

"Pearson never does anything directly. And we didn't part on the best of terms."

His eyes drop to the table and he says nothing for a minute.

"Why not? What happened?"

She's alert now, sniffs the importance of this.

"Steer clear of him, Danni." He uses her name as reinforcement, but the intimacy of it jars with her.

"What did he do?"

"Steer clear of him."

"I've got nothing to fear from him. I'm nothing to do with him."

Johnny shakes his head.

"When you've crossed his path once, you're in his life."

CHAPTER FIFTEEN

It is getting late. She is running out of time.

"Did you ever kill a man?"

Danni picks up her glass to cover the rush of emotion she feels asking the question. She has to be sure. The ice has made the glass cold and her fingers are chilled. But when Johnny looks at her, his expression freezes her all over.

Not like that, he thinks. Not in the way she means. Pearson was the one who liked killing. Though Johnny certainly knew anger. He didn't fully understand his own anger.

He closes his eyes and he can see them all at fifteen, the way they were, him and Pearson and the boys. A fug of smoke. Twenty Embassy and four one-litre bottles of cheap cider. Down the graveyard, sitting on the dead, curved bark of a lightening struck tree, the dry whitened remains resting on the sodden ground. He can remember it so clearly right now that he shifts slightly, as if he can feel the gnarled stump in his back still, the rough hewn edges where one of the branches has sheered off. Him and Pearson, Brendan Murphy and wee Seamy. Seamy got on his nerves that night, getting giggly and stupid after just half a bottle of cider and continually pushing him off the log of the tree.

"Quit it Seamy," Johnny had said, until the fourth time when the anger flared in him, seized the inside of his head and rattled it, and he grabbed hold of Seamy by the collar and banged him up against a nearby tree.

"Fucking quit it, I said," he hissed, and he looked into Seamy's surprised, watery grey eyes – eyes so vacant that Johnny felt his anger shrivel into nothing. He could feel the silence of the others at his back rather than hear it, a silence that prickled the base of his neck, and he let Seamy go abruptly, left him sprawling at the base of the tree.

Jesus, where did the anger come from, anger that flared from his belly and shot into his veins like an injection? It scared him sometimes, what he might be capable of. Other times it made him feel powerful, seeing the wariness in the eyes of others. He turned back and took a swig out of a bottle of cider to cover his confusion. Pearson was smoking a cigarette and watching him, his eyes lit with curiosity and relish. A ghost of a grin hovered on his lips and Johnny felt a rush of repulsion.

"Got something to show yous," said Pearson.

Johnny lit a cigarette and took an opened bottle of cider to a grave stone slightly away from the others. The grave had a marble slab set into the ground as well as a head stone and he sat on it, the stone cold and slightly damp through the seat of his trousers. He sat with his legs stretched out in front of him, the bottle held between his thighs. He could feel Pearson's irritation that he had removed himself, diminished his audience.

"Fuck, where d'you get that Pearson?" he heard Brendan ask. He glanced up. An air pistol. Pearson grinned.

"No questions, no lies," he said, with a self importance that made Johnny draw deeply on his cigarette. He leant his head back on the headstone. His backside was numb already. He shouldn't be sitting here, he thought. Sitting on the bones of the dead. He turned and looked at the stone. Padraig James Mulvaney. Aged 88. Y'd a good innings Padraig, he thought, swallowing a mouthful of cider. And I'm sorry if you think I'm not showing much respect for the dead. But maybe Ireland needs a bit more respect for the living and a bit less for the dead, he thought bitterly.

"Cheers man," he muttered.

"Bit o' huntin'," he heard Pearson say. "C'mon Johnny boy!"

The three of them headed off, Pearson flanked by Brendan and wee Seamy, Pearson glancing back at Johnny to see if he followed. Johnny sat perfectly still, light fading, barely watching them leave. His bones felt hard and sore and brittle against the cold stone but he couldn't be bothered moving. He was still there, like a statue, when they returned, shadows looming towards him, the three of them pushing and shoving and laughing over-loudly.

Johnny saw the rabbit corpse slung over Pearson's shoulder, then the body hurtled towards him, landing with a thud at his feet.

"Present for you Johnny!"

Johnny reached out a foot and kicked the body away instinctively, repulsed, a little fearful of the open eyed corpse.

Pearson grinned. He took a torch out of his pocket.

"Need to get used to blood in our business boys," he said, looking straight at Johnny. Johnny took a puff of cigarette and blew it upwards, ignoring him.

Pearson stretched the rabbit out on the grass and took a knife from his pocket. Johnny felt his eyes reluctantly pulled towards it.

"Here," Pearson said handing wee Seamy the torch. "Shine it on there."

The steel knife glinted, the point of it indenting the soft flesh, then he sliced cleanly with the tip of the blade up the length of the animal's abdomen. The muscles were thin, easy to cut through.

"Fuck!" said Brendan, screwing up his face as blood spurted over Pearson's hands.

"That's the liver," said Pearson, pulling the right and left segments of the organ out of the cranial end of the abdominal cavity. His face glowed cold in the torchlight, Johnny thought, lit with an unquenchable curiosity. Pearson looked at wee Seamy and Brendan, hard, intelligent eyes sharpening into focus.

"Put your hand in there," Pearson said to wee Seamy. Brendan's face was still twisted into a grimace and he looked at wee Seamy who burst into an explosion of nervous laughter.

"Aw Jesus no ..." he said, half laughing, half horrified, jostling into Brendan to move back.

Pearson looked at him.

"Put your hand in there," he repeated, with such calm calculation that they all went quiet. "Do it."

Wee Seamy's eyes darted to Pearson, gauging with an animal instinct how much choice he had. None. He moved forward, his hand hovering over the bloodied mess in Pearson's, Pearson watched him intently. Wee Seamy reached out an arm stiffly, his hand almost disembodied from the rest of him, his fingers paddling blindly as if being dipped into water. Pearson grabbed hold of his wrist and pushed it in to the open abdomen of the dead rabbit.

"Properly," he said. "C'mere you," he said to Brendan and Brendan lumbered forward warily. Pearson still had tight hold of Wee Seamy's wrist and he yanked his hand towards Brendan, smearing the blood on his face.

"Aw fuck, Pearson!" Brendan spat.

"Get used to it," Pearson said. "Imagine it's the belly of a soldier!"

It struck Johnny that he had never seen Pearson more animated, more alive. As he watched him, Pearson caught his eye.

"Johnny," he said. "Your turn." His eyes are vicious now, lost inside his own fantasy. Johnny is the only one he avoids confrontation with normally. Johnny can feel it sometimes, a wall that's made up of interlocking bricks of wariness and regard. He doesn't want to force their parting. He wants Johnny there. But sooner or later Pearson has to assert his leadership.

"Johnny …" The three of them are watching him but he feels detached from them already. Johnny picks up the cider bottle from between his thighs and drains it, then turns with the sudden speed engendered by instinct and hatred and anger and he smashes the bottle off the side of the gravestone. The bottom of the bottle shatters into pieces on the stone below and he's left with the jagged neck in his hand. So fast, so unexpected, that even Pearson starts, then his eyes narrow warily.

Johnny springs to his feet, the cold stiffness of his locked position on the stone sending lightening forks of pain through his buttocks when he moves. He holds the bottle like a weapon, not waving it because he doesn't need to.

"You're a fucking psycho, Pearson," he had said quietly, and he moved past them and out of the graveyard, the open, glassy eyes of the rabbit locked in his memory …

Johnny opens his eyes and sees Danni watching him. The memory of the graveyard, of Pearson, fades.

He is not listening, Danni thinks with frustration, putting her glass down on the table.

"Did you ever kill a man?" she repeats.

Johnny stares at her without answering for quite some time.

"Yes," he says, eventually, his eyes never leaving her face. "I did."

CHAPTER SIXTEEN

He will not be drawn on who he killed. Not yet, Danni thinks. She thinks she has her man. But she has to be clever. Sure footed. She will not be careless.

"Is the struggle over?" she asks. "Do you have sympathy for the Real IRA, the Continuity IRA?"

"I am not part of it now, Danni."

"Your views have changed?"

"Everything has changed."

"Why?"

"I was a young man then, for a start."

"That makes a difference?"

"Of course it makes a difference! Are you the same as you were in your twenties? Young men are …" He does not finish the sentence. It is too obvious.

"And there is a peace process," he continues. "There was no peace process when I joined. There was violence and prejudice and victimisation. You can't judge a moment in history by what's happening now."

"Why did you really join?"

The word 'really' changes the question, demands a kind of honesty. At first, he resents the implication that he has not so far been completely honest. But maybe she is right.

Within a minute, within the same thought even, Johnny alternates between believing no explanation is possible, even desirable, and searching longingly inside his head for a way to make her understand. He wants to see the hardness in her eyes yield, but he will not justify himself. Not to her; not to anyone. He says nothing for a minute, looks at the table, like he's searching through mental files in his head for explanation.

"You've got to understand," he says finally, softly, "what it was ... you know ... what it was like to be a teenager here at that time. What we'd seen growing up. When I was a kid, I was watching the civil rights marches going on ... people out on the street ... ordinary people like my dad and my Uncle Gerry, out marching for the first time in their lives. They weren't political. They weren't agitators. They were ordinary, working-class guys who worked hard all their lives and just wanted the best for their families. But they couldn't get the best for their families in the system that worked here at that time. What jobs you could get. What houses you could get ... that depended on your religion."

"So your dad and your uncle ... they were terrorists too?"

"What's a terrorist?"

"Oh don't play with words," she snaps.

"Nelson Mandela was a terrorist. Now he takes tea with the queen."

"Did they join the IRA?" she says insistently, ignoring him.

"Who, Nelson Mandela and the queen?" he demands.

"Oh fuck off!" she says.

They both stare into their drinks.

She becomes aware of a background noise that is gathering momentum, then the doors of the nearby function suite burst open and a conga line straggles through reception towards the bar. Oh please God, not now, she thinks. A wedding party, all of them singing loudly with the ' look at me' exhibitionism of too much booze. Embarrassment grips her, and she takes hold of her glass and sips it. Johnny glances up and away again. The line kicks its way past their table, back out into the foyer, and disappears through the swing doors of the function suite leaving a pregnant, surreal silence.

Then Johnny says quietly, "No, my father and my uncle did not join the IRA."

"So why did you?"

"Because ... because of what I've been trying to tell you," he says exasperatedly. "Things were *different* for my generation. It wasn't just Ireland that was changing in the 1960s, everywhere was changing. Britain ... America ... and who was pushing that change? It was young people. You had student marches and demonstrations ... anti-Vietnam protests ... and we were part of that change over here too. My dad, my uncle ... they had accepted a lot but it all got simply too much to accept. And it was my generation that was really going to challenge it in sufficient numbers. We were young and we were energetic and we wanted change. We wanted a future."

He's looking at his hands on the table and her own gaze is drawn to them. They are folded together, long white fingers intertwining.

"I've brought a document with me," he says slowly, deciding to say the words only as they emerge from his mouth. "I brought it in case you really want to know what this is about. But it's a document that means a lot to me. And if you're playing at this, don't bother taking it."

She looks at him uncertainly, eyes flickering as his hand moves to the inside pocket of his jacket. The pages are folded.

"What is it?"

"My grandmother wrote it. Mary Seonaid O'Connor."

She starts to unfold the pages.

"No, read it later."

She hesitates, then reaches for her bag and tucks it inside.

"I can't tell you any more than that can," he says. There were three things happened to me one after another when I was a teenager. The first was my mother giving me my grandmother's words to read at the height of the protest marches. The second was the British army moving onto the streets of Belfast and Derry. When they came, there were plenty in our streets who stood to cheer them in. We thought they had come to protect us. And then we realised they weren't there to protect us at all. And that's when things changed for me, Danni. That's when things changed."

He takes a long drink from his glass. She watches the creamy head settle back on the Guinness, then looks up at him questioningly.

"And the third thing?"

He is silent for so long she begins to wonder if he heard her.

"The kids in the streets where I lived began running battles with the British soldiers," he says, eventually. "My young brother, Pat, was at it all the time. Pat ... och Pat just liked the adventure of it as much as anything, you know? There was this day I saw him and an old school pal of mine called Joe Breslin stoning the army trucks as they passed. They weren't the only ones. There was a whole crowd of them. It was what happened, just the way things were. But I couldn't be bothered with the pettiness of it, steered clear. I walked back down the street I had come up and turned down another way to get out of the scheme for a bit. I don't know how long I was away ... twenty minute maybe, half an hour, something like that. When I came back, there was this car parked down the bottom end of the street near my house, with a crowd round it."

She finds herself drawn to his face in spite of herself. Her eyes scan the angular contours, watching the emotions that flit and dart in the shadows of his face.

"It was Pat," he says, looking up at her, as if all these years he still can't believe it. "It was Pat," he repeats.

What was Pat? Danni thinks uneasily, watching him silently.

"Somebody had opened up their car to lay him on the back seat while they called an ambulance. I was trying to see but at first I couldn't see for the crowd, and then somebody moved and I caught sight of the sleeve of his jumper. I was pushing my way through then, shouting to let me through and somebody said, 'That's his brother, let his brother through.' And I could see the blood seeping into the car upholstery, spreading out you know, creeping out like it was alive, and I was thinking, they're never going to get that out. They're never going to get that blood out."

"Wait a minute," Danni says. "How did ...? He was shot for throwing stones?" Her voice rises incredulously.

"You know nothing about this place," he says. He cannot keep the bitterness from his voice. "People like you are why people like me had to join the IRA."

She should hate him for that, Danni thinks in the silence that follows, and yet in a strange way she understands this better than anything else he has said. A sense of rage for his loved ones.

Johnny exhales deeply.

"Sorry."

"What happened?"

"I grabbed hold of Pat's hand but he didn't open his eyes. There was this siren wailing in the distance. It felt like it was wailing somewhere inside me, inside my head. Someone had called an ambulance."

She can see he's remembering it in his head, playing it slowly like a movie reel, the way she replays the bomb blast. She knows what that feels like, the way the scene runs and reruns in your head, and you just can't switch it off. Marco on his hunkers. The arc of Angelo's bag in the air.

"It got louder and louder. I heard someone muttering, 'It's too late' and I looked up to see who it was, but everyone had parted to let the ambulance men in. 'It's his brother,' somebody in the crowd said to the ambulance men. One of them came and lifted me by the shoulders and said, 'Come on then, young fella' – I always remember the way he said that because it sounded odd – 'we'll look after him for you now.' The next thing my mother came running out of the front door in her slippers. Someone had knocked the door to tell her. Blue floral slippers. She had this wild look on her face, you know. Her eyes were just crazy.

And then she saw Pat on the stretcher as one of the men was covering his face with a sheet and she started to scream. Somebody grabbed hold of her on one side and somebody on another and she just screamed that street down."

His forehead creases with the memory and he looks down at the table.

"It was like she howled for everything she'd ever lost. Her father. Her son."

Then he lifts his head to her and says flatly.

"I'll never forget that sound as long as I live. I've spent my whole life trying to wipe it out."

CHAPTER SEVENTEEN

Her own father, she's thinking, as she watches him. Was he one of them? The soldiers who bludgeoned their way into Northern Ireland? The soldiers the boys threw stones at.

"My father was a British soldier," she says.

She will never understand, he thinks.

In the silence between them, she sees her own father the way he was. Suddenly and vividly. The stranger in army uniform coming home, upsetting the way things were between her and mummy. She remembers running behind her mother's legs, gripping hold of her skirt and peering round the side. Her father, kneeling on the floor laughing, holding out his arms to coax her. Her mother pulling her gently round, bringing her over. "Daddy's home, Danni. Say hello." Her father smells vaguely of beer and she does not want to hug him. His soldier's uniform is rough on her skin.

She watches resentfully from the side of the sofa as he kisses her mother on the lips. Her eyes widen as his hand slips onto her mother's backside and then her mother pulls away and murmurs something but he's not having it. He's laughing and pulling her close and Danni runs out suddenly from behind the sofa and kicks him on the shin.

"Oi!" he shouts, and Danni mother's swoops her up protectively.

"I can see you've been spoiling her," he says. "Just as well I'm back."

"Don't be silly, Jimmy," her mother says, "she's only a baby still." And Danni feels the gentle press of her mother's lips against her head.

He is home from a long tour of duty and she cries for the first week. She can no longer climb into bed in the early hours of the morning when she wakes, seek her mother's warm body and drift back to sleep with her damp head resting against her mother's back. She does it so automatically she is barely awake any more. Until she feels her father lifting her and returning her to her room and then her eyes are open suddenly with the cold harshness of morning and a world that does not cradle her gently as it once did.

"I'll see to her," her mother is saying and her father snaps back,

"For God's sake Marie, just leave her or she'll never learn."

Danni howls until her mother creeps in and slides into bed beside her.

"Hush, honey," she murmurs and Danni sniffs back tears and gulps for air before she grabs a fistful of her mother's nightgown and her eyes droop again into sleep. Her mother chose her. Her mother always chooses her.

Danni's father believes in discipline. It's just his way, her mother tells her as she gets older. But Danni never gets to understand his ways. He wanted a boy. She always knew he wanted a boy. Her mother chose the name Daniella because she thought it pretty, but her father was the first to call her Danni and sometimes Dan.

He and Danni eye one another with a kind of watchful resentment. They move home often and she blames him for that. New schools, new friends, new houses. A sequence of drab army properties with radiators that give out more noise than heat, and damp patches on the walls, and flecks of fungus on the bathroom walls. Kitchen wallpaper than has peeled back above the spot where the kettle has steamed for years. At first she cries each time they leave. "Why do we always have to go?" she frets. And her father says she must be a good girl and not a baby now; she's far too old for tears. She must help her mum. Eventually she no longer cries when she hears they are to move. She becomes adept at making acquaintances and avoids making friends.

She is ten when the knock on the door comes. Two army men with uniforms that do not look like her father's. Her mother sends her to her room to play. Just for a few minutes Danni, she murmurs. Her mother's face has blanched with fear. Much later, when Danni hears the door close, she listens for her mother's voice calling her but it does not come. She tiptoes to the sitting room, looks round the open door to where her mother sits shivering, pulling her cardigan round her body like she will never be warm again.

He did not die in action, that was the irony. Her dad, the soldier. Not in the posting to Northern Ireland. He had a heart attack, they said, fell straight and stiff and heavy like chopped timber. He simply never opened his eyes again.

They shake hands perfunctorily, neither of them concentrating. Each of them has their own secrets, their own preoccupations. Danni does not flinch at the touch of his hand now; she barely registers it. Somewhere inside her, she is aware that should she stop to examine what she feels; he has stirred some kind of emotion in her. Not pity, nor compassion. Not empathy nor sympathy. Not understanding. Confusion perhaps comes closest but she has not the will to work it out tonight. There are other thoughts to occupy her.

They will meet again, they both know it. So sure are they, that they make no formal arrangement, each eager to retreat back into their own world, alone, to examine memories that have been dug up and left like bones in an open grave. She stands behind the glass door of the foyer, watching Johnny walk into the grey smirr, turning his collar up against the damp. When he disappears, she watches the space where he was, then turns back into the light.

A father who was a British soldier, Johnny thinks. She will never understand. An IRA man, Danni thinks. He will never understand.

It is hopeless.

CHAPTER EIGHTEEN

"On the floor! Now!"

On the long walk back across the city from Danni's hotel, Johnny can hear the words in his head like they're being shouted now. See the place it all began. The office door of the old disused warehouse banging open so violently it bounced off the wall behind.

"What the ...?"

"Get down on the fucking floor! Move!"

Johnny had wriggled face down against the concrete floor, feeling the cold stone and grit against his cheek. Three men stood above him, each with a gun, their faces hidden beneath black balaclavas. Where was Pearson? He tried to turn slightly and caught Pearson's jacket out of the corner of his eyes. He must be on the floor on the other side of him. A foot roughly pushed Johnny's face back to the floor and a small flurry of dust rose up and caught in the back of his throat making him cough.

"Shut up!"

"What are you doing?" Johnny yelled. "What the fuck is happening?"

"Tie him!"

A thin blindfold was yanked over Johnny's eyes, tied so

tightly at the back of his head that he saw shooting stars in the blackness. It felt like his eyes were going to be pressed so far into his skull that if they were released, they would ricochet like a pinball machine.

He couldn't hear Pearson's voice. What were they doing to Pearson?

Cold metal pressed into the side of his head and he heard a click. Christ! This was it. He screwed his eyes tight and realised he'd never felt any emotion as primitive as this in his life before. Fear and adrenalin surged in explosive bursts, unstoppable, like water from a burst mains pipe, and in those seconds he looked for escape possibilities, even where reason told him there were none. He'd have crawled on his belly, slithering like a snake and licking dust from the concrete floor to survive. Grab the gun at his temple and turn it on the man who held it if he could. Blast his brains out. He always wondered if he could kill a man and now he knew. He could kill three if it meant he lived. His eyes stayed screwed shut, waiting for the blast. He was going to die.

"Jesus, Mary and Joseph ..." he prayed mechanically inside his head. "I give you my heart and my soul ..."

A hand grabbed at his leg, another at his belt. They were trying to remove his jeans and a sudden surge of anger over-powered his fear.

"Fuck off!" Johnny's hands were already being tied behind his back but he kicked out with his feet. "We're here to enlist!"

"You want to join the IRA?" a voice said into his ear. Johnny could smell the talker. Old sweat. A jumper that smelled fusty, like it had been locked up in an old damp cupboard. He tensed, listening.

"You want to join the IRA?" the voice said again. The voice was so close to his ear, the soft, whispering tickle of it on his skin made him shiver.

"That's why I'm here, isn't it?" Johnny said belligerently.

"I think maybe that's a story," the voice continued. "I think you want to infiltrate our unit so that you can tell tales to the British army. I've heard stuff about you, Johnny. I know all about you."

Johnny's legs were cold against the stone and a piece of grit was digging painfully into his thigh. They had tugged the jeans off over his shoes and he felt ridiculous lying here in trainers and socks still, vulnerable as well as scared. Who had been telling lies about him?

"How old are you, Johnny?" The metal at the side of his head dug further into his skull. He realised he recognised the voice whispering in his ear. He and Pearson had been going to a Republican bar for the last year. They wanted to volunteer but it was a slow process even getting to talk to someone who was really involved and not just full of bullshit. There had been a conversation … Pearson introduced them … Gerry … a senior figure in the local unit. The pain behind Johnny's eyes was intense. Strange patterns of coloured light formed blue lagoons and shimmering green rivers behind the blindfold. He felt faint.

"Nineteen. Now fucking get that thing away from me!"

"Nineteen? A baby. Shame we're going to have to snuff you out already."

"Jesus, Mary and Joseph, assist me in my last agony …" The words were long buried but surfaced in his head, gasping.

A door banged loudly. Pearson. What was happening to Pearson? Shit. They were separating them.

"We've fucking done nothing!" Johnny roared and suddenly wriggled violently against his ties, thrashing like a landed fish in a net. Gerry had asked him to come here, him and Pearson, to discuss volunteering. They'd been given an address where they were to meet, this old disused warehouse. Now they were going to blast their brains out because of some crazy misunderstanding.

Johnny heard a bang, like a gunshot, and his struggle froze.

"Pearson!" he shouted. Then suddenly the room became full of movement, a door banging, figures bending over him, voices shouting, and he struggled to make sense of the noise and movement and direction.

"On your feet! Fucking on your feet!" he heard someone shout, and a pair of hands hauled him up from the floor. Johnny stood swaying, disorientated, uncertain which way to face.

A strange sound, filtered through to him, like a strangled laugh. Someone untied his blindfold and the pressure eased but he was still left stranded in a blackness that only gradually lightened. He rubbed his eyes and heard the laughter swell.

"Jesus, did you see his face when that door banged!"

Initiation rite, Johnny thought bitterly. Blinking, he peered ahead and saw the three men's balaclavas being discarded. But there were four men laughing at him. One of them was Pearson.

The rain begins to fall heavily again and Johnny quickens his pace through the streets. Old, half forgotten, unwelcome memories. She is, he thinks, turning his life upside down already.

CHAPTER NINETEEN

Back in her room, Danni does not switch on the harsh overhead light but flicks the switch on both the bedside lamp and the television. She wants only the light from the television and reaches for the remote control to turn down the sound. "John James Callaghan, Northern Ireland's Director of Public Prosecutions," the newsreader is saying, "has given a lecture to a legal conference urging zero tolerance of prostitution in an effort to clamp down on Belfast's rapidly expanding red light district ..."

As she starts to turn the sound down, a picture flashes on the screen that is vaguely familiar. She searches the face knowing that somewhere in the unfamiliar is a face she knows, though she cannot immediately place it. Of course! Myra. The prostitute at Pearson's office. She is younger in the picture, unmarked yet by life. Danni turns up the volume, stands transfixed by the report.

"His remarks come following the brutal murder last night of a Belfast prostitute. The victim has now been named by police as Myra MacIntosh. Originally from Glasgow, Ms MacIntosh was hit on the head with a blunt instrument and stabbed repeatedly before being dumped in a rubbish bin in the city's red light district. Police have appealed for witnesses. They are particularly anxious to talk to a petite, dark haired woman, thought to be in her thirties, who was seen talking to the victim in the city's Ormond Street around 9.30 p.m."

The shock that Myra is dead, the woman she so recently walked with and talked to, prevents her realising the obvious. A single tear for a woman she barely knows gathers in her eyes and then suddenly the other lines from the report finally seep through her consciousness and she realises that she, Danni, is that other woman the police would like to talk to. She was the last person to see Myra alive.

CHAPTER TWENTY

The electronic card to Danni's room flashes red when she tries to return to it the next morning after an early morning walk. She slept a deep, exhausted sleep until 4 a.m., then lay gazing into the darkness until her eyes stung, thinking about Myra and whether or not she should go to the police. If she doesn't go, it's like saying Myra didn't matter, that her life was worth nothing. But she doesn't want to get involved and anyway what's the point? She would be going only to tell them she knows nothing. And how can she explain what she was doing there? Yes officer, I was trying to track down the man who killed my husband and son fifteen years ago so that I can blast a hole through him with a shotgun …

After a few hours she gave up trying to sleep, leaving the hotel to walk for an early breakfast at a local deli. Right now she wants to lie down on the bed, seek refuge in a couple of gins from the minibar, drift into unconsciousness. There is a certain liberation in loneliness. Who is there to see her having gin for breakfast? The card flashes red yet again and she tuts. What's wrong with the bloody thing? Perhaps the cleaner has been in. She turns it again, twisting, turning, until finally the light flashes green.

She opens the door with a sense of surprise that the room seems to be in darkness. She drew the curtains first thing this morning, sat with strong black coffee and watched a mottled red dawn creep slowly over Belfast like a rash. In a second the door has swung out of her hand and closed sharply behind her, pushed by someone behind the door.

"Oh my God," she says, and the light flicks on.

"Morning Danni."

"What the fuck are you doing here?" she asks, her heart hammering in her chest. Pearson smiles coldly.

"That's no language for a lady, Danni."

On the long desk that runs along the wall, a movement catches her eye. Coyle is sitting on top of it, legs outstretched and crossed at the ankles. What the hell does he have in his hand, she thinks, and then realises it's a chocolate breakfast muffin. He pulls the paper case from the sponge intently, showering fine crumbs over himself and barely glancing up at her.

Danni looks from one to the other, calculating her next move, wondering whether to risk shouting out.

"How did you get in? How did you know where I was? Did Johnny tell you?"

Of course, it must be Johnny. She fell for it, all that stuff about not seeing Pearson for years. The two of them are tied up. Must be.

"So you've seen Johnny?" says Pearson curiously. "How is he?"

She is out of her depth. Pearson's eyes are like a mirror, bouncing images back rather than absorbing them. In the glassy superficiality of them she sees a sudden reflection. Her father in his uniform, square jawed, eyes that have seen too much, her link to this country before she even realised she had one. She feels the same impotence now she always felt looking at him then.

"You can't just go breaking into people's rooms."

She stays still but her eyes follow Pearson as he walks to the window and pulls the curtains again. He says nothing.

"What do you want?"

She throws her bag on the bed, trying to fake nonchalance.

"Just a chat, don't we Coyle?"

"Hmm-mm," says Coyle mid-bite, and another flurry of muffin crumbs snows to the floor.

He brushes some off his tightly fitted lavender blue shirt and leans across to flick the switch on the kettle.

"Make yourself at home," she says sarcastically, a sudden flash of temper emboldening her.

"You heard about Myra?" says Pearson.

"Yes."

"Unfortunate. But we need to make sure it doesn't get even more unfortunate."

Up close, the ridges down the back of Pearson's head seem to have taken on a life of their own, as if something lives under the skin, a small animal that moves like a foetus in a belly. He turns to Coyle, who's pouring coffee into a cup.

"Here. Did you order the wreath?"

"Eh?"

"The wreath, I told you to order a wreath."

"Not yet."

"Do it. Won't be many other flowers for the poor bitch."

"What kind?"

"Lilies for funerals, isn't it?" He turns back to Danni. "Should be lilies, Danni, shouldn't it?"

She doesn't reply.

"You were seen last night," says Pearson. The police want to talk to you."

"I know."

125

"It wouldn't be a good idea."

"I'm not sure … I think I ought to but …"

"No Danni, you don't understand," he says quietly, and he reaches out and takes hold of her chin in his hand. His fingers against her skin are warm, strong. He holds the outline of her bones in his hand so firmly that she has the sudden sensation that he could crush her entire skull if he squeezed his fingers together, that the bones would simply crumble to dust. She holds very still.

"When I say it wouldn't be a good idea," he continues, "it's not an opinion. It's an instruction. I mean, don't do it. It's unfortunate for all of us that you were seen last night. Bad luck. But they won't trace you if you don't come forward. As far as the police are concerned, Myra was working alone and it's simpler for all of us if it stays that way. I don't want any connection with her. You see my point Danni?"

"Yes, I … I …"

"Good. It's a waste of time anyway, isn't it? I mean you can't help them or anything so there's no point."

"No."

He sounds almost reasonable but his closeness overwhelms her with raw fear. Pearson drops her face abruptly.

"Give us all a cuppa then pretty boy," he tells Coyle, "Danni could do with one."

His voice is mocking, like he doesn't understand Coyle's campness and is amused by it, but she isn't convinced. She can't help noticing the appraising way his eyes slide down Coyle's slim hipped, jean clad outline.

Pearson shakes his head.

"He doesn't half wear poncey colours, doesn't he, Danni?"

Her hands shake as she tries to turn the lock on the door. Not that there seems any point now they have gone. How did they get in in the first place? Sleep is the last thing on her mind now. She sits on the edge of the bed, breathing deeply. Her sense of panic is aimless, stirring up the agitation inside her with nowhere to take it.

Traynor. Perhaps she should phone Traynor for some advice. She reaches tentatively for her mobile then sits with it cupped in her hand, hesitating. She can't phone Traynor. She just can't. Because what she said to him was true: this is *her* journey. Traynor would tell her to come home, and if she didn't he would be out on the next flight, and then where would she be? She'd be following his agenda and not her own.

She needs out of here but where is there to go? There's no one to run to. Unless ...

She grabs a sweater, stuffs it into the top of her bag. A new packet of complimentary biscuits ... so the cleaner HAD been in the room. Maybe Pearson simply told her they had left their key inside the room by accident, got her to open the door ... maybe they *can't* get back inside whenever they want, she thinks hopefully. She throws the biscuits in her bag ... an umbrella ... looks round wildly for anything else she will need. A knock at the door makes her gasp.

"Who is it?" she demands, rooted to the spot.

"Room service."

"I haven't ordered anything," she calls, then peers through the spyhole on the door into the corridor. A young man with a tray stands outside. Cautiously, she open the door. He smiles.

"It was ordered for you ma'am. There's a card with it."

She looks at the small gift-wrapped bowl of grapes. Invalid fruit. The card is printed, "With Compliments". Underneath a handwritten scrawl says simply, 'Keep Well. Mr Wasp.'

She bangs the door behind her, half runs down the

corridor, eager to be out of here. Outside, she hails a taxi and sinks down into the seat, burying her mouth in the woollen folds of her scarf.

CHAPTER TWENTY-ONE

He climbs the stair knowing she's there. Every day since he rounded the corner and saw her sitting on his doormat, he has half expected her to be there again, like Polly Flinders, her legs outstretched in front of her. Each time, he has been uncertain whether the feeling he experiences when there is no one there is disappointment or relief. But today he feels the surge of adrenalin when he sees her, his heart thumping deeply, blackly, against his rib cage.

She is leaning against the wall. Her back is flat against it, her arms folded, dark eyes feverish. He says nothing. He fishes the key from his pocket, opens the door and walks in silently, turns to look at her with the door open. He waits. She waits. Then she moves from the wall and walks into his hall, turns into the living room and hovers in the middle of the floor. Johnny flicks the light switch, glances at her as he puts a notebook and a pile of books on the table, then takes his jacket off and throws it onto a chair.

"They broke into my room."

"Who?" he says, though he knows. He feels, with a sense of despair, the click of the trap behind him, the metal cage closing round him. It was a mistake to come back here to Ireland. He thought with the peace process it could be different now, a new beginning. It pulls him always this country, yet sometimes he thinks he hates it too. Already he is sinking back into a world that he thought he had left behind, a world that when he was away from here he thought could surely no longer exist. But he looks at her standing in the centre of his room, this stranger whom he feels he has known all his life, and he knows there is no turning back.

"Pearson," she says. "Coyle."

He nods.

"Sit down."

But she walks to the window, unable to settle, and looks out, arms folded.

He watches her intently.

"They roughed the place up?"

She shakes her head.

"They were waiting in the dark for me."

He starts suddenly, his body tense and alert.

"They ... did something to you?"

"No ... no ... they ... no."

She watches as he turns to sit in the armchair. He grimaces slightly as his leg twists under him.

"What happened?" she asks suddenly. "To your leg."

"It fell out with Pearson," he says acerbically, and lifts his leg straight out in front of him to rest on the coffee table.

She looks questioningly at him.

"Another time," he says. "Tell me what happened."

She tells him about meeting Myra outside Pearson's and he listens without interrupting, his elbow resting on the arm of his chair, cheek resting lightly on the tips of his finger. But he looks startled, sits up suddenly when she describes hearing the news broadcast. The police are looking to speak to her? She's sure? He lowers his leg from the table and bows his head slightly, his hand reaching up to run slowly through his hair.

There is no danger for Danni in talking to the police but there is danger for Pearson. And when Pearson thinks he is in even the slightest danger, he tends to simply remove the threat. Danni needs to remove herself first. He glances up at her and he knows she is frightened. He also knows that she does not yet realise how much need there is for her to be frightened.

"Danni," he says quietly, and she feels a sharp tug inside her every time he uses her name, the unwelcome intimacy of it. Just a couple of days ago they were strangers, anonymous, and now they are not. It unnerves her. "Whatever brought you here, it's time for you to go home."

She looks out of the window and he watches her chew the inside of her cheek. Her eyes flick over to him. He wonders about the battle inside her. Some kind of understanding is growing inside him, but it has not yet sharpened into clarity. She knows what loss is, of that he is sure. Is that what brings her to this country? Is that what fuels whatever she is writing?

"I am not ready to go home."

"I know."

She shoots him a look he does not understand, a mixture of hostility and desolation and sadness.

"Danni ..."

"No," she says. She looks tired today, her eyes dark smudges in the paleness of her face. "I am not finished."

He has a sense, as he did the first time she came here, that this room is no longer his, that it has become invaded by a force bigger than it is used to. It makes him uncomfortable and yet excites him too. In a way he has tried to walk away from life but it has followed him, forcing itself into his meagre existence, widening the parameters of what he can say and think and feel.

"You can't stay there," he says.

She turns from the window now. The irony of him try-ing to protect her is farcical, makes her feel stupid, like a child playing at something beyond her understanding and experience and capabilities. What made her come here to his flat when she was in danger? What was she thinking of? And yet, there was something that was formed last night, something that rose out of his desolation and his grief, and met with her understanding of despair, and fused into an unwelcome bond between them. A bond she does not want, she thinks.

"It was silly of me to come to you," she says, as much to herself as to him.

"No ... no... it's ..."

"I'll be fine. I panicked."

She picks up her bag.

"I'm in a hotel, a public place."

Johnny raises his eyes and looks at the ceiling.

"Don't ever underestimate what Pearson is capable of."

She looks at him with such coldness that a frisson run through him.

"I know exactly what men like him are capable of," she says, and walks to the door.

When she has gone, he opens his notebook on the table, places his books carefully in front of him. The essay title is written in his small squashed hand, the letters huddled together in heaps, leaning this way and that against each other, whisper-ing secrets, jockeying for room. He reads the words, but his mind is elsewhere. He can make little sense of the concepts.

Perhaps he is too old now, he thinks, has left it too late for serious learning. But he does not feel old. He leans back against the plastic framed chair he bought from a charity shop, wriggles against the discomfort of it on his back. A wave of despair washes over him.

He is hurtling towards fifty and has achieved nothing. Meeting someone new makes him look at his life as an outsider would. A man with a criminal record, released as a result of the peace process, living in a rented flat with no career behind him and few prospects in front of him. No wonder she's hostile. He frowns at the page in front of him. Or is there something more? He closes his psychology books over.

After he left school, there had been an aimlessness about him that, combined with an anger over Pat's death, made him dangerous. His ma sensed it. Go away to university, she urged him. Sure, didn't he have the qualifications to do it? She wanted him out of Belfast, he knew that much, wanted to break the spell of this place. "I've lost one son," she told him. "Don't make it two."

But he couldn't leave Pat in a Belfast cemetery, stiff in the cold ground, leave British soldiers patrolling his streets. Inside, he knew his ma was right, that to make something of his life he had to get away from here, and away from Pearson, and live in a place where the horizon was further away, not closing in on top of you. And part of him wanted to. But he couldn't do it, leave this place he loved for other people to save or destroy. He had a right to have a life here and he would rather stay and demand it than sell out for an easy one someplace else.

He got a job in a warehouse for a while, humping boxed electrical goods into lorries for delivery. Pearson was curious about the job, Johnny's movements there– even asked if there was other work going – but he never seemed to work regular hours like the rest of them. Yet he always had more cash. His life seemed to expand constantly while Johnny's shrivelled.

"I've got a proposition for you," he told Johnny one day, and as he outlined his plan, suddenly the reason for all those questions became clear. He wanted Johnny to help with a job at the warehouse.

"No," Johnny said instantly.

"Nobody will know it's an inside job. We'll tie you up, threaten you with a gun ... all that stuff."

"No chance, Pearson."

Pearson's eyes hardened, shrivelling into glittering little raisins, the way they always did when he was denied.

"You've got a brain, Johnny, but you'll always be a small town boy."

Pearson did the warehouse anyway, without warning him, on a day Johnny wasn't working. He was heart-sick of the job and had been on the point of jacking it in but he didn't dare give in his notice for a few months. It would stink of an inside job. He had Pearson by the throat up against the wall over it.

"Don't shit in my back yard," he told him.

Pearson brushed him off. It was to fund an IRA weapons consignment, he said. And maybe it was, but it was to fund Pearson's flash car and his fancy apartment first. Work with me and I'll give you a cut, Pearson said. We're good together. Fuck off, Johnny had retorted.

The truth was that after joining the IRA, Johnny's life was mapped out. You didn't live a normal life when you were a volunteer. The police knew his every move. He was searched constantly, sometimes twice a day. He became unemployable. Even Pearson got pulled in sometimes, though the others joked he was Teflon coated. It was years before Johnny figured out why the police didn't trouble Pearson more. Hard to believe how slow he was to recognise the truth.

All those wasted years, he thinks.

He gets up listlessly, walks to the kitchen and flicks the switch on the kettle, stares through the window until the sudden rush of heating water fills the room. He makes a coffee he has no real appetite for, takes the steaming mug back to the table.

And now he's back. Full circle. He wants to make a different contribution to Belfast now. He thought the time was right. But maybe the time is never going to be right. On impulse, he reaches for a volume of Yeats in the bookcase behind him, flips to 'Easter 1916'. How many times did he read it during the years inside?

> *Too long a sacrifice*
> *Can make a stone of the heart.*

He murmurs the words aloud. He thought his own heart had petrified long ago. And maybe it was easier that way. An image of Danni flashes into his mind. Easier than this.

He loves words. He looks at them sometimes on the page in front of him, lines from a new novel, or from an old familiar, favourite poem, and he feels they are almost mystical. So individually insignificant; together so powerful. Small squiggles that can amuse or arouse or anger or inspire, that pull your emotions in every direction.

The first time he heard 'Easter 1916' was in that ridiculous school meeting of Pearson's. What twisted charisma Pearson had in those days. More charisma than insight as it happened. Pearson had no idea Yeats was against violence. Johnny picks up his pen and doodles, writing elaborately in the middle of the page, the words that he read over and over in prison.

> *All changed, changed utterly;*
> *A terrible beauty is born.*

CHAPTER TWENTY-TWO

Danni tries to remember the name. Susie? No, Sarah. Something with S. She stops trying, lets her mind go blank. When she was with Myra that night, Pearson asked about a friend, another girl … where she was. S. S. S. Stella! Stella. Where was she, Pearson had asked, and Myra had replied that she was outside the pub.

When she returned to the hotel from Johnny's flat, a bouquet of flowers had been waiting for her. Plain white funereal lilies. A white card. Mr Wasp. She takes them and breaks the green stems in the middle, watches the white gummy fluid run over her fingers, then crams them into the bin.

She has told herself that it is no great loss for the police if she does as Pearson has told her to and stays silent. After all, what does she know? But alongside that insistence, there has been something in her head all day, fighting to be remembered. A detail about that night that may be important. The Vauxhall car with the baby seat, the man who toured round and round and round. The last thing she saw out of the back of the taxi, the car slowing again as Myra stood under the lamp, smoking.

What if that detail is important? What if another girl

dies and she knows she has done nothing to prevent it? She could, after all, speak to the police without mentioning Pearson. But if they ask her what she was doing there in that street, what does she say? Why is she in Belfast? And she knows one thing: she cannot get to the police without Pearson knowing. And he will not believe that she has said nothing about him, even if it's true.

Back in the hotel room, she lies on top of the bed, thinking, thinking. How can something so simple as being in the wrong place at the wrong time cause her so much danger, so many rippling repercussions? But this isn't only about her. It's about Myra. Dumped in a rubbish bin, the entrails of a life flowing into potato peelings and empty milk cartons. Disposable woman, disposable life. There is a debt to be paid to Myra, she thinks, a woman whose life didn't matter. Her death *will* matter. Danni of all people knows how much death matters.

Stella. That was it.

She knows she shouldn't do it. She also knows she will.

Pearson was wrong. There *are* flowers for Myra. Out in the lane propped against the wall, a small assortment of posies and single blooms, and a bouquet from the supermarket, wrapped in rain-spattered cellophane. She hears the rustle of the paper as the wind ripples through it, a whispered elegy in the dark back alley for a woman who died amongst rain and mud and human ugliness. Danni bends forward to squint at the inscriptions in the fading light. "Myra, you are with the angels now. Watch over us all from heaven. Sleep tight. Stell."

All those euphemisms. They stir her up. Make her feel cynical and embarrassed and alienated all at once. And yet somehow compassionate too. On some level she wants to feel those things, to believe in angels. Angels and heaven and long sleeps. People who would never talk that way in life start tiptoeing round that kind of language when confronted by death, because how else do you make it bearable? How else do you pretend that there's order and reason and purpose? Heaven and angels, thinks Danni, watching rain drops form a small puddle on the bouquet wrapper.

And when it's a child … Jesus, when it's a child. A week after she buried Marco and Angelo, she went to the cemetery for the first time. She had placed a wind chime on Angelo's grave, and she heard the ethereal tinkling from the rain-strummed chime as she rounded the hill. It pleased her somehow, as if Angelo sang to her as she came near. The bouquets lay in a mound. One of the messages she read talked of heaven's playground, and being the smallest angel and the brightest star, and suddenly the sentimentality of it became unbearable, and she looked at the mound of flowers, browning now and beginning to fester, and felt more desolate among those words, kindly meant as they were, than she had ever felt in her life.

"Danni …"

His voice is gentle but she jumps.

"Shit!" Her hand flies up to her chest.

"Sorry …"

"What are you doing here?" she demands.

She calms slightly.

"How did you know I was here?"

"Danni, you need to understand how easy it is for someone like you to be followed without knowing about it."

"You followed me?"

"Pearson will have someone watching you. You should go back to the hotel now."

She glances round instinctively.

"There's no one here."

"You thought that when I was here. What are you doing?"

138

She tells him about meeting Myra, that first night she went to see Pearson and he shakes his head.

"Don't get involved."

"I *am* involved."

"Go back to the hotel."

"No."

The rain begins to fall afresh, tip tapping on the cellophane, sparkling in the street lighting.

"I have to speak to her," she says. "I have to ask about the Vauxhall."

She notices that, just as he had back at the flat when she told him she wasn't going home, he tries his best to persuade her but accepts her answer. She frowns. He is a man who understands compulsion.

"I'll walk you."

"No need."

But they walk anyway, to the end of the road, see the lights of the pub on the opposite corner.

"Perhaps she won't be out … after what's happened," says Danni.

"And perhaps she will," he says quietly. "When you have a habit to feed …"

There's a young girl, no more than nineteen, standing just down from the doors. She has long blonde hair, spiked softly round her face and huge doe eyes. It's obvious she's on the game and yet her face … her expression …

She watches as Danni approaches, Johnny beside her.

"I don't do couples," she says tensely, her eyes flicking uneasily between the two of them. She looks like a child, thinks Danni.

"No, it's okay," Danni says. "I'm looking for someone called Stella who works round this patch. "Just wondered if you knew her."

"What do you want?"

"Do you know Stella?"

She hesitates.

"Why?"

"I need to speak to her. Do you know her?"

"I'm Stella."

"I want to talk to you about Myra," Danni says.

Stella's eyes well up instantly.

"You were good friends?"

She nods silently, wiping a tear roughly with the heel of her hand.

"Myra looked out for me," she says eventually. "She was like a big sister to me."

"Aren't you frightened being out here?" Danni asks curiously. "After what happened to Myra ..."

"It's the first night I've been out since," says Stella. "I said I wasn't going back but I need the money. I'm only out for a couple of hours. I told Pearson. Another forty quid and that's it."

Danni takes out a wallet. "I need to talk to you. I'll give you the forty if you'll come into the pub and talk to me."

Stella shakes her head.

"You don't need to give me money."

Danni hold out two twenty pound notes.

"Time's money. I'm stopping you earning. Take it."

Stella hesitates, then reaches out. "Thanks," she says.

Johnny goes to the bar while Danni ushers Stella to a corner table. Stella sits on a bench seat, her back against wooden panelling, the overhead lamp casting a warm, orange light over her face. She is shaking slightly and despite the glow from the light, her skin is grey and pasty with black smudges underneath her eyes.

"Stella this is really important. I don't want Pearson to know about this conversation."

"I wouldn't tell that bastard anything."

Danni nods.

"How long have you been with him?"

"Year and a half. Myra said we were going to get out soon." Her eyes fill with tears again and she puts her elbows on the table, covering her face with her hands.

"How old are you Stella?"

"Eighteen."

"Haven't you got family … a home …?"

"I can't go back to my mum, you know? It would break her heart. I'm her wee girl … she …" She shakes her head.

"She doesn't know?"

"No. Well … sometimes I think she does, somewhere inside her … but she hasn't admitted it yet …"

She looks at Danni, ignoring Johnny.

"My mum's a decent woman," she says defensively. "Dead respectable and everything. It's not her fault what's happened. I couldn't bear if she looked me in the eye and said she knew. I just couldn't …"

Her voice is full, so full it's liquefying, brimming over. Out of the corner of her eye, Danni sees Johnny look down at the table. She clocks his body language, the emotional tension, thinks, fleetingly, that he is finding it too painful to watch Stella for some reason. She forces her attention back to Stella.

"She cried when she found out about the drugs," Stella is saying. "She kept saying to me, what did I do wrong? And I said you didn't. It's me. It's always been me." She sits back in her seat and looks at Danni, a look that is bare, stripped of artifice. "And now Myra's gone …" she says.

Stella's desolation closes in on Danni. It has happened so often this week, that sudden feeling of becoming caught up, emotionally entangled, in things that had seemed so logical and uncomplicated, snared in a net of feelings that trap her like a wriggling fish, helpless and gasping.

"Stella, I don't know how to help you …"

"You're not here to help me," Stella says, with a rush of such brutal clarity that Danni is silenced.

Johnny glances at her and Danni meets his eye, then immediately looks away, ashamed of such an instinctively conspiratorial exchange. They are not together, here. They are strangers, just like she and Stella are strangers. Her life is her own. She is not responsible for anyone and in turn, they can expect no part of her. She owns nothing and owes nothing.

Stella gazes morosely at her drink. Danni looks bitterly at the wall, aware that she may have removed her gaze, but Johnny's rests unwaveringly on her still. It makes her feel naked.

"I need to ask you about Myra," Danni says quietly. "About her clients. I spoke to Myra that night. The night she died."

Stella glances up quickly.

"I met her on the street outside Pearson's. She showed me the way."

Stella looks at her as if searching for something she missed.

"You were seeing Pearson …?"

"It's a long story. But I'm the woman the police want to talk to. The thing is, Pearson has warned me not to go anywhere near them or …"

Stella laughs, a short brittle laugh.

"Yeah, yeah …" she says. "I know Pearson …"

"The thing is Stella, I probably have nothing to tell the police except … well there's one thing I wanted to check with you. When I was with Myra there was this car that went round and round and round and the guy was just staring at her … and if I thought it was the person who killed her, I just couldn't … I'd need to go to the police. I couldn't just leave it … I …"

"What kind of car?"

"Vauxhall."

"Oh him. Baby seat?"

Stella barely waits for an answer.

"Tosser," she says dismissively, taking a gulp from her glass. "He's down all the time, just watching …"

"Could he be …?"

"I doubt it."

"How can I be sure?"

"You can't."

Danni rubs her face with her hand. She doesn't know how she has got into this mess, how one thing has led onto another so quickly. She looks at Stella who by the minute fluctuates between being a helpless child and a woman who knows so much of the wrong kind of stuff that it has begun to destroy her.

"You know you said Pearson can't know about this conversation?" Stella says.

Danni nods.

"Well I can tell you stuff he can't know either."

She has begin to shake more noticeably. She wraps her jacket round her front, a gesture so reminiscent of Myra the night she died that it gives Danni a pang. It makes her think of watching a child shuffle in her mother's shoes.

"What is it, Stella?" Johnny asks. He has been silent but is suddenly alert.

"Myra had a client that she said was our path out. She was biding her time."

"What did that mean? Was he in love with her?" asks Danni.

Stella shakes her head almost impatiently.

"It's not bloody *Pretty Woman*," she says scornfully. The only ones who fall for you are dirt poor. Myra had her share of them all right. She had this guy who used to pay her to

143

talk. Just to sit and talk. He'd bring her flowers and stuff. Said he wanted to marry her."

"What happened?"

"His mum said he couldn't," says Stella, with a little splutter of a laugh.

Even Johnny smiles, Danni notices.

"Myra said he was frightened of being rejected. He went to prostitutes because they were the only women he felt superior to. Then he fell for Myra. Men often fell for her. She's even got this Catholic priest who is a client. But she said the trouble with him was that he had no money to buy her silence. There wasn't enough in the collection plate."

"So who was the man who was going to be her path out?"

"It was someone really, really senior in the legal profession. Not the usual job. Some guy Pearson arranged for her to go and see. He told Myra she had to be specially nice to him."

"What was his name?" asks Johnny.

Stella hesitates.

"I don't know. Myra said it was safer if she didn't tell me. She didn't want Pearson to think I knew. But I could tell from the questions he asked me yesterday that he thinks I *do* know."

"And you really don't?"

"No."

"What did Myra tell you?"

"She said he was reckless, that he didn't touch alcohol or drugs but he got drunk on adrenalin and danger, on the buzz of risk. Arrogant too. He thought he could get away with it and nobody would find out. But Myra found out."

"Found out *what?*" says Danni.

"Who he was." She pauses, shivering. "Myra reckoned he would pay enough for her silence to get us out and cleaned up and get a new start. She was sure him and Pearson had some kind of arrangement. Scratched each other's backs. He turned a blind eye to some of Pearson's business stuff and Pearson protected him. But Myra was pushing it."

"Trying to get money?" says Johnny.

Stella nods.

"She told me the day before she died that she had confronted the guy, told him she knew who he was and that she wanted enough money for me and her to get out."

"How did he take it?"

"Furious, Myra said. She said she thought he really thought prostitutes would be too stupid to know who he was. But Myra had seen him once on the news on telly. There was a public awareness campaign about tightening up the prosecution of prostitution and he headed the press conference."

"But he was going to a prostitute himself?" says Danni.

"Myra said he got his kicks from that. She reckoned that was the whole point for him, being in a position of public power but pushing the boundaries in private."

Stella drains the vodka and coke in her glass.

"Can I have another of these?" she says.

Johnny picks up the glass raises his eyebrows in silent enquiry at Danni's glass. She puts her hand over it, shakes her head. Stella watches him as he walks to the bar.

"Is he your man?" she asks, nodding at Johnny.

"No." Danni can't help sounding brusque.

"He will be. There's something between yous."

Danni says nothing.

"He's quite good looking in a funny kind of way," Stella says eventually. "I think he's nice. You kind of trust him."

Danni looks over her shoulder, watches Johnny at the bar, the stillness of him. A whirl of confusion spins inside her. She turns back, sees Stella's eyes on her.

"Myra was certain who the guy was?" Danni asks.

"Positive. She said he was familiar right away but it took

her a while to realise where from. Guys like him, she said, they get their kicks bungee jumping off their careers, taking risks. She said that's the way men are."

"She didn't like men?"

"They let her down. Any guy she ever had cheated on her. She didn't think they were worth much. She said to me once that the punters looked at her with disgust after they'd done it to her. They didn't know she looked at them with disgust from the minute they stopped their cars for her." She looks up, a bit apologetically, at Johnny who has returned to the table with her glass and stands listening. He sets it down on the table in front of her, sits back down quietly, saying nothing.

"Myra told me not to tell anyone I knew anything," says Stella.

"And certainly not Pearson. She said it was too dangerous for me. The less I knew the better. She said she would handle it and then … and then we'd get out …"

"What were you going to do?" asks Danni.

Stella looks helplessly at her, eyes filling like pools. "I don't know," she whispers. "Just get out of here … I don't know, really …"

A dream without shape or definition, Danni thinks, a fairytale of escape. Things would be better. They would no longer be drug addicts. No longer be prostitutes. And the reality of that, the way of making it happen, was just a shadow behind the wall of longing.

"You have to get out immediately," Johnny says. "Away from Pearson."

Both women turn to him, Stella eyeing him fearfully.

"You think …"

"If Pearson thinks you know the identity of this guy, leave. It puts you in too much danger. It doesn't matter that you don't if he thinks you do."

"Stella," Danni says, "what do you think happened to Myra that night?"

Stella shrugs, but Danni knows she is simply too frightened to say what is inside her.

"Stella …"

The tears are trickling down Stella's face now.

"Stella …" Danni reaches across the table and clasps the girl's hand.

"I'm scared."

"I know."

She strokes Stella's hand to calm her. Johnny is tense beside her. Danni can feel it. It's like a heat emanating from him, his body taut like stretched wire. She looks at him. He's looking straight ahead, straight out of the window and somewhere beyond them. He's working on his own theories in there, she thinks, turning back to Stella.

"You think this legal guy killed Myra?" she asks softly.

Stella shakes her head. "Well … not personally …"

"Who then?"

Beside her, Johnny turns his head.

"You really need to ask, Danni?" he says, and his voice is hard and marbled with bitterness.

CHAPTER TWENTY-THREE

They walk together but apart, Danni conscious of leaving a gap between her and Johnny. He seems lost in thought, his hands thrust into the pockets of the black coat that he wears open, a scarf wrapped loosely round his neck and trailing. His cheeks are dark with evening stubble. The buckle of his knee as he walks is barely noticeable to her any more, a slight dip, a soft roll in his gait. There is something so companionable about their walking together that it angers her. She increases the distance between them.

She has no knowledge of where they walk, past rows of suburban housing, curtains open, lit by flickering televisions and the soft glow of table lamps. A young boy on a bicycle emerges fast from behind, making Danni jump, swishing inches from her, the tyres hissing in the wet of the rain soaked streets. She is following Johnny unthinkingly, until suddenly she finds herself somewhere she recognises. A row of shops, a launderette like an overbright beacon of light, a single occupant pulling strings of clothes from a machine. A newsagent, window lit with Halloween faces. She looks round, gets her bearings. They are close to Johnny's flat.

Her phone rings. She takes it out, looks at the number. Traynor. She switches it off and tosses it back into her bag. Johnny has walked on. He turns.

"I'll get a taxi to the hotel," she says.

Johnny walks back towards her.

"I'll make you a cup of coffee then take you back in a taxi to the hotel, check your room."

"There's no need."

"I think there is."

"I don't need you."

He shrugs.

"Maybe not. No harm though, eh?"

The soft Irish cadences of his accent wrap around the words, caressing them. She looks at him and realises she has lost sight of why she came here. There have been so many competing emotions. Why is she getting caught up in all this? She came for Marco. For Angelo. But they're dead, she thinks suddenly. And Myra's dead. But Stella's not. Yet.

"You shouldn't have told Stella which hotel you were staying in."

"Why not? It was the least I could do. We shouldn't have left her."

"We couldn't do anything else."

"Yes we could."

"We had no choice."

"There's *always* a fucking choice," she spits at him. If he had chosen differently, she thinks, her life would be different.

Angelo, she wants to scream when she looks at him. A silent wail spirals inside her from her guts, a physical force ripping through her like a tornado. Ang ... e ... l ... o.

He understands the pain but not yet the reason for it. His eyes drop. He frowns at the pavement, his hands still thrust deep in his coat pockets.

"We need to talk. Come inside."

She stands mutinously watching him as he walks forward to the stairs up to the flat. At the top of the steps he opens the door and leans against it with his back. He does not coax her, nor even look at her. She moves forward out of the dark street into the light of the stairwell.

Upstairs, they remain silent as he turns the dial of the gas fire and it clicks, hisses into life cheerlessly. There is a grey patch on the wall round the fire. She wonders if he notices any more. When he makes coffee, the noises seem magnified against a background of silence: the bang of the cupboard door, the sound of water on metal as he fills the kettle, the hiss of steam, the scrape of a teaspoon against the cup.

"We can't do anything with Stella until she's ready to help herself," he says, setting down a mug.

"We could get her out of there for a start."

"And take her where? Here? Your hotel room? Stella's an addict, Danni. You'd be living with her habit. And she'd be asking you for money and when you reached the stage beyond politeness where you said no, she'd end up taking it from you anyway. Oh she wouldn't *mean* to at the start. She wouldn't *want* to. But she would."

"How come you know so bloody much?" Danni folds her arms. "How come, smart ass?"

"Because I lived with an addict."

She sits up instinctively. His tone is not aggressive and yet she senses challenge, emotional challenge. He watches her, as if waiting – with a neutral kind of interest – to see how she responds to that challenge. As if he is curious but not personally invested in the result. She wonders if detachment is a trick he plays. On others. On himself.

"Who ..."

"A woman."

His right leg is crossed over his knee in a wide triangle. He reaches out, dusts imaginary flecks of dust off his trouser leg with his index finger.

"A woman?"

"A woman very much like Stella. Young. Messed up." He licks his finger and rubs it against his shoe.

"What …?

"I lived with her," he says.

Despite herself, she is interested. What kind of lover does a terrorist make? Can you compartmentalise a personality? In this drawer is his capacity to blow her child into the air, to drown a mother in the rivers of her own child's blood. In this drawer is his capacity for tenderness, for whispered intimacy rippling through his life, like a breeze through tangled grasses.

"What happened?"

"She died."

He clears his throat in the silence.

She cannot bring herself to say she is sorry.

"Overdose?"

Johnny shakes his head, readjusts himself in his seat, sits back.

The possibilities flip through her head … Car crash? Tragic illness? Should she ask? Stay silent?

"Pearson," he says, and underneath the jolt of fear that shoots through her, she is aware of the creak of his chair as he stands up. He lifts his cup, takes it to the sink. She hears the running water as the cup is rinsed out, the bang of it being placed on the draining board. She is sitting motionless when he comes back in the room.

"What did he do?"

Johnny walks to the gas fire hanging on the wall, reaches out his hand for the dial.

"Are you cold?" he says, turning the dial further so that she hears the surge of gas hissing through the fire.

"What did he do?"

He sits down again.

"It's hard ... that's ... not the place to start."

"Start where you like."

He tilts his head back, blowing out a sigh almost in defeat at the challenge of giving shape to his thoughts with words.

"Pearson and me ... our lives have been kind of tangled up together. He's made sure of that. It's like different strands of a rope that are wound round each other. And every time I've tried to extricate myself from that, he's made sure that I'm brought back into the knot. I suppose ... I suppose it started after ... You remember I told you about Pat?"

"Your brother?"

He nods.

"It was after that I joined the IRA with Pearson."

"Because Pat died?"

"It was the first time I'd seen a dead body. I was terrified. I couldn't ... I just couldn't get my head round it ..." He pauses. "Then a week later there was another dead body. Two streets away. I only knew the boy vaguely, but he'd been shot by the soldiers and I looked down at the chalk white of his face, the terrible stillness of a body that had been walking that morning ... running ... and I knew things had changed. I'd changed. I still felt frightened but I felt more angry. Furiously angry. The British army had moved into my streets, were killing my people ... They had no right ... no right ..."

"I don't understand how you could look at a dead body and want to kill someone."

She is thinking of her own first dead body but she does not want to go back there. She was too young to see her father but she saw her mother, cold as marble, and the sick fear of incomprehension had overwhelmed her. Where was she, her mother? Her body lay empty, like a burned out shell in which there had been some kind of electrical implosion. All wires dead; all movement impossible. And it had been so utterly enormous that she could not imagine wanting to create that state in somebody else. Death, in all its terribleness, affirmed your own sense of being alive. The last thing it did was make you want to take life away.

"Why would you do that?" she persists.

"Because we were at war. This country was at war. And when you are at war … things … you know the rules change."

"Land is worth killing for? Possession is worth the loss of others?"

Johnny shakes his head.

"It's not just about land, Danni. Yes, land is part of it and this land … my parents, my grandparents, my great grandparents are all buried in it. I have a stake in it."

She moved around too much as a child to understand that feeling. Home was temporary, an army base, a rented flat. A place where her mother tried to make old curtains fit new windows.

"But it's about politics as well as land," Johnny continues. "And sure, politics is only the way you want to live. The way you want to organise yourselves as a community. This struggle has been about ideas and principles. It's been about more than the living and dying of a single generation."

"If you are prepared to die for your principles, that's your choice," Danni retorts. "But what about the people who weren't prepared to die for your principles? The ones who had no choice? What about the innocent people caught up in it all?"

"That includes my grandfather, Danni. The innocent aren't all on one side." He catches her eye and holds it fiercely, wills her to come clean with him. "What are we talking about here, Danni?"

"The things you have done."

"How do you know what I've done?"

"Pearson …" She hesitates, wrong-footed.

"Oh Pearson … right …" His hair has fallen forward onto his face and he pushes it back exasperatedly with one hand.

Of course, Danni thinks suddenly. Why should she believe Pearson? Perhaps … She looks at him and is surprised by the surge of emotion that blossoms inside her. Why is she feeling this? Perhaps, she thinks, he is merely a terrorist and not *the* terrorist. Whatever else he is responsible for, perhaps he was not responsible for the deaths of Angelo and Marco. That would mean that her journey here had been a waste of time. The ordeal of this last week would be for nothing. And yet this emotion inside her means that is exactly what she hopes. She recognises it as a tiny surge of hope, a tentative fluttering, like the wings of a tiny bird inside her.

She cannot deny it. There is something that draws her to him. "I asked Pearson to put me in touch with someone who had been involved in bombings on the British mainland. He put me in touch with you because he said you had been involved in the 1992 December bombing in Glasgow. He thought that since I came from Scotland, I would be interested in that."

She watches every flicker on his face as she talks. His tiger stained eyes watch her back, absorbing her. He says nothing.

"He said … Pearson said … that you had been involved."

Still he says nothing.

"So were you?"

She holds her breath.

One lie, he thinks, one small lie is all it would take.

"Were you?"

"That's obviously not a question I would be advised to

154

answer," he says and though his voice remains unapologetic, there is sadness in it. "You must know that nobody was ever convicted for that operation."

"Were you there?" she repeats.

"Yes Danni," he says quietly, not dropping his gaze. "I was there."

She turns from him, the beating wings inside her stilling, the fledgling bird shot in a flurry of blood and feathers.

CHAPTER TWENTY-FOUR

He does not tell her, when she turns from him, that he had argued with Pearson about Glasgow.

"Why Scotland?" Johnny had said, his irritation obvious. Pearson always wanted to build empires. Even when it came to death.

Pearson had eyed him with a kind of venom. "There are no limits to the fight, Johnny," he said softly.

"Pearson, you're beginning to enjoy the scrap so much you're forgetting what the fuckin' fight's about."

Johnny scraped back his chair on the linoleum and looked round at the bare walls, streaked with dirt. In the corner of the ceiling, a black ball of spider had rolled itself up, the broken strands of fine grey web draped round it. Where the hell was this place, anyway? A safe house, Pearson had said, as their car lumbered up a pitted track. There could be no pattern to cell meetings, Johnny accepted that. But he had become increasingly uneasy lately. It wouldn't surprise him if one of these days a bullet blasted his brains out when he arrived at one of Pearson's 'safe' locations.

Across the table, Pearson never took his eyes off Johnny's face.

"Oh fuck off, Pearson," Johnny said, kicking out viciously at the leg of the table as he spoke. Pearson's attempts to intimidate him, to exert control, always riled him. The table shook on wobbly legs. Why did Pearson always want to be puppet master?

He could feel the uneasy ripple run through the others seated at the table. Five of them, he thought. Big Joe Devine on his right, his seventeen-stone frame wedged into a too-small wooden armed chair that dug into the wall of fat beneath his checked flannel shirt. Peter MacBride, a quiet, watchful man who worked as a labourer on building sites, on his left. Pearson opposite. And wee Seamy, wide-eyed and stuck to Pearson's side. Five of them whose lives depended on each other's silence. Yet how many did he trust? Only MacBride.

Devine coughed, shifting in his seat so that it creaked.

"Oh c'mon," MacBride said impatiently. "Let's talk properly about this."

It's freezing in here, Johnny thought in the silence that followed. He buttoned his long black coat over, re-tied his scarf round his neck.

"Scotland isn't what we're about," he said.

"What are we about, Johnny?" Pearson said. His voice held a whisper of mockery.

"I tell you what we're *not* about. We're not about killing innocent civilians. We're not about taking the fight onto neutral streets. We fight the British army. We fight the police. We fight the British government."

It wasn't that he was against violence. This was a legitimate war. He had been involved in IRA operations at army barracks and RUC stations and he knew what he was doing. But he always argued against operations that he felt put civilians at too great a risk. The minute you lost your regret about the necessity of violence, the minute death

157

became just business, your soul was lost. You weren't an IRA man, you were a thug. You were Pearson.

A picture of his grandmother's house in Donegal sprang into Johnny's mind, the dark basement that harboured its secrets for a generation. Guns shipped in from America via France. Explosives. Violence was part of his story. It was part of Ireland's story. He accepted that. As a child, when Mary Seonaid had wanted to read him fairy tales at bedtime, he had urged her to leave the book down and tell her own. The night four IRA men were sent to defend a meeting of the Catholic Working Men's Club at a private house in Dublin. He knew every word of it. They had surrounded the house, two in the lane that ran down the back of the street, two at the front. The armoured cars of the Black and Tans had swept silently into the street shortly after.

The night was dark, Mary Seonaid said in that low voice of hers, a voice that seemed like it had been dragged down an octave over the years by hardship. Johnny watched her face intently. The volunteers were shooting at shadows that moved from the armoured cars, she said. Sparks flew from the ground: bullets jumping from the pavements and lighting up the darkness, like shooting stars lighting a midnight sky. Johnny was enthralled.

An adventure story it was, full of bravery and daring. The four men who took on the might of the black and tans. Only three of them survived, but four of the black and tans were shot dead and the meeting of the Catholic Working Men's Club dispersed safely into the night. But Mary Seonaid also created tales out of the nights when ambushes of the police and army had been cancelled because civilians were in the way. It was a question of discipline.

Johnny looked round the table.

"Do you want to give us that talk of yours about the gentlemen of the early IRA, Johnny?" said Pearson.

Johnny ignored him and looked at Devine.

"One bomb over there is worth five here and we all know it," said Devine.

"How do the people of Glasgow fit into this? You're probably related to half of them."

"Maybe that's the point," retorted Devine.

"Related?" Pearson said. "If the queen visited Scotland, half of them would be out with their fuckin' flags. They don't give a shit what's happening over here. People need to be taught to give a shit."

"What do you give a shit about, Pearson?" Johnny said.

"What's the target in Glasgow?" asked McBride.

"We're not aiming for civilian deaths," said Pearson. "It's a warning."

"Where?"

"Just off Argyle Street."

"Argyle Street! How the fuck do you avoid casualties in the city's main shopping street?" said Johnny.

"Johnny, this has been passed by the Chief of Staff," said Pearson evenly.

"Did he pass last week's warehouse job an' all?"

Pearson sat back, putting his hands behind his head.

Devine and MacBride exchanged a glance.

"What robbery?" said MacBride.

"Quarter of a million pounds of alcohol and tobacco," said Johnny.

Wee Seamy laughed nervously. "Jeez," he said, and looked at Pearson.

"What's your point, Johnny?" The light from the bare light bulb above Pearson's head was shining on his bald head, glinting off his gold rings.

"I'm just wondering what the split is. How much the IRA gets and how much you do."

"The finances of the unit are none of your concern."

"It's not the unit's finances I'm thinking of," said Johnny. "It's what's siphoned off into your own fat bank account I'm thinking of."

"What's going on?" said Devine.

Pearson shrugged.

"Sorry, you know how it is. There are things I can't talk about."

"I'll fuckin' bet," said Johnny quietly.

"You know," said Pearson. "you're beginning to worry me, Johnny. I'm not sure about your commitment any more."

"Pearson ..." said McBride.

Johnny sat forward in his chair, hands in his pockets still. "Go on, Pearson," he said.

"No, shut up ..." said MacBride,.

"I don't know what side you're working for any more," said Pearson softly.

"Pearson, shut up," repeated MacBride.

"No," said Devine. "I want to hear ..."

"Did you hear that even the Chief of Staff's driver turned out to be a British agent?" said Pearson. "They're everywhere."

There was a second's silence before Johnny moved, a second's stillness. He could feel it inside him, the bit of himself that he couldn't control, roaring like a thunderous wave inside his head. The momentum of that wave lifted him so fast his chair toppled sideways to the floor as he moved across the table, grabbing Pearson by the throat, lifting him from his seat. That a shit like Pearson should question him ...

"Christ!" said Devine, making a lunge for Johnny and pulling him backwards.

MacBride wrapped his arms round Johnny's chest, pinning his arms to his side.

"Johnny, sit down. Come on, sit down," he said quietly.

Johnny couldn't bear it, the feeling of being hemmed in, held down.

"Let go, Peter."

Tentatively, MacBride dropped his arms.

"We're not leaving it at that," Devine said. "We're not leaving here until we know what we're dealing with."

Johnny shook his head. Pearson knew what he was fucking doing. Feeding the IRA beast, the paranoia that burned inside them all. Who was legit. Who you could trust. The fear destroyed you if you let it.

Devine looked at Johnny.

"So what's goin' on?"

Johnny leaned across the table.

"Careless fuckin' talk, Pearson," he spat.

"Johnny," said Devine, "if there's any truth in it you know what's going to happen here. I am going to break every bone in your body with a brick, before I blast enough bullets in it to make it sink to the bottom of the Lagan."

He was standing stock still, poised to spring. If Johnny was an informer, Devine knew everyone in this room was finished. Pearson sat back, arms folded, watching.

"Christ, Joe," said MacBride. "Johnny's credentials are better than any of us."

"Aye," said Devine, "and them's the ones they go for." He hovered over the table, forehead shiny under the light, looking in edgy anticipation round the table. Despite the cold, Devine's bulk had begun to sweat lightly.

He leant over Johnny's chair.

"Which road do you want closed, Johnny?" he said in his ear.

Johnny looked straight ahead, only the muscle in his cheek moving.

"Which road? When we dump your body."

"You've got nothing to fear from me," Johnny said and stood up.

"You're going nowhere." Devine was in front of him in a second, faces inches apart.

"You know the rules," he said. Any breaches of the code, whether desertion or betrayal, must be dealt with on the spot. Green book."

"I'm not having any kangaroo court."

"You've got no choice."

Johnny looked across at Pearson. He had barely reacted in the last few minutes, was watching quietly. Only Johnny knew him well enough to sense the satisfaction rise like a vapour from him as Devine spoke.

"You need to prove yourself, Johnny," said Pearson.

"I want to see him do Glasgow," said Devine, looking at Pearson and jerking his head at Johnny. "Alone. And if for any reason, it doesn't go ahead – any reason – I'll take it as a sign that he has friends in the wrong places." He turned to Johnny. "And then you can choose your road, Johnny, because believe me – I'll take you out."

Johnny couldn't get rid of the smell under his nose for days. It was there when he went to sleep, when he woke, when he ate. The damp, fusty smell of fertiliser combined with diesel. It was Devine who was the explosives expert in the cell but he insisted Johnny get involved this time. Later, Johnny realised that insistence had Pearson's hallmark all over it. Pearson knew how Johnny's mind worked, how the guilt would come to destroy him.

They travelled south to buy fertiliser because the fertiliser pellets in the north were coated in plastic to prevent them being ground. They barely spoke in either direction but Devine wouldn't let him out of his sight. Johnny couldn't bring himself to ask questions. He would not give

Devine authority, make himself apprentice, but simply did as he was asked, mechanically. In the next few days, he went through two coffee grinders reducing the pellets to powder. The fertiliser simply rotted the inner mechanism. And the dust … his clothes were permanently covered in fine pink dust. It stained him.

His mind was elsewhere. When he wasn't grinding fertiliser, he was organising the logistics, getting hold of a car from one of his garage contacts, fitting false number plates, creating a concealed section in the boot. They all had their areas of expertise and that was his. Not explosives. He had to move fast when the bomb was completed, Devine told him. Fertiliser was highly sensitive. If it got damp it wouldn't go off at all and it would remain potent for only around a week. He was to take the car on the ferry to Stranraer and drive the long, tortuous road to Glasgow. By the time he got safely off the ferry, he needed that drive to calm himself.

In his hotel the night before the bombing, he pored over maps of the city centre yet again, trying to bring the nervous excitement, the sick fear, the shivering, sweat-inducing anticipation, under control. He had looked at himself in the mirror as he cleaned his teeth and seen his own hand tremble, like it was separate from the rest of him. And his mind trembled too, shuddering to release the energy inside him, the surfeit of thought and confused emotion.

The next morning, he spoke to Devine briefly to go over the technical details.

"You are certain this will be a small, contained explosion?" he asked Devine.

"It's idiot proof," Devine insisted. "The only thing you have to do is set the timer and get the hell out of there."

The end of hope, Danni thinks as she turns from him, a surge of the old bitterness rising in her. But what's bitterness but misshapen sadness? Sadness that takes root and grows twisted inside you, that branches into spaces where it should never be.

Everything has stilled inside her: a kind of defeat. She feels drained. Just days ago she would have been convulsed by her hatred. And yes, she feels it still but she is also still sitting here, still listening. Still compelled to ask why, to find reason. Why is that? She rests her head back against the seat and closes her eyes against the light.

CHAPTER TWENTY-FIVE

He dreams about it still, though less often. The terrible transformation from abstract concept to concrete night-mare. The smell of pain hanging like a vapour above a river of blood, a vapour that he absorbed and never managed to eradicate afterwards. You think you understand something fully, the reality, the implications, until it happens and sud-denly you realise that you saw nothing. You saw as much as a blind child stumbling in the darkness. Some realities can never be prepared for.

He knew things sometimes went wrong. You did not join the IRA to play tiddlywinks. He used to think it was like drilling in a road; there was always the possibility of accidentally hitting a water main, sending the water spray-ing everywhere. But that had been only a metaphorical explanation in his own head. He couldn't believe it when the real mains burst in the explosion and the water and the blood mingled.

He had been a street away when the car bomb exploded, sweating in his haste to move quickly from the scene. He felt the boom, the vibration, and in the split second before he realised the enormity of it, there had been a momentary surge of elation that what he had helped make was successful. Then he realised this was no warning, no symbol. He was aware of a wall of noise in the distance and a corresponding silence in the street where he was, a pause in activity, a slow-motion stupor before everyone started to run. He couldn't help himself. He moved with the crowd back towards the explosion and stood at the top of the street, watching as the fountain of water shot spectacularly into the air. It was like a sick ballet set to a sound track of screams. Water and fire, element against element, and bodies everywhere he looked.It was when the first screams died out and the low crying started that he ran, banging into passers by as he went, pushing them to one side in his need to be out of that place.

He had jumped on a train and in a small town in the north of England, phoned Pearson at a pre-arranged number.

"You bastards," Johnny said, leaning his head against the glass of the box. "You fucking bastards."

"Fertiliser bombs are always the hardest to control," Pearson said. "Don't try and tell me you didn't know that, Johnny."

"You planned that," said Johnny. "You and Devine."

"You made it," Pearson said, his voice suddenly dropping venomously. "Don't try and wash you hands of it now. Don't try and make out you're not part of it. Take the glory, Johnny. You're part of history. But just remember. Your hands are as dirty as the rest of us now."

It was true, Johnny thought, smashing the receiver down, When everything had gone up, when the inferno came, and the smoke and the screaming and the running and the vapour of pain, everything he was went up with it. He lost a part of himself that day that never came back.

There is an echo of that pain now as he looks at Danni's wide, brown eyes. He saw the way she held her breath while she waited for him to answer the question. He wanted to answer differently. For her. For him. For all the wasted years. He wanted to lie and for it not to be a lie.

It would have been possible. How could she have ever known? His word against Pearson's. And something tells him that had he lied, she would have accepted his lie gratefully, that she would never have done anything to expose it. Because had he lied, there would have been a future. He knows that, though he is not sure she does.

But it was inconceivable. He cannot ameliorate his part. He will not bleat that he didn't mean it. What was he doing there if he didn't mean it? Nor will he say sorry. The word sorry seems somehow insulting.

He disappeared for a while afterwards. For his own safety. For the cell's. In the rented caravan on England's south coast he read every report. Listened to every news bulletin. Faced the enormity of what had happened. Of all of it, of the tales of tragedy and courage and heroism and self sacrifice that emerge in every tragedy, there was one detail he found harder to face than the others. A three-year-old child had died with his father. He could list the names of the six people who died that day, their ages, their occupations. The fact that one had been a single parent (what happened to her child, Johnny wondered repeatedly), that another had died just two days before her wedding. But the three-year-old was just a child who had not yet lived, who had no details to give, who took up only a few lines next to the long paragraphs of the other victims, and the blankness of his existence, the fact that it was all still to write, was the most unbearable thing of all,

Angelo's picture was used on the front page of every paper. Every child. No child. Cherubic smile, the pink apple blush of babyhood still on his cheeks, the curiosity of a world as yet unexplored embossed in mischievous eyes.

Eighteen years ago, he was three. He would have been twenty-one this year. Back then, and in the years since, he has had so many days to remember the boy who never grew up. The child's foreign name had emphasised to him that the fight had drifted too far from home. What did he have to do with any of it? Angelo Piacentini, the boy who has haunted his waking and his sleeping for eighteen years, the boy who never grew up.

CHAPTER TWENTY-SIX

"How did you feel?" she asks, her head still back against the cushion and her eyes closed. "The day of the bombing?"

Perhaps, she thinks, a little sliver of hope beginning to flicker again, he was only there with others, swept along with something he had no control over. Perhaps that was how it was.

He takes so long to answer that she opens her eyes. He is sitting hunched forward, arms resting on his knees, hands clasped together.

"I can't answer that," he says.

"Why not?"

He shakes his head impotently.

"I don't have the words."

"So you regret it then?"

"I regret certain things that day. I don't regret being part of the struggle. I don't regret … but there are things that … Danni, all I can say is that words are an inadequacy. I won't use them for excuses. There are no words that can tell you what I really feel. What do you want me to say … that I am sorry people died? What's that but a ripple in a great big ocean?"

She should applaud him, really, she thinks lethargically.

Applaud his refusal to give her empty words. Wasn't that what had made her so furious watching that reconciliation programme, those expressions of easy regret? How do you know they're easy, a voice inside her head asks, and she turns in impatience from it.

She notices suddenly how very thin he is.

"The woman …" she says, "… the addict."

Like an ascetic monk living on berries, she thinks, living his life separately from the world around him. Living his own rules. His skin is grey white, taut over the bridge of his nose, almost transparent, except under his eyes which are smudged a purpley black. His body is a series of elegant angles. He is a triangle, she thinks, not a circle. No round soft edges, but sharp clean lines.

"Roisin," he says.

"Tell me …"

She wants to know. Why does she want to know? Why does it matter?

"She was one of Pearson's girls."

Shock winds her.

"A prostitute?"

"Eventually."

He gets up.

"Do you mind if I turn that down?" he says, nodding at the fire.

She shakes her head, watches the purple flame diminish to a peep.

"Is that how you met? Through Pearson?"

"God no."

He sits down again, not looking at her.

"Were you in love with her?"

His eyes flick to her instinctively, as if reading her face, as if he wonders why she asks the question. She wonders herself.

"I don't … maybe … not by the end. I'm not sure if I ever was. I was certainly in lust with her."

"What was she like?" she asks and the simple question seems to silence him completely, makes him look at her with eyes that see nothing but the past. He looks so intently that she sees herself reflected in his eyes, her image drowning in dark grey and bottomless mirrors.

What was she like? Jesus, what was Roisin like? She was the sexiest woman he'd ever seen. Willowy but curvaceous, in heels not far off 6 feet. He sees her in her green dress the night it all went wrong, a green that simply illuminated her, switched her on like a string of lights. Chestnut curls tumbling to her shoulders, greeny grey eyes that glinted like a cat's. She was capricious that night, flirtatious, wilful, the way Roisin could be. There was an inner restlessness about her that never quite disappeared. On the nights she was most beautiful, he noticed, she was also at her most self-destructive, like someone who knew this light that cascaded from her was temporary, that she needed to grab it, experience it, before it dimmed. Nothing was ever enough on those nights.

He was almost scared of her when she was like that, at the crest of the roller coaster of her moods. But it was undeniable that he wanted her more too. No, maybe not more, just more jealously if he is really honest. Other people's desire for her fed his, that was the truth. All eyes would be on her and he'd watch quietly, never moving to her, never placing a proprietorial hand on her back, or steering her from the centre of attention, to his quiet corner. He had too much pride for that. Sometimes he thought she would have liked it if he had, that it would have been a kind of triumph. Sometimes he thought she taunted him with her vivacity.

That green dress. She wore it like a glove. She'd only worn it once before that night. He'd peeled it from her within seconds of arriving home, when they were still in the hall, and she'd laughed as she kissed him, the dress rustling to the floor. It made her feel powerful that he wanted her that much. It made him feel powerful that she was his.

The second night she wore the dress was different. There was no beauty in it. Everything felt tarnished. Pearson had moved in on her, full of plans. Just because she was Johnny's. Just to show he could. Roisin was easy prey. She was interested in life, in new things, in experiences, and Pearson with his pills to pop, and his constant stream of stuff to snort, offered all of that. But he never touched any of it himself.

Johnny knew how it worked. The lines until you were hooked were free. After that, they came at a price. Roisin had no idea how high a price. Sometimes, when she was at her most vulnerable, when she hit the lowest curve of her moods, she was like a needy child. But tonight she was brittle, petulant … and eager for somewhere to invest her energy.

She leaned on Pearson's shoulder, because she was taller than him, and whispered something in his ear and laughed. And Pearson had said, away now and don't listen to Johnny He has no idea how to have fun. He had put his hand out to pat her backside, and Johnny had wanted to pat him in the guts with his closed fist. What really got him was that Pearson wasn't sexually interested in Roisin in the least, it was games, always games, with Pearson. Control. Time for me to go, Johnny had told Roisin, and she'd hesitated but stayed. She never came back in the same way.

"What was she like?" he repeats, looking at Danni so intently that he sees an image of himself reflected back in her serious brown eyes.

"She was … she was …" And for the life of him he cannot finish the sentence.

He has put some music on, given her a glass of white wine. The warmth of the room is acting like a cocoon, wrapping her up, inuring her. She has kicked her shoes off, put her feet up on the edge of his table.

"You said she died."

"Yes."

"How?"

He tops up her glass from the bottle. The fire on the wall hisses in the stillness.

"She became a cocaine addict."

"But you said it wasn't an overdose."

"No, it wasn't."

"Did Pearson …?"

"Yes and no."

He reaches for the bottle again.

"Maybe I'll have one after all."

She watches him pour, feeling her face glow pink in the heat from the fire.

"Roisin ended up owing Pearson for her habit. She got deeper and deeper into his debt, which is the way he wanted it. He didn't care about Roisin but it was his way of exercising control over my life, showing me he could pull my strings. She told me things were under control but they weren't. Money went missing but she always denied she had anything to do with it. She'd fly into a rage if I questioned her but I couldn't trust her. She sold jewellery then claimed she'd lost it. But then I discovered that she … she had started working for him."

"She was on the streets?"

He nods.

"She fell apart when she realised that I knew."

173

Danni thinks back to Stella talking about her mother, how she said she couldn't bear it if her mother knew the truth, and Johnny had looked like he couldn't listen to any more.

"Of course she denied it at first but then she was clinging to me, crying and begging me not to leave her," he says flatly. He takes a sip of wine, grimaces.

"Bitter," he says. "Do you want something else?"

"It's fine."

What she wants is for him to continue, but he does not want to remember, she can see that.

He sits in silence for a minute, sipping from his glass.

"Did you leave her?" she asks eventually.

"No."

He lapses into silence again and she asks no more. She takes her feet off the table and tucks them under her. The heat and the wine are making her sleepy and she lays her head back, content to leave him to his thoughts.

"She was very beautiful," she hears him say, and she lifts her head.

"But not by the end. When I discovered how she was funding her habit, I told her I'd do everything I could to help her but I didn't want a relationship with her any more until she cleaned herself up. She promised she'd do it but she couldn't. Pearson made sure of that," he says bitterly. "And the fact that I knew … she couldn't deal with it. She couldn't look at me properly. So I understand … in a way … why she did it."

"Did what?"

"I was late home. Didn't want to come back. I don't know if she thought … Anyway … whatever … The house was in darkness. I was glad. I thought she was out. I opened the door and reached out for the light and then …"

His voice is unsteady. Danni says nothing, waiting.

"When I switched it on, I saw her feet hanging down from the stairwell." He takes a sip from his glass then replaces it carefully on the table, seeking composure in the smallness, the neatness, of the action. He does not look at Danni. "She'd killed herself."

CHAPTER TWENTY-SEVEN

It is the early hours of the morning when he finally takes her back to the hotel. She tries to insist that she will go alone but he ignores her.

When she sees Danni the receptionist smiles and looks back down at a sheaf of papers before suddenly starting in remembrance.

"Oh Mrs Cameron!" she calls, reaching below the desk. "We have something for you."

Danni freezes. Johnny, a step ahead of her, turns.

"For me?"

The receptionist pulls out a paper carrier bag and smiles brightly.

"A gentleman left it for you a few hours ago. A present. Is it your birthday?"

"Oh … yes," lies Danni lamely. She takes the bag, retreats to her room, her stomach a bubbling cauldron of nausea and nerves. Johnny says nothing.

The box shaped parcel inside the carrier bag is gift wrapped in pink floral paper that says, "Especially For You" across it, between pink splodges of cabbage roses. A curled ribbon bow froths from the top, a confection of spiralling metallic pink. When she lifts the box, she can feel the corner of it is damp and sticky. Something is spilling out inside. A smashed bottle perhaps.

"Do you want me to …?" Johnny asks.

She shakes her head.

The paper is well taped, layer upon layer stuck over the edges so that it cannot possibly fall accidentally open. Danni tugs at the edge with a fingernail, trying to find a start. Her fingers shake slightly. Impatiently she reaches out to her toilet bag on the dressing table, rummages for a pair of nail scissors.

She cuts the flap above the tape, runs a finger under the rest, and the paper falls off revealing a shoe box beneath. The corner is stained dark and damp and she lifts the lid tentatively. Inside, a flash of darkness, a streak of red staining the white inner box, and then the series of impressions come together to make a whole picture.

"Jesus!" She half throws the box onto the table instinctively, looks down at the hand that held the corner of the box, sees the sticky pink hue on her fingers. She drags her hand across the table, desperate to clean it, then rushes to the sink of the en suite. She turns the tap frantically, watches a tint of pink appear in the water running onto the white porcelain. Johnny understands. You have to wash blood off quickly or the memory of it stains you forever.

He is standing over the open box when she returns. The lid is up, the body of a dead bird visible inside. Its head is tilted back at right angles, its neck almost dislocated from its body. One eye is open, black, dull and glassy. The body has stiffened now but the blood that seeped from it when its throat was cut is still moist and sticky in the box.

Johnny closes the lid.

"I'll deal with it," he says quietly.

Danni stands at the doorway of the ensuite still. She feels

cold all of a sudden, nauseous, stifles a shiver that threatens
to run through her.

"What does it say on the lid of that box?"

Johnny shakes his head.

"No more singing ..."

She runs her hand up her arm. Everything is surreal. Out
of control.

"He knows we spoke to Stella?"

"I told you there wouldn't be much doubt about it,
Danni."

He lifts the box carefully.

"Have you got a plastic bag?"

She moves finally, reluctantly, and rummages in the bottom of the wardrobe for a bag. The wardrobe door squeaks
closed. He puts the box flat on the bottom, ties the handles
carefully, and places the package back into the paper carrier bag. Danni watches, clamping her jaw to stop her teeth
chattering. Johnny glances up at her, but says nothing. He
puts the bag over at the door and sits on the edge of the
bed.

"Okay?"

"Yeah."

"Come and sit down."

Danni moves mechanically, sits on the bed leaving a substantial space between them, her shoulders hunched and
hands clasped between her knees. Outside in the corridor
a door bangs closed, voices ring in the corridor. Someone
laughs. Normal sounds out there behind a closed door,
normal lives. Her own life has moved so far from normality
so quickly. What is this room? Who is this man? She turns
sideways to look at Johnny, finds him watching her already.

"It'll be okay," he says quietly. He reaches out unexpectedly and takes hold of her clasped hands. She doesn't move
but sits stiffly, rigid as a rock, looking down at his hand

covering hers, like she's looking at an alien creature in a glass exhibit case.

She lies in bed after he goes, open-eyed in the darkness. She is frightened, cold frightened. It is not the bloodied bird that haunts her still; it is the sight of Johnny's hand on hers, the surge she stifled inside herself. That terrible mixture of searing anger and instinctive, unwanted chemistry that his tenderness prompted. For one awful moment she had wanted to grasp his hand back. There is nothing familiar here, nothing she understands.

There was, in that touch, something that released a tightly coiled spring inside her. As if all the years of suppressed physical longing simply pushed their way through the barriers she had created and let her know she wasn't finished with life yet, not by a long way. Not that her longing was directed at *him*, she thinks. Not really. And if it was, she has even more reason to hate him. Marco, she thinks. She wants Marco. She has always wanted Marco.

Her body tenses suddenly. She listens intently then lifts her head slightly from the pillow.

"Marco," she whispers into the darkness. "Marco?" He seems so close here in Ireland, as if he has followed her silently, simply watching so that she is never completely alone. And here, lying in bed in the darkness, the sense is so strong that momentarily, irrationally, she is deceived and lifts her head from the pillow.

When only the silence answers her, she lays her head back down into the pillow. How stupid she is! What did she expect? It is a long time since she looked for him in that way. After he died, she found at first that her instincts to talk to him were greater than ever. In the greatest ordeal of her life there was only one person she naturally turned to and of course he had gone. Faced with so many practical ordeals after his death, she was in the ridiculous position of wanting to ask Marco how she should organise his funeral.

And now, the same instinct. There is a reason why she feels him so close again here. There must be. Perhaps he is here to give her courage, to help her pull the trigger, to ensure she avenges his death. What do you want me to do, she whispers. "Marco?"

CHAPTER TWENTY-EIGHT

He walks into the darkness, glad of its cover. A sprinkling of stars pepper an inky sky. The night offers him an anonymity that always makes him more comfortable. Nightfall makes him feel like a shadow; he likes the distance it gives him from the world. Or gave him. She is under his skin. Under his skin and nothing feels the same. It's like he has become reacquainted with his nerve endings. Part of him feels exhilarated and alive for the first time in years but there is a sense too of foreboding, of resentment, even.

He does not understand her. Neither does he understand the effect of her. He only knows that she has invaded him insidiously, dangerously, put down a root system that is spreading inside him in every direction. A taxi trundles by, vacancy light blazing, but he does not hail it. He likes to walk. Sometimes, when he cannot sleep, he walks for hours, past sleeping houses that seem to breathe silently in the darkness, past padlocked garages and warehouses, past high-rise blocks with occasional windows lit like stranded planets in a galaxy of darkness. He often wonders who inhabits those lit windows, who embraces the night as he does, what lives they live to make them keep the same strange hours.

The smell of her. He breathes in deeply as if she's there and he can smell her perfume: a heady mix of exotic floral sweetness and heavy low notes of spice. He wonders what it's called. It's substantial. Like Danni herself. He pictures the way the short glossy curtain of dark chestnut hair falls against pale skin, the serious intent of her eyes. The almost cold passion of her. And then that part of her that is missing, that gives her both her toughness and her vulnerability. He imagines too much. He thinks about holding her, touching her, about breathing her in, about losing himself then finding himself again in her.

So many years of this existence that until she came here, he no longer even realised the lack in it. There had come a point in prison when he decided that the only thing you could control in life was your own mind. Own it, contain it, control it. Control your thoughts and your needs and your desires. And if you controlled it enough, you didn't need anyone else in the world. You could rely entirely on yourself; no one else mattered. That was strength.

He got used to suppressing everything. In prison it had been something of a comfort that even when you were locked up, your mind was your own. Even if they killed him, they couldn't own him. When the door thudded shut for the night, when he looked at the bars on the outer windows, he knew there was a part of him that no one could ever possess except himself. A space that no one could reach, a kind of infinity. Sometimes he thought that his mind was like space, a resource that not even he knew the limits of.

When the intelligence officers visited him, offering him a deal for information, he looked at them from a place far away. Inside his head, he counted bricks on the wall. "Is he on something?" he heard one of them murmur to the other. In the recreation hall later that day, Aidan McCann, who had been convicted with him for the Lands Road bombing, had sat down beside Johnny. "I heard you had a visit." Johnny glanced up at him but said nothing. "Have you ever wondered," McCann said, his feet splayed in front of him, "what Pearson said when those guys came calling?" Johnny's insides had tumbled in shock and when they settled, everything in his head was in place.

He'd always suspected he was banged up in here because of Pearson, but he'd assumed Pearson had done it just to prove he was in charge. Johnny lay back on his bunk that night, his arms behind his head. He wished he had a cigarette. It was hard tonight to keep control of his mind. The walls were closing in. He wanted to smash anything he could get his hands on. Pearson was an informer. He was sure of it. After they joined the Provos, Pearson had risen rapidly through the ranks, quickly being recruited to the nutting squad. Johnny remembered the story about him insisting on shooting some poor bastard who had sold petrol from his garage to military vehicles, but all the while it was a cover …

Yet, it was in prison that he learned not to hate Pearson. Of course it was almost impossible at first because if it hadn't been for Pearson he wouldn't have been in there, banged up for a terrorist attack he had nothing to do with. Typical Pearson. Bent even as an informer. But Johnny, his head scrambled with guilt over Glasgow, had to admit there was a kind of twisted justice in it: never imprisoned for an attack he did commit, incarcerated for one he didn't. Karma.

Anyway, hatred was too enormous an emotion to release into that space inside his head, in case it expanded, filling it all up and leaving nothing for him. It would leave him out of control and if there was one thing he promised himself it was that he would never again be in anyone else's control but his own.

Six years. A man can learn a lot of discipline in six years. He would set tasks, goals. Small, silly things. Tea without sugar. Toast without butter. Not eating for a day. No meat for a week. It was a drive for control, for self sufficiency, but there was another element to it. Perhaps an even deeper element. Making his life frill-free was a kind of atonement, a punishment that he knew he deserved. He couldn't have explained it but he knew in some vague kind of way that it was connected to a need to break free from the burden of his own guilt.

It was in prison that the studying started. He lost himself in knowledge and that, too, freed him. An enormous release when eventually he read Yeats and Joyce and Doyle with his own understanding, with the confidence of an educated man. Books were another discipline, a mind's training. He had his books and his music and most important of all he had himself. And in the end he decided there was no other option but to rely on himself.

It wouldn't be honest to say he didn't miss women, physically, emotionally. The soft curve of them, as elemental as the roll of this land he loved so much. The curve and the straight, not just physically but mentally: a different way of looking, a different way of thinking.

He misses the sensuousness, the colour and the scent, the feel of silk, the instinct for physical indulgence. He misses the sex. He even misses the arguments, the feeling that he has to take account of someone other than himself. Of course, women had the capacity to fuck him up, same as they did any man. But he missed being fucked up. It was hard not to feel castrated when there was no possibility of women in his life. The way he lived now, it was hard to feel like a sexual being of any kind. And yet until Danni came, until she turned up on his doorstep, it was just another discipline, another control. If you'd have asked him, he'd

184

have said he had it mastered. That he barely thought about it any more. The fire of the fight had gone out and maybe that's why Danni has taken him by surprise.

The streets are deserted, the puddles icing at the edges. The cold air cuts at his chest. Behind him, the low hum of the city's gritters cuts through his thoughts, the swish of their brushes as they spread salt.

She is not like Roisin, he thinks.

He wonders why he makes the comparison. Why should she be like Roisin? He loved Roisin in his way, though sometimes he felt as if he loved her like a child instead of an equal, with a kind of parental indulgence. Certainly by the end. He lusted after her; of that there was no doubt. He wanted to have her. But with Danni he wants to see inside her. He wants to understand her and absorb her. His yearning is beyond discipline.

The cold is beginning to bite. He walks faster, not hunching against the chill, but opening himself up to it. Trying to control it with his mind. Not far now to the flat. He is not consciously thinking about what he must do next about Pearson but he is aware that it is ticking over inside his head. He knows that there is no alternative. Pearson is protecting someone and that means that ultimately, he is protecting himself. And the thing about Pearson is that he will protect himself to the death.

Whoever Pearson was shielding when he got rid of Myra is important to him, to his business. Until Johnny knows who it is, he can do nothing and he and Danni – and Stella of course – are in danger. He needs to find out who it is. And maybe the only way to find out is to go and work with Pearson, the way Pearson always tried to get him to do. That would be the ultimate test of discipline.

He has boxed the thought inside his own head, unwilling to examine it, but he knows the reality of it. He closes the door of the flat, and switches on the gas fire immediately, pulling a chair close to it, allowing the heat to turn his skin pink but still feeling frozen at the centre. There will be no more requests to Danni to go home. He knows it is pointless. Something else keeps her here. He does not know what it is, but he does know it will need to run its course. He also knows he wants her here.

There is something between them. He knows it. She knows it. But she keeps fighting it and he doesn't know why. He is not imagining it. He knows he is not imagining it. It is as if she is simultaneously drawn to him and repelled by him.

Slowly he bends forward and takes his shoes off, capturing cold toes in his warm hands, massaging the feeling back into them. He keeps his coat on, tucks his feet up into it, then lays his head down on a cushion on the arm of the chair and gazes into the flame of the fire. He sees the curve of her lips as his eyes close, the sensual fullness of lips that he has yet to kiss. She is here in this room, in his sleeping, in his waking, in his longing.

CHAPTER TWENTY-NINE

He is wakened by a banging at the door, a closed fist thump that beats low like a distant drum. He jumps up, disorientated, heart thumping, neck stiff from sleeping in the chair. The fire hisses still, the room thick with heat. He squints at his watch as he hurries to the door. 8 a.m. The thumping continues steadily.

Danni. Stella. He looks from one to the other. Danni is paler than ever, dark eyes black-rimmed with shadows. Stella is shivering in a black miniskirt, long bare legs ending in a pair of pointed toe stilettos. They are plastic; the scuffed toes showing patches of white where the coating has chipped and peeled back. He is confused still with sleep.

"Can we come in?" Danni says.

"Sorry," he says, finally coming to and standing aside.

Stella follows Danni into the living room.

"It's lovely and warm in here, so it is," says Stella gratefully, and huddles over by the fire. Danni stands, arms folded, watching Johnny. He creases his forehead in a questioning frown at her but she doesn't respond.

"I'll get some coffee," he says. "Stella?"

"White," she says. "And can I have two sugars?" She asks like a child who might be refused.

He is aware of Danni following him into the tiny kitchen.

"I had nowhere else to bring her."

He nods, eyes scanning her face. She stares back at him, eyes serious, and he knows she is emotionally stripped. She wouldn't be here otherwise. He puts down the bag of sugar he's holding.

"What's happened?" he asks quietly.

"Stella came to the hotel last night. I got a call from reception at 2 a.m. saying she was there. I didn't want to go down at first in case it wasn't really her. But then they put her on the phone and I spoke to her, told her to come up to the room."

He barely reveals his response, but she knows from the tiniest movement of his body, the way his eyes lose contact momentarily with hers, what he's thinking.

"I'm *glad* I gave her the hotel name," she says defiantly. "Where else was she going to go? She doesn't have anyone."

"What did she say?" he asks, refusing to be sidetracked.

"That Coyle and Pearson got hold of her."

"Are yous two talking about me?" Stella's voice comes quietly from the doorway and Danni spins round.

"What did they say Stella?" Johnny asks.

"They wanted to know what I knew. If Myra told me anything before she died."

She breathes deeply. "That guy Coyle's a psycho. He took out a cigarette lighter and kept flicking it in my face, asking Pearson what would happen if he put the fire onto my hair. Would it all go up or would he need to douse it in petrol first?"

Johnny knows the way that goes. In his own way, Pearson knew how the mind worked and he trained the people round him to know. Fear grows in the mind, not the body; the brain makes a wonderful hothouse. Plant the idea in there that something really bad is going to happen and the seed takes root, watered by the imagination. Johnny had always thought Pearson liked that better than the actual physical violence. Once it became physical there may be a rush of adrenaline, but then it was kind of over.

On the other hand, Johnny thought, Pearson wasn't frightened to use violence either.

"Johnny?"

He glances up at Stella.

She's holding out her arms with her sleeves pulled up. Her arms are livid and sore, covered in burn marks from the cigarette lighter. Not bad enough to need treatment. Just like a series of burns you might get in an ordinary domestic kitchen. A warning shot.

He says nothing but the muscles in his jaw tighten as he looks at her arms.

"Did you tell them?" he asks.

"What?"

"Did you tell them what you knew?"

"I had to when he was burning me. I said Myra told me about someone really senior in the law but I didn't know the name, had no idea who it was."

"And ...?"

"They didn't believe me."

Johnny watches her silently. She doesn't know how lucky she is that they didn't believe her. Otherwise, she'd be dead by now. They needed to keep her alive and frightened until they found out exactly how much she knows – and who else she has told. They know she has talked to him and Danni. That puts them all in danger now. He turns from the two women, aware of their eyes on his back as he pours water into mugs.

"Here," he tells Stella. "You take these. I'll put some toast on."

Danni turns as Stella walks by her, as if to follow, but

Johnny lunges for her arm to stop her from following Stella. He wants to talk to her alone. She turns sharply at his touch. There is a moment, when things happen unexpectedly, when the truth simply enters the brain subconsciously, before the brain filters and censors its own emotions. And she feels it then, in that moment, a surge that floods her when she looks at him unguardedly, like her blood is trying to flow too fast through narrowed veins. He sees it, and she knows it, and she turns from his seeing.

"Danni," he says softly.

"What?"

She tugs her arms down out of his grasp.

"We have to get out of here."

He sees the fear flicker in her eyes.

"What are you talking about?"

"You are going to have to make a quick decision here, Danni. They will be back for Stella. You can be sure of that. It's not over. And they know we've been with her. We're next. And I'm telling you, Pearson won't stop with a few burn marks."

He watches her taking it in, calculating, but she makes no display of emotion.

"Are you sure?"

"Positive."

"I'm not going home."

"No."

"So where …?"

"Leave it to me. I'll take you. Don't ask me where it is, just trust me to take you."

"Stella …"

"You have to decide, Danni. Stella is a danger to you. She's a crackhead and she's going to bring you down."

"I can't leave her."

"That's fine Danni, your decision. But make sure you

know what you are deciding. You're going to be holed up in the middle of nowhere with Stella going through withdrawal. No drugs, no medical help, and Stella going crazy. Do you understand that?"

She puts her hands to her face, buries herself into them, guarding herself, her feelings, from him for a couple of seconds.

"Danni ..."

She does not move.

"Danni ..."

He starts towards her but becomes aware of movement in the hall and hesitates. Stella hovers at the doorway.

"The coffee's going cold ..." she says helplessly.

Danni's hands drop finally from her face.

"And you ..." she says to Johnny, ignoring Stella for the moment.

"Where are you going to be?"

"Here."

"How can you stay here?"

"What's going on?" says Stella.

"I need to stay here to keep an eye on what's happening," says Johnny.

"You can't ..."

"I need to go to Pearson."

"What do you mean?"

"Work for him. Or pretend to."

"Don't be so bloody stupid!"

"What's happening," says Stella plaintively. "Will you tell me?"

"Listen Danni, it's the only way. Once you've been in Pearson's life, he doesn't let go. He wrote to me all the time I was in ... all the time I was away from Ireland. Told me he wanted to see me when I came back, wanted me to work for him. That's why he sent you to me. He always finds connections, ways of burrowing back in. And if I go to him and say you've gone home, that I want to work for him, he's not going to think that I know anything, is he?"

"It's too risky."

She checks herself then. What is she doing? Why should she bother about him? That unguarded moment earlier ... the way she responded ... it was nothing. She looks at him coldly.

"Please," Stella says. "What ..."

"We need to leave in a couple of hours," Johnny is saying.

"Up to you," she says. After all, she doesn't care if Pearson tears his arms and his legs from him like the insect he is. It's all he would deserve.

She becomes aware of Stella then, shivering again, her teeth chattering, marking out a tattoo of fear.

"Come on," she says gently, putting an arm, round Stella and leading her into the sitting room. "We need to talk."

CHAPTER THIRTY

It occurs to her as she sits in the hotel bedroom with her case open but packed that she could simply head to the airport and go home. That she doesn't need to go any further with this. It's not her problem. But there's something about being on a path that makes you keep on going simply because it's there. It's human nature. Just to the corner to see what's round it. And then, when there's another corner to impede vision, just as far as that. Then to the tree. That would be a good place to turn and go back. Just to the tree. Well maybe to that big rock. And by then you've lost your way back. You keep on going because you have to.

Where is he? Her fingers tremble slightly as she pulls the zip on her case. She has slipped the pages Johnny gave her into a pocket on the front. There has been no opportunity to read them yet. She checks the room one last time, the cupboards, the drawers, underneath the bed. She looks at her watch. Only a few hours of daylight left at this time of year. She goes to the window and pulls back the curtain slightly, looks down on the hotel car park. She thinks about the way Johnny looked earlier when they talked about hiring a car. "Danni," he'd said, "I don't have any money but I'll borrow some. Give me an hour."

"No, the money's here." She'd pulled out a wallet and handed it to him and he'd looked at her strangely.

"Fancy job, Danni?" he'd asked quietly. "What do you do?"

"Fancy insurance policy," she'd said, unable to keep the bitterness out of her tone completely. Then she'd smiled tightly to cover it. "And you know what I do. I'm a writer."

"Insurance?"

His voice was alert, curious.

"I'm a widow."

"Jesus," he'd said softly. "I …"

He glanced at Stella who was sitting curled up in his armchair like a terrified child, lost in her own fears. Pearson isn't the only challenge for Stella. She knew there would be no chasing dragons where she was going.

"Not now," Danni said shortly and she'd gone to put an arm round Stella to get away from him. But he watched with his arms folded and she knew he'd ask again.

She lets the curtain drop. A bottle of water sits beside her case and she sips from it, despite not being thirsty. A quick glance at her watch. Back to the curtain. Her phone beeps and she makes a dive for her bag. What's happened? Text message. She flips open her phone. Traynor. She opens the message with some irritation, resenting the intrusion. *Worried. Why not in touch? Please phone.* She snaps the phone shut then thinks better of it. She'd better reply and keep him off her back. *No worries. Reception poor. All well. Call soon.*

She moves back to the window. A steel grey Fiesta turns into the car park and she is suddenly alert, like a runner on the starting block. Dark hair. It's him. She gathers her things, pulls the handle up on her case, half runs down the hotel corridor with it, the wheels trundling behind her.

Stella is already in the back of the car eating a sandwich,

looking more cheerful. She sticks her head out of the window while Johnny gets out to help Danni put the case in the boot.

"Johnny got us some food," she says, waving a carrier bag out at Danni. "Want a sandwich?"

"Maybe later."

Stella has kicked her shoes off and stretched her legs out in the back seat. She empties an open bag of sweets into her lap.

"What colour do yous want?"

"Where are we going?" Danni asks quietly.

Johnny swings out into a stream of traffic.

"Somewhere in Donegal. Best you don't know names," he says.

"How long will it take?"

"Couple of hours."

Stella falls asleep after an hour, head lolling back, mouth slightly open. When a soft snore rumbles from the back, Johnny glances at Danni and they both smile. Danni turns to the side window, looks out at the light dripping slowly from a bleeding sky. The hills pass, the grey roll of the land, tree branches skeletal spectres waving in the semi-darkness. She hears the rush of water, peers out at a frothing fall tumbling down steep rockface. Johnny switches on the radio low and it hisses and splutters.

"A fifty-year-old man was shot dead in a remote part of Donegal last night in what is believed to be a reprisal killing by the Real IRA, a splinter group of the Irish Republican Army. James Patrick Feeney, a Belfast based electrician, was accused of being a British informer in the 1980s. Sinn Fein leaders have distanced themselves from the shooting, saying it was the work of dissidents and would not be allowed to railroad the peace process. Violence has escalated recently with a sharp increase in both small bomb explosions and the number of punishment beatings in both Catholic and Protestant communities." The radio crackles loudly and Johnny reaches out and snaps it off tersely. Silence fills the car.

"What *are* punishment beatings exactly?" Danni asks.

Johnny glances from the road to her face.

"My leg," he says wryly. "That's a punishment beating."

"What?"

"Pearson."

"He attacked you?"

"No. He organised it."

"I've never really understood ..." she says, and then breaks off. That's not true exactly, she thinks, looking out at the speeding darkness. She's never *wanted* to understand. She's never before wanted to subdue her grief enough to understand this country and its troubles because if she understood then ... No. There's never been room in her grief for understanding. For knowing. Still isn't.

"What do you get beaten for?"

Johnny shrugs.

"Something. Nothing. Everything."

"But you ..."

"Nothing." He screws up his eyes against the headlights of an approaching car.

"Get them down," he mutters, and then he slows to let the car past.

"Is it like that guy on the news?"

"Sometimes. But sometimes it's just another layer of so called justice. Areas where people don't trust the police and they leave it to the paramilitaries to sort out what they call the anti-social element." He smiles wryly. "Joyriders, burglars, that kind of stuff. And sometimes ... well, sometimes it's just people in a mixed marriage or ..."

"Are you serious?"

"Then there's people like me. Where it's just a grudge attack really, wrapped up in something else."

"What did you do?"

"I didn't do anything. But two of the boys in our cell were picked up by the police with explosives in the boot of the car before they used them. How did the police know? Pearson hinted that it was me who tipped off the police. Of course, there was no proof but the suggestion was enough for a warning."

"So why did he drop you in it?

Johnny shakes his head dismissively, as if it's a question of little significance. "I have my own theories on that. But control mainly. To show he's boss. Just Pearson being Pearson."

He takes his eyes off the road for a second, glancing at Danni. He can tell she doesn't understand.

"I have no proof but I think at that time, he had done a deal with the British intelligence services."

"Pearson! But that … that doesn't make sense."

"It makes perfect sense. The intelligence services were working constantly to get inside the IRA. They used whatever they could to get volunteers to become informants. It wouldn't have been that hard with Pearson. If he was taken in for some bank or warehouse job, there's no question he would trade information to get himself off the hook. He had lots at stake and few principles."

Danni leans her elbow on the car door and rests her head. There are so many layers to this. In the back, Stella stirs, half lifts her head.

"Are we there yet?

"Not yet. Go back to sleep," Danni says softly over her shoulder. Stella's head rests back down on the seat.

"I'm cold," she mutters.

"Here," says Danni, and hands her over her jacket. "I'll put the heating up a bit."

Stella snuggles down into the jacket.

"You know what you're in for there, Danni?" Johnny says sombrely, jerking his head back towards Stella.

Danni shakes her head impatiently.

"How can I? Anyway, there's nothing I can do but deal with it as it comes."

She stares into the tracks of the headlights, reluctant to admit even to herself how frightened she actually is. She changes the subject.

"What happened the night … when your leg …?"

For a minute she thinks he won't answer, that he is ignoring the question.

"We were at home … Roisin and I …" he says eventually, changing down a gear to negotiate a bend. "The doorbell rang. Roisin went to answer it. I heard her scream. Next thing, four guys in balaclavas are in the room."

She says nothing, waits. Is that all he's going to say? She tries to steal a glance without turning her head. His face is set like stone.

"There's always a group …"

She can hardly hear him, reaches out, with a glance over her shoulder at a sleeping Stella, to turn the fan down on the heater.

"Always a group?"

"In punishment beatings."

"What happened?" she asks.

"Roisin was screaming. One of them grabbed hold of her and wrapped his arm round her mouth. I made a grab for him but two of the others pinned me down."

He makes it sound matter of fact, like there's no emotion left to be had in the telling of this tale. Somehow it only serves to emphasise the fact that it's pulled from his guts.

"One pulled a gun."

Danni holds her breath.

"I heard the shot ring out …"

"They shot you?"

"Roisin first. Made me watch, pinned down with my arms behind my back." The muscle flexes in Johnny's cheek but his voice is steady. "You've heard of kneecapping."

"I've heard of it …"

He nods.

"They don't actually shoot your knee, usually. They shoot you on the back of the thigh. That's what they did to Roisin. Trouble is, sometimes it ruptures a major artery."

"And you …?" she asks, her voice barely above a whisper.

"I was struggling so hard I managed to move, just as they shot. They actually did get me in the knee. There was so much noise and movement and speed that …"

He frowns, remembering.

"Roisin," she says. "What happened to her?"

"She nearly died. It was after that she … it was the final straw really."

Danni looks at him curiously.

"He must hate you. Pearson, I mean."

Johnny smiles, a half smile.

"Yes and no. You don't understand Pearson yet."

"What do you mean?"

"Love and hate are part of the same thing with Pearson. I'm like family: I'm his. Or so he thinks."

CHAPTER THIRTY-ONE

Danni's head is resting against the car window, her eyes shut. Exhausted, Johnny thinks glancing at her. His eyes feel strained with the onslaught of car headlights, his head bombarded with memories.

How old were they, him and Pearson? Eight maybe. Nine. Ten. Johnny had watched, wide-eyed, when Pearson had run past his da as he sat in the garden in a deck chair with a bottle in his hand, and a pile at his feet. The auld man had shifted his foot marginally, with malevolent subtlety, and Pearson had been decked in a rugby tackle fall, landing on the grass winded, belly first, like a mis-timed dive on water. His chin had slid painfully along the grass, grazed with blood and mud, and he'd looked up, howling, with *that* look, a silent plea urging him to say it wasn't deliberate.

"Stop your bawling," his auld man had said, "and let it learn you something." He pointed a finger at Pearson. "Always be on the watch."

Pearson's ma, tiny, thin as a pipe cleaner doll, wired rigid through the centre, came out.

She had led Pearson away silently, neutrally somehow, without reproach but without tenderness, dusting him down and cleaning him up. On the outside anyway. She barely glanced at her husband.

"There's something not right about you," Pearson senior muttered at his son's retreating figure, his face contorted. "Not right," he repeated, stabbing a finger into the air after each word.

And Johnny had wandered off home, puzzled at the ways in which the world seemed different in Pearson's house.

He saw an old photograph of Pearson's ma when she was young once and was shocked. Laughing into the camera, the face animated, lit from the inside somehow. She was actually pretty. The strange doll-like quality was daintiness then. God knows what optimism had drawn her to her husband, what misguided hope of protection, but it faded over the years with the bruises. All that was left of her by then was a frame from which everything had been stripped: all flesh, all colour, all spark, all hope.

But it was Pearson's auld man he could never forget. He sees him like it's yesterday, a summer's Saturday afternoon, emerging from the bookies with his shirt sleeve rolled up to his elbows, forearms like tree trunks, weathered brown and solid. Lumbering through the arched alleyway from the courtyard at the back of the pub, stiff-legged, like his body is too big to carry, too inflexible to bend. His fists carried viciously, rolled, like they're permanently ready for action.

Four sons and all of them the same as the auld man except Pearson, the runt of them, the small one whose power had to come from inside his head. Johnny got a shock when he saw Pearson's father near the end, when the cancer had devoured him, the bulk gone but not the viciousness, the power shrivelled into a darkly glittering hatred. And at his funeral, the hulks of his boys lined in confused bafflement, the pipe cleaner doll in their midst, grey hair stiffened with lacquer, back stiffened with resolve, tight lipped and dry eyed.

She was glad, Johnny knew. And Pearson was glad, and his brothers were glad, and Johnny wondered what kind of damage that did you inside when you felt glad your auld man was dead. At the funeral, he stood beside Pearson outside the church, and it was that day he realised that Pearson would never be normal, that he would always confuse love with ownership, and that somehow he, Johnny, was caught up in that twisted, car crash of confusion inside Pearson's head in a way that he couldn't fully understand. Pearson would never willingly let him go.

CHAPTER THIRTY-TWO

The cottage is half a mile up a track off the main road. It sits angled in a dip, like its shoulders are turned from the wind. The white walls are grubby and paint peels from the flaking window sills, revealing chipped red paint beneath. The garden is neglected, swathes of dead ferns and grasses, withered and rotting, straggling into the metal fence that is bowed by time and wind and straying sheep. It's the silence that strikes Danni first when she emerges from the car, only the sound of the wind in her ears, the closing car door sounding like a gun shot crack in the quiet. From far off, she hears the bleat of sheep carried on the wind.

She turns back to the car to see Stella's face at the window, white, agitated, disorientated from sleep. Stella knocks on the window, frowning at Danni as if she's locked in.

"It's open, Stella," she says, but she opens the door for her anyway.

Stella slips her feet into her shoes. Stands out shivering in the cold.

"Where the fuck is this?"

"I don't know, Stella."

Johnny takes a key from his pocket and unlocks the front door.

"It's not going to be hotel standard," he warns.

Inside it's cold and cheerless, the light in the sitting room half hearted and blocked by a thick, dark lampshade that is coated in dust. The carpet is beige with a black pattern, threadbare and dreary. They all stand in silence. Johnny switches on a black standing lamp. Stella throws herself onto a beige corduroy two-seater and stares morosely around. She's rattling now, Danni thinks.

Danni walks into the kitchen, little more than a cooker, a sink, and a few cupboards with a small fridge tucked into a corner. She turns the tap. It takes a minute but the water coughs and splurts after a few seconds, splashing up on her. The air is so cold in here she can see her own breath when she breathes out.

The cottage is traditional, originally all one on level but later renovated to give bigger rooms downstairs and create an upstairs with two small bedrooms, barely bigger than box rooms, and a bathroom. The walls of the bedrooms are grubby white and there's little in them but beds, though one has a small table and a lamp.

"I need to go soon," Johnny says from behind her and she spins round. He has brought some bags from the car.

"I'll put the shopping in the kitchen," he says. He rummages in one for a box of fire lighters.

"I'll light a fire before I go. You'll need to keep it topped up. There is a load of wood by the back door."

"You're leaving tonight?"

He glances up at her.

"I have to Danni. I need to be there when Pearson realises neither you nor Stella is there any more. I need to drive straight back tonight, be there to see him in the morning."

"You are putting your life in danger getting mixed up with him again."

He doesn't even look at her.

"My life's not worth much, Danni," he says flatly, and walks from the kitchen to lay the fire.

Not worth much. And how can she disagree with that?

It feels like abandonment driving off. He can't do anything else but he is aware of her watching from behind the curtain, following the line of the headlights rising and dipping all the way down the track to the road. He wonders at what point she lets the curtain drop.

Little over six months ago, he thinks, he was in England. He had no intention of ever coming back to Ireland. Why is he here? He looks out at the humped silhouettes of hills in the darkness, a lick of silver moonlight on the river that runs by the main road. His mother's death brought him back. And this. Ireland. A land, a love, a dream of a life that was. Nostalgia and longing and a hurt that could only be healed in the soil where his parents and his grandparents lay. This brought him home.

He loved it and he hated it, but it was his, his dreams that vaporised over the hills, disappearing like sea haar in the warmth of sunlight. There comes a stage where it feels like all of life is looking back, that everything now is memories and nostalgia, a long goodbye to what has been. Except … except … that Danni feels like a new beginning in a morass of yesterdays.

He drives the road faster on his way back, hugging the bends, seeing her face in every mile.

CHAPTER THIRTY-THREE

The cupboard doors are banging in the kitchen, shuddering on the walls, the noise reverberating in Danni's head like slamming coffin lids. Stella, sweating and shaking, slams them one after another with increasing anger. "There must be," she mutters as Danni watches silently. "There fucking is. I know there is. Jesus, Danni, give me something."

Stella's eyes are feverish but the agitation is punctuated by uncontrollable yawns.

"Please Danni." She grabs hold of Danni's arms and Danni has to resist a sudden desperate panic, an urge to shake her off as she might shake off a spider that suddenly startled her. "Please Danni!" She is wheedling now but the thin bony fingers are vice like in their grip.

"Stella, there's no booze. Johnny didn't leave anything like that."

"It would help, Danni, please. Something to take the pain away." A watery mucous runs from her nose but she seems oblivious to it.

"Stella, I don't have anything."

"You do. You know you do. You could get it. Couldn't you Danny? You could get it. There must be a shop."

"There's no shop for miles. Anyway, I can't leave you.

Yes you can. Yes you can, Danni. I'll be okay. I'll stay right here. I promise. I …" Her fingers are gripping harder and harder.

"I can't."

"I fucking hate you," Stella says venomously, digging her nails into Danni's arms. She lets go suddenly, pacing the floor anxiously, kicking out at the cupboards with her feet. Danni watches silently as Stella suddenly doubles over with stomach cramp.

Danni opens the back door and leans against the frame, wrapping her arms round herself and breathing deeply. She daren't leave Stella. This is as much escape as she can allow herself. The air is chilled, damp, tinged with the mild, sweet fustiness of rotting vegetation. A soft mist rises eerily from a sea of bracken in front of her, the bracken bowing wearily, heavy with dampness and singed brown at the edges with decay. She thinks longingly of walking through it, into the anonymity of the mist, tries to imagine what's beyond it, beyond the enclosed world of this house.

Bang! Behind her, Stella has uncurled herself and is throwing open cupboards she has already checked, rattling pots and knocking over bleach bottles, slamming them closed again. "There is," she mutters. Bang! "There is." Bang! "I fucking know there is …"

Danni closes the back door quietly, with a soft click, and removes the key, slipping it into her pocket.

Screams in the darkness. Danni hears them, like a distant echo of the screams inside her own head. She snaps on the bedside light, heart pounding. 4 a.m. She only got to bed an hour ago because Stella wouldn't sleep. Couldn't sleep. She left her eventually on the sofa in the sitting room, curled up with stomach cramps, white and sweating and her hair sticking damply to her forehead. She'd left the lamp on for her, and the television, though she wasn't watching it. The sound of voices might make her feel like she had company.

When she throws open the sitting room door, Stella is standing on top of the two seater screaming, her feet drumming hysterically.

"Get them away!" she screams at Danni in terror. "Get them away!

"Get what away? What is it Stella?" Danni walks towards her, baffled.

"The rats! The fucking rats! They're all over the floor! Oh my God you're walking on them." She throws her head back and screams, like there's another force inside her, something separate from herself.

"Stella, it's okay. There aren't any rats. Stella. Shhhhhh. Stella, it's okay."

"It's not. They're everywhere. The tails …" She's pointing to the swirls in the carpet, trembling and crying.

"Stella listen to me. There are no rats. I promise you. They're in your head, Stella. It's the smack … remember? Stella …"

"They're there," she screams. "Under your feet. Why can't you see them?"

"I promise you Stella …" Danni tries to keep the desperation out of her voice, reaches out to her with her hand. Stella won't have it. Putting her hands behind her, she backs away on the sofa.

"Keep away from me. You put them there. You let these rats in. You did this. KEEP AWAY FROM ME!"

Danni stays still.

"Stella," she says softly. "Stella listen to me. You're not well. There are no rats here. Don't be frightened. This is what happens when you get rid of all the junk in your system. Remember earlier when you thought there were spiders on the walls. There weren't, though, were there?

Remember? I promise you Stella. Everything's going to be okay. Just tell yourself the rats are not there. Not real. They can't touch you or harm you. Just remind yourself they're not real. See?" She runs her foot over the carpet. "Nothing there."

"Not there?" Stella is staring at her in confusion. She runs a hand over her tear-streaked face and shudders.

"Deep breath, Stella," Danni says. "Listen, I am going to come up there on the sofa and look after you. Okay? Okay Stella?"

She walks tentatively towards her, holding out a hand. Stella doesn't move.

"I am going to step up there, now. Okay?"

The sofa wobbles slightly as Danni climbs up.

"I'll look after you," she says. "Come here. Come on now, kneel down here and then you won't have to step on the carpet if you don't want to. That's it. That way you won't fall. That's it. Well done Stella."

Stella is on her knees, her head on Danni's shoulder like a sick child. Putting her arms round her, Danni feels the slightness of her, the wasted skeletal outline beneath her clothes. It's only been two days since Johnny left. The longest two days of her life. She finds it almost hard to conjure him up now, the exact curve of his mouth, the set of his jaw, the quiet stillness of him. It was a bit like that when her mother died, that inability to hold on mentally to physical outlines. It gives her a strange jolt. What happens now if he never comes back?

A sly voice inside asks if she misses him but she silences it immediately. What if Pearson has got hold of him, the sly voice retorts. What if Pearson kills him? A panic rises inside her. It is not, she tells herself, the idea that Johnny might be dead that distresses her. It is the idea that some-one might get to kill him before she does.

CHAPTER THIRTY-FOUR

Belfast, November 2010

He knows himself with a cold kind of precision. How icy his blood flows when the bars begin to close around him. When the body is being starved, it shuts down to protect the vital organs. When Johnny is threatened, he shuts down his emotions to protect his psyche. It is his default survival mode.

He tore up every one of Pearson's letters in jail. They meant nothing to him. But here he is in the same old street, looking up at the light in Pearson's office, ready to walk back in there. For her. For Danni. Fire and ice, battling inside him. The outer door bangs shut behind him. His hands are thrust deep in his coat pockets and he takes the stairs two at a time, long legs swallowing them up.

He has the satisfaction of seeing Pearson start in surprise when he opens the door without knocking.

"Johnny!"

Johnny manages a half smile. In the corner, Coyle, hands thrust deep into a bag of salted crisps, look startled, then stiffens almost imperceptibly when he takes in the situation. He has heard about Johnny. He doesn't want him back here, interfering. Coyle is Pearson's top man now. "Johnny, me old fox," grins Pearson. He stands up from behind his desk and moves towards him.

"How're you boy?" he says, slapping Johnny's proffered hand rather than shaking it.

"Good," nods Johnny. "Good."

"What's this?" says Pearson, tugging on Johnny's long hair and laughing. "Jesus, if your ma could see you now!"

Johnny smiles tightly.

"Ah Pearson, do you want me to cut some off and stick it on for you?" he says raising his eyes at Pearson's bald pate. "Sure, you could be doin' with some."

"Always the joker," says Pearson, patting Johnny's face sarcastically, just a little too hard. "Always the joker." He turns.

"You'll need to watch this man for me, Coyle," he says.

Coyle lifts his head morosely, licking salt from his fingers.

"So this is Coyle," Johnny says, and he looks at him unsmilingly, with cold deliberation.

Coyle's long dark lashes flutter upwards, and he matches Johnny's stare. Pearson moves back to his desk and opens the drawer, pulling out a bottle of whisky.

"Sit down man," he says. "A wee glass of the red diesel." Johnny watches the peaty whisky swirl in to the glass.

"What about Coyle?" says Johnny, glancing at him. He turns to Pearson. "Or is it not legal for him yet? He looks like he should be on the fizzy pop still."

Pearson laughs.

"So Johnny. How you been? What brings you here?"

"A lady called Danni," says Johnny.

Same old Pearson, he thinks. His eyes have hardened into granite slits at mention of Danni.

"Yeah?" says Pearson.

"She said you asked me to call."

"Oh yeah, yeah," says Pearson. "Just social, you know? I heard you were back."

He takes a sip from his glass and smiles benignly at Johnny.

"What happened to her?"

"Who? Danni?" Johnny shrugs. "Dunno. Said she was going home. I'm afraid I couldn't help her. With her research." He makes sure to hold onto Pearson's gaze longer than necessary. "In fact, that's partly why I'm here. I'd rather you didn't put anyone like that in touch with me, you know? I didn't really appreciate a stranger turning up at my door."

Pearson grins.

"No problem, Johnny," he says. "She was just ... two birds with one stone, you know?"

"I've moved on."

"Course you have. We've all moved on." He takes a swig from his glass. "Though you don't ever move on from Ireland really do you?"

"Not when you've been inside for it, no."

"That was unfortunate."

"It was for me."

"Still," says Pearson, "you're out now. You need to come round, Johnny. See my club. I'm in the entertainment business now. Did you know?"

"Zoo," Johnny says, picking up his glass and swirling the rest of the whisky over in a oner. It burns all the way down. The walls of this place are closing in on him. He needs out. He glances over at the corner. Coyle is watching him with a sneering hostility.

"That's the one," says Pearson. "You been?"

Johnny shakes his head, stands up.

"Tomorrow. Nine," says Pearson.

"Maybe," says Johnny. "You know me, Pearson. I'm not very sociable."

"Course you are," he says. His eyes seem to shrivel, like the pupils have been burned out in their sockets. "Why else would you be here?"

CHAPTER THIRTY-FIVE

Danni opens the kitchen door and looks up into a darkening, moving sky, clouds solid as ship hulls floating in a gunmetal sea. The back step has become her refuge. She shivers. It is cold out here but she doesn't want to go back inside with Stella. Loneliness is familiar to Danni; it doesn't frighten her any more. It's just a background ache she learned to live with years ago. But being alone with Stella is different. Loneliness is worse with someone else present; there is something with which to measure the gulf. Above her, the clouds form and reform in an ocean of shifting shapes. She rubs her arms, feeling the cold gradually ripple through her body, steady as a breeze through barley fields.

She closes the door quietly at her back, longing for a feeling of distance from the house. It isn't just Stella. It is Stella's fear. It rises out of her like a grotesque separate entity, a ghastly dismembered hand reaching out of a lake. Danni is frightened. It is going to grab her, that hand: drag her in, drag her down, drown her. She lets her back slide down the door, until she crouches on the step, her head leaning against the frame. It is out of control. Everything is out of control. Out here, against the vast expanse of sky that wheels round her, she feels tiny and insignificant and powerless

"Danni! Danni!"

She closes her eyes as the voice reaches out to her from behind the door.

"Danni!"

She doesn't answer.

The letterbox moves.

"Danni ...?" Stella's voice seeps through the opening, whispering almost, Danni, crouched on the step still, turns her head to the opening but doesn't answer.

"Don't leave me, Danni. Please." The metal flap drops with a bang. Slowly, Danni stands up, her legs locking in cramp. She opens the door tentatively. Stella is sitting on the floor, her back to a cupboard, knees drawn up to her chest, shaking. Her hair is damp, stuck to her head with a light glue of sweat. Danni watches her silently, but Stella refuses to look up. Danni slides down beside her. She can smell Stella faintly, the staleness of several days without a shower, of illness, and it surprises her, the strange, distant tenderness that wakes in her. Stella needs her. Like a child needs, wholeheartedly and selfishly. It is a long time since Danni has felt her existence matters this much. You can endure so much for someone who needs you, she thinks.

A light fluttering noise above her makes her look up; a plain brown moth battering itself against the grimy inner rim of the old, white, dust-coated lampshade. It hurts her eyes to look but she is as mesmerised by the moth as the moth is by the light. There is nothing it can do but hurl itself frantically into the burning bulb. Danni looks away, still seeing patterns of light in front of her eyes. In her semi blindness she can not see, but can feel, Stella's head dropping lightly onto her shoulder, and she lifts her arms, wrapping them round Stella's bony frame, rocking her gently like a weeping child.

CHAPTER THIRTY-SIX

Johnny puts the lights on in his bedroom first, so that he will be seen at the lit window, then closes the curtains. He looks down out of the corner of his eye to the black Ford sitting on the opposite side of the road. Bloody eejit, he thinks. He might as well sit under the lamppost with a surveillance sign painted on the side of his car. Pearson must have lost the plot getting kids to work for him. Slim-hipped, pretty boy kids. Johnny switches the bedside lamp on and the main light off, as a person would if they were getting into bed, then moves back out of the room and into the darkness of the sitting room, looking out into the road from behind the curtain. Coyle looks up, starts up the engine, drives off.

Being in the room with Pearson, smelling the old rank scent of claustrophobia – it was too much. He can't do it, can't pretend to work with him unless there is no other possible way. He thought that being older would change things, that he would cope with it differently, but maybe the advantage of being older is not coping differently with the same old things but doing them in a different way completely. He sits down on the sofa in the darkness, feels the ridge of broken springs beneath him. The light of his mobile glows as he punches Danni's number in.

"Hello?"

Her voice silences him, hearing the low, rich tone of it. He misses a beat.

"Danni."

She says nothing.

"Is everything okay?"

"Yeah fine."

"Stella?"

"Fine."

"Hard to talk?"

"Yep."

He sits forward on the sofa.

"I've told Pearson you've gone home but it's been too risky to come straight back in case they follow. They're watching the house. Well Coyle is. My best bet is to leave late one night and be back by early morning."

"No need. We're fine."

The snub of it pierces him keenly. The trouble with beginning to need people is that you need them to need you too.

"I need to talk to Stella," he says.

"Right." She pauses. "So … so should we expect you?" she adds diffidently.

He rests his head back staring into the darkness.

"Yes," he says. You should expect me. Some time."

"I'll put Stella on."

He hears low voices, then Stella.

"Johnny?"

"How're you Stella?"

"Yeah okay. Okay Johnnie. Danni's been … she's been amazing."

"Yes." He believes that.

"Listen Stella, I need to ask you about something. You remember you said Stella spoke about her two important clients … one in the law and one a priest."

"Yeah?"

"Well, did she ever say who the priest was?"

"'The Right Reverend Father McConnell' she called him when she was taking the piss and giving him his full title."

"And when she wasn't?"

"Holy Jim, the failing Tim," she says, and her voice gives away to a small laugh. "When she was taking the piss but *not* giving him his full title."

Johnny smiles in the darkness.

"I think she quite liked him in her own way," says Stella. "She talked to him. Told him what she wanted to do, how she was going to get out."

"Did she say a parish?"

"No, never said. Why?"

"Doesn't matter. It would take too long to explain. Listen Stella, I need to go but you take care, y'hear? Danni will take care of you there. I know that. I can't come back yet … there are … there are some things I need to take care of first … But I'm rooting for you and I know you can do it. Okay?"

For a second he thinks she's gone already.

"Stella?"

"I'm here," she says, her voice breaking.

"You can do it Stella," he repeats. "Keep going."

"I will," she says, "Bye." And the line goes dead.

He looks at the phone for a minute then moves over to his computer, and switches on. It shouldn't take him too long to track down Father Jim McConnell of Belfast.

CHAPTER THIRTY-SEVEN

Her first day beyond the back step. While Stella sleeps, Danni walks through the edge of the woods behind the house. Yesterday's rain has passed. The day is crisper, cleaner, with a light wind. She breathes in deeply, feeling the cold, sharp air cut into her chest as her lungs inflate. Out of the corner of her eye she sees movement: a rabbit darting into the undergrowth. She stands on tiptoes trying to see where it's gone. It's cheering to see something move. Life-affirming. Sometimes in the last week it has felt like there's no one else in the world alive but her and Stella. The last survivors on earth after a nuclear explosion, clinging to a fading reality.

Sometimes when life felt bleak back home, she thought there was no existence that could be worse than the one she was living. But there was. There was this. Trapped inside a world that is constantly shrinking, a world with no view or vision, one that can only look inwards and not outwards. It's as if there's an invisible boundary line drawn round this property. Back home, she thought she wasn't part of the world any more. Now she sees she was and she wants to walk back into it. She wants to walk right through these woods, hear the rustle of her feet in fallen leaves, run her fingers over the pine trees and sniff the sticky resin on her fingertips. For a long time, life has seemed inconsequential; now it seems precious. She didn't know how much she wanted to live.

The wood is surprisingly shallow, opening out after only a few minutes' walk. She'd had no idea, standing mainly in the dark on the back step, of the shape of the landscape round her. Gentle hills that roll into a sheltered glen, a white house, a fairytale house with a bright yellow door, clinging to the side of it in the distance. A secret world, opening out unexpectedly from the darkness of the trees. Ireland. She sees it for the first time, brushed with the decay of autumn, the land hunkering down against the onslaught of approaching winter. Ireland. This is what he fought for. She breathes deeply.

She wants to hate this land but she can't. The hills roll in front of her and the wind sings round her, whistling its tune through the stillness. The song is an invitation to love and there is something immediately old and familiar about this landscape that draws her in and makes her part of it. The rash of yellow gorse across the horizon. The stain of browning pink foxgloves, withering in the ditches, delicate bells ringing silently in the breeze. Beautiful but deadly poisonous. A bitter combination.

She becomes aware suddenly of a distant noise, looks round trying to locate it. A ruined farmhouse sits in a dip below her and she realises it's the thud of the wooden door, banging rhythmically against the frame. She scrambles down the incline. The loose, corrugated iron roof rattles as the wind ripples through it and out into the rustling braches of the trees waving at its side. Danni gently pushes the front door open, stepping over a jumble of rotting wood and piles of fallen masonry into an old sitting room. A fireplace survives, the cracked floral tiles edging round the base and damp stains rising high on the walls, spreading like spilled tea across the remnants of faded, peeling paper.

Danni looks through the glassless windows at the panoramic sweep. Who had lived here, in this beautiful wilderness, had farmed it and tended it, had eked out a survival until there was only ruin left? Who had loved it until love was no longer enough? A country was its people as well at its land; they were a unity. The word grated in her mind. Unity. She would not think of it. She closed her eyes in the stillness and when she opened them again, a brief winter sun caught one side of the glen and the world seemed both strange and lovely all at once, pulling her in a way she could never have imagined, so that for a moment, a fleeting moment, she understood why beauty and ugliness stood side by side, and how a landscape could pierce you clean until you wept blood and water from the wound, and vowed to die for it.

In the living room, Stella is lying on the two seater, eyes open and fixed on the slumbering fire. Danni goes and sits on the floor next to her. Only then does she see Stella's cheeks are wet. A tear runs silently and plops into the groove of the corduroy sofa beneath her face. Danni takes hold of her hand.

"You're doing well, Stella," she says softly. "The worst bit is over." Stella has stopped hallucinating, stopped being sick, but for the last day she has been in the grip of a lethargy that is almost as alarming.

"It won't ever be over."

"You need sleep and food and normality, Stella and then …"

"I can't have normality," Stella interrupts. She drags her eyes from the fire briefly, a flicked glance in Danni's direction. "The shaking has stopped but the craving hasn't. And I'm still me, Danni. When I leave this place I'm going to go back to where I was and who I was. I can't stop being me."

"You have choices."

"You don't understand."

"Tell me, then."

"I've been on the game since I was fourteen. Nothing can ever wipe that out. Nothing can take away what I feel inside about it. You can't change what you have been."

The words pierce Danni. Hasn't she said them herself? Isn't that what this journey is all about? What does she say to Stella?

"Yeah, but you can change what you *will* be," she hears herself say.

Her stomach lurches at her own words. Are they true?

Stella shakes her head. "I'm going to need to wipe it out again. I know that. Myra and I used to talk about escape but you can't ever escape what's inside your own head."

Ain't that the truth, Danni thinks. She should be combating this, convincing Stella that she can do it. Giving her a reason to try. She just can't think of one.

"What happened when you were fourteen?" she asks. "How did you get involved?"

"It's a long story."

"I'll check my diary but I don't think either of us is going anywhere."

Stella gives a wan smile.

"I'll give you the short version. My mother ran a brothel. When I was fourteen one of her clients said he wanted me. So she sold me to him. She said I'd better get used to giving men pleasure because if I couldn't do that, I'd have no use in life."

"But you said your mother was …"

"I know what I said …"

Danni, still holding her hand, gently rubs her fingers.

"It's what you wanted her to be?"

"I suppose so."

"Did you love her?"

"My mother? Oh my God, yeah. Yeah, I loved her. Your mother's your mother isn't she? I mean, she can do what she wants but somehow you just keep on creeping back, hoping that this time things will be different. You know, that she'll love you back. You can't accept it as a kid, can you? That your mother doesn't love you, I mean."

"Maybe she did love you in her own way."

"No." She shakes her head but doesn't look up. "I don't think she was capable of it, to be honest. No surprise, I suppose. My father was one of her clients. Said she should have had me aborted but she left it too late."

"Do you still see her?"

Stella shakes her head.

"She's dead."

"I'm sorry …"

"I cried for days. You know, because … nothing could make it right now. And she would never see me make it. There's not the same incentive any more."

"Do it for yourself, Stella."

Stella closes her eyes tightly, shutting out the world.

"I kid on …" she says, and her eyelids flutter, "I kid on it doesn't bother me … doing this. But it kills me. My head's done in with it. Can you imagine what it feels like, to say to yourself that you can't go any lower? A junkie and a prostitute."

Danni looks at her ashen face, poor and wasted, and thinks she could be both ten years older than she is and ten years younger. Just a child.

"Stella, you're not even twenty. You can be anything you want to be. Nothing's fixed in life."

She believes that. She suddenly realises she believes it. And how does that change what she's doing here?

"It's okay for you Danni. You haven't had to deal with this stuff," says Stella.

Danni finds herself smiling inwardly, ruefully. She can't even be angry. Stella is so young.

"We all get dealt different hands, Stella. I've had my own things to deal with."

Stella's eyes open and she looks at Danni tentatively.

"What things?"

"Just …" she says and stops, shrugs. The fire is dimming. She kneels in front of it and stokes the ashes, puts more peat on top, and a log, and watches the flames lick round it.

"Please don't do that," Stella's voice comes from behind her, quiet and pleading.

"What?"

"Don't have me tell you everything and then refuse to say anything yourself. Please. It makes me feel like … like nothing."

Danni sits back, leaning against the two seater.

"It's not you Stella … it's just … I never … I guess …" The room falls silent. She senses Stella waiting. "When I was twenty-two, I lost my husband …"

"Oh Danni I …"

"And my three-year-old son …"

"Oh my God …"

She is aware of Stella sitting up slowly behind her. She glances round briefly at her. The corduroy pattern from the sofa has left an imprint on Stella's cheek she has been lying so long.

"What happened?"

"A bomb … IRA …"

"I wondered why … what … How long ago …?"

"1992. Eighteen years."

The flames have begun to build into a blaze. A spark spits outwards, landing on the carpet and Danni quickly brushes it with her fingers, leaning forward to put the grate over the fireplace.

"My little boy's name was Angelo," she says suddenly, sitting back and wrapping her arms round her knees. "And he had the most beautiful eyes you've ever seen."

"You must miss him," Stella says, with such poised simplicity she seems suddenly grown up.

"Like a limb," Danni whispers. "Like a space that never gets filled." She puts her face on her knees, her dark hair falling forward. Stella stretches out a hand, strokes her hair gently just once, a gesture of such exquisite tenderness that Danni thinks she will simply break into tiny fragments, too small ever to be pieced together again.

CHAPTER THIRTY-EIGHT

Belfast, November 2010

He wakes with a headache, a throbbing behind his eyes that becomes a thump on the top of his head. Banging like a broom on the ceiling, the way ould Mrs Chisholm used to bang on their ceiling to quieten them when they lived in the old Keswick Street flats. Before they moved. And his mammy would look harassed and shush all the children then and tell them to stop their squabbling. Johnny was always the quiet one. He'd watch when the thumping started, mesmerised by the way it reverberated in the room, the way the floor shook beneath their feet.

He turns over in bed, feeling dismal. He's coming down with something. The room seems bare and chilled, the bedclothes that he barely noticed before are dead and insipid, the colours spilled beyond their boundaries from frequent washing. The walls have the pistachio wash of an institution and he doesn't even have a single picture on them to brighten the place. A bed without a headboard, a chair with a lamp on it, and a chest of drawers. Jesus, it's just as well he's never brought anyone in here, he thinks. Like Danni … He shuts the thought down.

He sits on the edge of the bed. He is tall, broad, but every curve of his ribcage is visible. His skin is bleach white. Dark hair falls almost to his shoulders. He pushes himself up, head thumping dully, pads naked down the hall to the kitchen despite the cold. The frost has gone. There's rain hurling at the windows. He pours himself orange juice and swallows over a couple of paracetamol, wipes the spill from the carton with a cloth that he chucks into the sink without rinsing. No discipline today. Other things on his mind.

Our Lady of Fatima is a modern church at the edge of a Belfast housing estate. From the outside it's squat and ungainly and inside it's everything he would hate if he ever stepped foot regularly inside a church. Which he doesn't. In here there are none of the soaring roofs and grand arches of the churches of his childhood, none of the fine figures captured intricately in the electric blues and purples of elaborate stained glass. In here, a wooden cross, a square-jawed, modern Madonna. Didn't people know what beauty was any more?

He stands at the back like a visitor, all the instincts of his childhood fighting with adult resistance. He's not sure whether to dip his finger in the holy water font and make the sign of the cross. Or whether to genuflect at the pew end. Instead, he stands at the back with his arms crossed. He gently massages his temples, the pain still pulsing behind his eyes. He thinks he's alone at first until he suddenly realises there's someone sitting in the corner of the very front pew, reading. A man in his fifties, the soft flab of indulgence straining the black shirt and suit, spilling over the neck of his white clerical collar. Johnny walks to the front of the church, stands waiting. The priest looks up.

"Hi," he says, smiling. "Can I help?"

"I'm looking for Father Jim McConnell."

"Well you've found him, so you have." He looks at

Johnny and the smile becomes more tentative, fading gradually from his lips.

"Can we have a talk in private?"

The priest stands up.

"Come through," he says leading him into the sacristy.

They walk in silence. Johnny stands in the middle of the room and folds his arms. McConnell looks at him expectantly.

"Myra MacIntosh," says Johnny quietly, watching him. The pale flabbiness of McConnell's face seems to blanch further, then, momentarily, crumbles inwards: quivering, gelatinous, amorphous, before he tries to regain control. He says nothing, but Johnny sees his breath quicken.

"You knew her then," says Johnny sardonically.

McConnell sits down suddenly on the chair and Johnny eyes him. He looks like he could have a bloody heart attack in front of him.

"Who are you?" says McConnell. "Police?"

"Jesus, no," says Johnny with a short, instinctive burst of amusement. He watches the change of expression on McConnell's face sharply. "I wouldn't look too relieved yet," he says.

"What do you want?"

"To talk to you about Myra."

"I don't know you," says McConnell gruffly, standing up, "and I barely knew Myra MacIntosh either so I think it's best if you go."

"If you know what's good for you," says Johnny with such quiet menace that it halts McConnell in his tracks, "you will get your arse back down on that seat, or your bishop, your parishioners, and everyone else will know exactly how well you knew Myra MacIntosh."

McConnell hovers uncertainly.

"That's blackmail."

228

"Ten out of ten and three Hail Marys, Father." Johnny crosses to a small radiator and leans against it. He feels cold and shivery and his head is thumping. He looks at the priests podgy hands, sees the tremor, and feels a certain pity.

"Look," he says, "I'm not here to judge you. God knows I'm in no position. I need information and then I'll go away and I won't come back."

"I only had sex with her once," says the priest, refusing to look him in the eye. He covers his face suddenly with his hands, pushing them up onto the top of his head and halting there, his fingers knitted into his hair and his head bowed. "Bloody stupid weakness."

Johnny watches him, saying nothing.

"Bloody stupid weakness," he repeats to himself. He glances up at Johnny.

"It's alright when you're twenty-five and full of it," he says bitterly. "Full of your own sense of vocation. Full of God and self sacrifice. And you look at women and know you could have one if you wanted to. Then you get to thirty-five and you're spending your evenings with other men's families. Baptising their kids. Officiating at their sons' and daughters' weddings. Wanting their wives. When you go home it's to a parish priest who's half sozzled on whisky and loneliness and you look at the future and get scared. Really scared. You end up thinking, what have I got of my own? Nothing. At forty-five you're beginning to turn into that parish priest and at fifty-five ... well you look at women now and know you couldn't have them any more even if you wanted to."

There's something stirring in Johnny as McConnell talks, an uncomfortable half fear, the memory of his grey, faded old bedding this morning, the curve of his emaciated ribs, the sense of isolation that made him feel he was in a bubble world, inhabited only by himself. He wants McConnell to stop talking.

"I was just curious the first time," McConnell is saying. "You know? I was driving by quite innocently the first time. And I saw Myra ... and she looked ..." he shakes his head. "I kept thinking about it ... about her ... and I just couldn't get it out of my head. I went back a week later and then ..." His voice trails away into nothing. "When you spend your life denying sex, sexual provocativeness is kind of ... irresistible," he adds.

"So you became a regular?" Johnny asks.

"No ... well yes ... but I ... at first I told myself I only wanted to help her. Talk to her. And I did the first few times. Told her I was only in the area to try and help any girls who wanted to be helped. I wanted her to come to the church."

"What happened to change things?"

"Typical Myra ... she made sure things changed. She was so direct." He looks distressed for a moment. "I genuinely liked her," he says, his eyes appealing to Johnny for some small sign of forgiveness. "But she saw right through me, you know? She said to me, Father ... She always said Father so sarcastically ... Father, you're going to have to make up your mind if you want to save me or fuck me." He shifts uncomfortably. "I apologise for using that language but that's what she said."

Johnny smiles faintly.

"I took her number and one night I called her. Arranged to meet her. We had sex in the car. I'm not proud of it but I'm not ... not a *bad* man. Not a bad priest, even."

Johnny looks around the room at the accoutrements of the church, the prayer book, a statue of Our Lady on a sidetable with a rosary in front of it.

"How do you square it with all this?" he asks curiously.

McConnell looks at him with the first flash of belligerence.

"You think it's the worst thing I could do? Who lives up to what they aim to be? Do you?"

"No, but I don't tell others what they should do."

"I tell people they shouldn't be selfish but nobody would expect that I was never selfish in my life. Nobody would be shocked if I was. Why is celibacy so important?"

"It's not. It's the pretence that's important. You lot tell everybody else how to run their sex lives while doing something else. You don't publicly claim that you're never selfish but you do publicly claim never to have sex. How can you have sex and still be a priest?"

"I went to confession."

"And promised never to do it again?"

"Sometimes we fail. In all sorts of ways, we fail. Anyway, I told you I only had full sex with her once ... though ... though I admit there was ... there was ... sexual contact ..."

Johnny has gone from feeling cold to feeling the sweat glistening on his back. He moves from the radiator. What the hell difference does it make, these grades of intimacy? Full sex, half sex, simulated sex.

"Look none of this matters," he says, a bit impatiently. "I told you I'm not here to judge you. I have no right." He wipes his forehead. He's burning up. "Anyway, I don't actually care if you have sex." Johnny leans his weight against the wall. "But what I do care about right now is whether Myra talked to you about her other clients."

"No," he says, a little too quickly.

Johnny raises his eyes to the ceiling, clicks his tongue impatiently. He waits.

"I'm going to make an educated guess, here," he says eventually. "I think she did. I think she told you about another important client of hers, knowing that you couldn't afford to ever tell because you would give yourself away. I

231

think that would have appealed to Myra. Anyway, I think in your own strange way you became friends. I think she might have asked your advice."

"I cared about her," McConnell says quietly. "I was devastated by her death."

"Well if you cared about her, you have to tell me about this other client. I can't tell you why but it will help friends of hers. Otherwise, someone else is going to die here and you're going to have to take your share of the blame."

"Oh my God," says McConnell and he puts his head back into his hands. "What have I got into?"

"Sometimes life gets out of hand, eh Father?" Johnny says, and his tone is not without its own compassion. "But I'm telling you that other people need protecting and the only way I can do that is if I know who Myra was seeing."

"I can't. I can't get involved."

"Because you need to save your own skin?" Johnny looks at him and shakes his head. He's losing patience now. "Well, let me make it easier for you Father McConnell. If you don't, I make your name public. After all, for all I know, you might have killed Myra."

McConnell looks wildly at him, like the world as he knows it is falling apart. "What? Of course I didn't kill her! I lov ... I was fond of her. I'm a priest for God's sake!"

"Yeah? Well give me the name or everyone gets to know the story of the priest and the prostitute. Ask your God and see if He can help you with that one."

McConnell squints at him. "You're putting me in an impossible situation."

"Moral dilemmas," says Johnny brutally, "Who'd have them?"

He watches as McConnell gets up from his chair, walks over to a table and tears a bit of paper from a notebook. Above him is a picture of the Sacred Heart, the anguished face of Christ staring down from the wall. Silently, McConnell writes something on the paper and hands it back to Johnny.

Johnny glances at it, then stands in silence for a few seconds just staring at it. No wonder Myra's dead. He looks at McConnell and nods.

"You don't need to worry," he says, walking past him. "You won't see me again." He lets the door swing closed behind him with a bang.

Shit. He has been careless. This thumping head has put him off his stride. Johnny wipes the sweat from his forehead and glances again in the car mirror to see the black Ford turning off the main road. How long has that been following? God, had he led the car straight to McConnell? He slows as he approaches traffic lights that are turning red. In the side road to his right, he sees the Ford slow half way up the street and wait. A few minutes later, it has rejoined the main road and is sitting a couple of cars behind him again.

He'll have to go to the club tonight. Keep things right. Then he'll head back to Donegal. He parks outside the flat, and out of the corner of his eye sees Coyle pull in further down the street. When he steps onto the pavement, his legs feel like they'll give way beneath him. He needs to sleep for a while. Back in the flat, he swallows some more paracetamol and heads for bed. But there's something about the bedroom he can't face. He packs a few things in a bag for later, then takes a blanket and lies down in the sitting room with the fire on low.

Pearson said 9 p.m., so he'll make it 10. How quickly he has slipped back into that old pernicious relationship where everything is competition or confrontation, everything is about scoring without even admitting you're playing the game. It was the hardest thing about prison. Not thinking that Pearson had won, but knowing that Pearson would think he had won. Then Pearson became so inconsequential it didn't matter any more. Until now.

CHAPTER THIRTY-NINE

Zoo is located in an old converted church with a double flight of steps leading up to the main entrance. It's on two levels, the old upstairs choir loft converted into a bar area surrounded by thin silver slats running floor to ceiling, like an ornate cage. Downstairs, the main area is given over to a dance floor with a bar at one end, the supporting columns of the original church now painted in black and white zebra stripes.

Johnny sees Pearson in the upstairs gallery, sitting in the corner of a cordoned off area of the cage, with an entourage. Johnny recognises one or two of them. Still hanging on, he thinks. Pearson looks like a dodgy car salesman with his black shirt and fitted jacket pulled over his stocky figure, the trousers straining over chunky, muscular thighs when he sits. Gold jewellery round his neck and his wrist, sitting like rocks on a stubby, bald, Buddha's fingers.

He hears a roar of laughter from above, Pearson with a glass in his hands, holding forth. As Johnny moves further in, he sees Coyle at Pearson's side, watching him. Pearson catches sight of him, waves a hand at him to beckon him up. Johnny nods. Points to the toilet. A few minutes to get his head together.

He has his back to the door when it happens. Hears nothing above the roar of the hand dryer and the thump in his head, until the arm is round his neck and he hears the clinical click of a blade flicking out next to his ear. He tries to turn but feels himself being slammed up against the wall, his cheek turned against the cold, unforgiving tiles, his arm held up his back.

"Stay still Johnny," a voice whispers, forcing his arm tighter, further. Johnny winces with the pain but says nothing. Coyle, he thinks. He recognises the voice ... the tall, slim build. He could take him if he could only fucking move.

"What were you doing today at the church?"

"Prayin'."

"Don't fuck with me, Johnny, or you'd better start praying now."

He feels the cold metal blade pressing against his neck.

"Think you're a big shot? Not any more. You're yesterday's man."

In a sudden burst of anger he grabs Johnny's head and thumps it against the wall. The pain comes in a wave that washes over him, reaches a crescendo, then recedes, leaving a wash of minor ripples in its wake.

"What did McConnell tell you today?"

"Nothing," Johnny says through gritted teeth. Pain spirals him upwards until he hovers somewhere above himself. "He wouldn't tell me anything."

Thump. His head cracks sickeningly against the wall It's amazing how many computations the brain makes in a single second. Johnny knows he has no choices any more. Coyle hasn't the experience to walk that fine, beautiful, brutal line between torturing his victim until he cracks, and killing him. Johnny either does something here or he risks dying. That knowledge, along with a second wave of pain, unleashes a burst of energy, a torrent of pent up anger. And just as it's unleashed the door opens and a startled clubber freezes in the doorway.

"Fuck off out of here," Coyle screams looking up, and Johnny, thankful for the slight hesitation the interruption prompts in Coyle, throws everything into releasing himself, jerking his leg up backwards into Coyle's groin, twisting round and bringing his elbow into his stomach. The door bangs shut again.

Johnny was never a pretty fighter. He wraps his arms round Coyle and hurls him into the wall, watches him slide down it, cracking his head off a basin. The knife slithers along the floor. Johnny grabs hold of it, sees blood running down his hand. He's been cut as he twisted out of Coyle's grasp but he doesn't even know where because he feels nothing yet. Later he will feel the keen sting of pain in his right forearm, see the knife is so sharp it has sliced him open, lifting a wafer thin slice of flesh. And there's a gash down the palm of his hand, blood oozing slow and thick and sticky. He has a sudden image of the bird in the cardboard box in Danni's hotel room.

He closes the blade of the knife over. Coyle is flat on the floor, semi-conscious, and Johnny bends over him, grabbing hold of his shirt, lifting his head off the floor by the collar.

"I should finish you off," he whispers. He feels a dangerous surge inside him, the years of controlled aggression beginning to crumble into an explosive dust that will take only a tiny spark to ignite. It's always been inside him, that unpredictable roar inside his head that drowns out his reason. But since prison, he's controlled it. Now he feels the control slipping away into darkness.

"You hear me?" He lets Coyle's head bang back to the floor.

He has lived with what it feels like to kill a man. To kill a boy, he thinks, the dark eyes of the child that have haunted him so often for so long, rising unbidden in his mind. After that, killing Coyle would be like accidentally standing on a spider. Unfortunate, but hardly a tragedy.

"Let me give you some advice Coyle," he says, speaking directly into his ear. "If you want to pick a fight, don't pick one with a man who has nothing left to lose."

The door creaks behind him. Pearson stands inside with two of his henchmen at his back.

"Ever travel alone, Pearson?" Johnny asks aggressively.

"What's going on Johnny?"

"Your wee playmate got above himself."

"He saw McConnell today," Coyle says groggily from the floor.

Pearson takes a step forward.

Johnny lifts Coyle's knife and flicks the blade out, staring at Pearson.

"You know, Pearson, I don't really fancy my chances against three of yous." He glances at Coyle still sprawling on the floor. "Three and a half," he adds. "But you know what? I could do a bit of damage to a few pretty faces on my way down."

Pearson lifts his hands.

"Hey Johnny, calm down. Come on now, we're old friends. Come and have a drink."

"Some other time," says Johnny. He can feel the livid heat of his cheek bone where it smashed against the wall. He puts one hand tentatively to his head where a lump is forming. He motions with the knife.

"Move over there," he says to Pearson.

"Come on Johnny."

"Move."

He knows Pearson is calculating. He can't get rid of Johnny here. It's too public. He wants him to come and have a drink so he can keep an eye on him. Dispose of him later.

Pearson sighs.

"Okay Johnny," he says soothingly. "We'll move here. You go out there and wait for us."

He's keeping up a façade but he'll be furious, Johnny thinks. Forced into a position of weakness. That's when Pearson's at his most dangerous. Johnny walks with his back to the wall, the knife held out in front of him. He closes the toilet door behind him and walks swiftly to the entrance of the club, slipping the knife into the inside pocket of his jacket. The bouncers eyeball him on the way out. He has maybe half an hour before Pearson will send someone after him to his flat.

The night air is cool on his fevered, swollen cheeks. As soon as he is outside the club, he runs as best he can, trying to ignore the pain in his limbs, sprinting round the corner to the sidestreet where he parked. He turns the ignition immediately, pumping the accelerator with his foot, and turning on the fan. There is no need to go back to the flat. His bag is in the boot and he's going to Danni.

He drives one handed, the gash on his left hand making it painful to hold the wheel. Changing gear makes him wince; he tries to use the tips of his fingers only. Blood stains his shirt. He accelerates hard, the engine roaring as he pushes it to its limit, braking hard on bends. The adrenaline surge of the last hour makes him reckless. He has to be fast. He doesn't want them to follow him, to lead them straight to Danni and Stella. And the fact is he needs to be there. Nothing to lose, he'd told Coyle. No, that isn't true any more.

He puts his foot to the floor, careless of speed, blanking out his thoughts in the blur of the white line, the endless curve of the road. When he reaches the track to the cottage he turns fast off the road but immediately brakes, wincing. The rutted track, covered in bumps and potholes, sends lightening forks of pain through his body. There's sweat on his forehead again, glistening beads of fever from the flu that has been building through today, combined with the sick pain and inflammation of his injuries. And the sickness in his head, he thinks. Sometimes he fears what he is capable of.

CHAPTER FORTY

He sees two figures at the window as he approaches, Danni and Stella watching the headlights move slowly towards the house. He notices it's Stella who comes to the door, Danni holding back in the sitting room.

"Hi Johnny," Stella calls softly into the darkness. He takes his bag and as he walks towards her, he feels his leg buckle more than usual and then, moving into the circle of light, he sees Stella's face freeze, her hand flying to her mouth.

"Oh my God," she says.

"What is it?"

He hears Danni's voice rising high and then he sees her standing next to Stella as he reaches the door. Stella has stepped out, taken hold of his arm.

"My God Johnny, what's happened,?" she whispers.

"Danni," Johnny says, looking at her. His head is fuzzy.

"Stella, get some ice," Danni says urgently.

She holds out a hand to steady him.

"Take my arm," she says. She cannot look at him. It is the first time she has touched him deliberately.

"I'm okay," he says.

"Bloody well take my arm, will you?" she says sharply.

He lies on the two seater. Danni listens intently to his stumbled explanations as she puts icepacks on his head and cheek.

"Sorry," she says, her voice low, as he winces at her touch.

She puts a hand on his forehead. Burning up. His eyes are closing in exhaustion.

"Stella, can you bring some paracetamol and help me get him to sit up," she says. "Johnny. Johnny," she says close to his ear and supporting his neck to raise it, "you need to sit up for a minute."

His eyes open, unnaturally bright, liquid and glistening with fever. He is somewhere between consciousness and sleep, acquiescent in his confusion.

Afterwards, Danni lays his head back. She pushes the two chairs together for herself to lie in as she had ended up doing with Stella when she couldn't leave her.

"Danni, you go to bed," says Stella. "You've done enough of this."

"No, you need to get stronger. I'm fine." She throws down a pillow and a blanket. "I'll stay here."

When Stella goes to bed, Danni watches Johnny's face while he sleeps. She stares, frowning, at the livid swelling on his cheekbones, the dark curl of his lashes, the thin, fine, bow of his lips. For the first times she can really examine him without anyone knowing she is doing so. Why does she feel this way? She has not forgotten why she is here. Everything that has happened has swept her up like a whirlpool but surely there will come a point where she is spat out again into the reality of her hatred for him.

There is no need to panic. It is only human to feel a temporary shock at his injuries. This strange tenderness will go. But right now she watches his face quietly, confused by the fact that, for the moment, she is confused.

There are, in the next forty-eight hours, only small crests of lucidity in great crashing waves of surreal fantasy as the fever takes hold. Stella, Danni, swimming towards him, noises muffled in the pull of an underwater tide. Danni tangling in seaweed that wraps around her like green limbs, frilled growth clinging perniciously to her throat, creeping tighter and tighter till she's choking with it. And him, tearing at it with his bare hands, trying to free her, release her, stop it tightening round her windpipe.

At the height of the struggle a brief moment of consciousness, cool hands freeing him from the sheet and blanket that he has been thrashing in, that tangles now around his legs like a vine. Stella? Danni? A cool cloth pressed onto his forehead, heavy with water, soaking into him, taking him back to the brine of the sea, the smell of salt carried on the wind, the tang of it on his tongue. He can taste it, the salt cracking his lips till they sting, bitter and bloodied.

The eyes come out of the sea like a monster, dark and dreamy and haunted. Eyes like arms, that can reach out, lift and roll in agony and supplication. He carries them everywhere, the eyes of a child who drowned in him, who rises constantly from the deep towards him, the eyes of a child betrayed. Angelo, whom he never knew but who stays with him constantly. A boy, a boy, a forever boy who never looks to adulthood, but only looks to him who destroyed him.

He tries to sit upright, his eyes still closed. A woman whispers, "Johnny it's okay. Lie back."

"I killed him," he says, sinking back into a pillow, sweat on his back. He needs to tell Danni. She needs to know, to understand, to forgive. But who is this woman he is talking to?

"Killed who?"

"The boy. The child. He's dead."

"You're dreaming."

"No. He died. The bomb … but I didn't mean … I didn't … Pearson …"

"Shh. Lie back Johnny. Shh. Shh." Her hands are cool. Her fingers brush his skin like chilled silk.

Who? he thinks.

"How did the boy die?" she asks softly.

"In the bomb. With the others. Pearson … he made sure … I killed them all." He grips her hand. Danni? he thinks. "Mistake …"

"Of course," she says. "Of course …"

His hands sweep frantically over his chest. "Get the powder off," he says.

"It's okay, Johnny, there's nothing there …"

"Yes … yes … it's pink."

"No there's nothing."

"The fertiliser powder."

His hand continue sweeping over his chest, trying to brush it off, until she grasps his hands and holds them still.

He is engulfed in heat. Only her fingers can absorb the fire. She presses them to him with a secret tenderness. Then he drifts into the heat, Angelo's eyes rising towards him again out of the flames. He has to tell Danni the worst. He has to tell her about the child.

"The boy," he says. "He's here … looking …"

"No," she says. "Not here."

Perhaps she's right, he thinks hopefully, and slips back into the centre of himself, from where he can no longer fight to emerge.

"We may need to get a doctor soon," he hears someone say urgently, a long way off.

And then it's gone. The storm blown out. The wind dropped. The eyes back beneath the sea. His eyes flicker open and he sees them, Stella and Danni, talking quietly together. He stares at them, eyelids flickering, stinging with the effort of keeping them open. He does not move his head but moves his eyes, swivelling them slowly to take in the panorama of the room. The movement hurts, the light burning his eyeballs, burning like an acid wash. He closes his eyes again. His body is heavy, his limbs weighted like rocks.

"Johnny." The voice is a soft caress. He opens his eyes, screwing them up against the light. "You're awake." She sounds pleased. He wishes it were Danni who had spoken.

CHAPTER FORTY-ONE

He knows they will come eventually. It's only a matter of time before they track him down. He is uncertain how long he has been ill – twenty-four hours? Forty-eight? He is too weak to get up yet but he has decisions to make. The first is to tell Danni about the gun. He waits until Stella goes for a bath. He is still lying on the two seater, barely awake.

"Danni," he says. "Can you come over here?"

She sits on a stool beside him and he tells her, describing where it is hidden, the position of the box in the loft. It is only partly because he feels so weak that he asks her. More importantly, he doesn't want it to be a surprise to her. He knows what will happen next and he needs to include her. She watches him gravely, her dark eyes absorbing him blankly, until he feels eaten up by her, exhausted with the effort of trying to read her.

"Will you get me the box?" he asks.

The fire spits and crackles in the silence.

She leans forward mechanically and thrusts a poker into the grate, shifting the burning wood with a controlled hostility.

"Whose house is this?" she asks stiffly.

"It was my grandmother's."

She looks at him coldly, as if he's lying.

"She moved here from Dublin," he says. "Remember I told you – that first night we had a drink at your hotel? She moved after she lost her husband. They were only just married."

She says nothing but he catches an almost imperceptible physical reaction, a slight stiffening, a movement inwards into herself.

"And now?" she says eventually, dumping the poker with a clatter on the hearth.

"It was left to me. But you can see, there's no way to live here and make a living. It was a small community even back then but now there's almost nothing left."

"Why haven't you sold it?"

"Because it was hers. Because I loved her."

His mouth is bone dry, his lips cracked.

"Can I have some water, please?" he asks.

As she moves to get a glass, he says, "You haven't read it yet …? What I gave you – about my grandmother?"

She shakes her head. She had forgotten. She remembers now how she slipped the sheets into the front pocket of her case in the hotel room.

She brings a glass over and holds it to his lips but he takes it for himself and drinks.

"Slowly," she warns.

"Thanks."

He hands it to her and sinks back with some relief, his eyes roaming round the room. A shell, that's all this house is now really, but he remembers it in his childhood, filled with the smell of peat smoke and the all encompassing presence of his grandmother. The tall, straight-backed stance of her when she moved. Many people thought her haughty. But Johnny always understood that she held herself so stiffly with the effort of trying not to crumple. Being a widow was her identity; it wasn't just a part of her, it was what she was, a whole life summed up by the loss that defined it. She rarely spoke about it but she carried it physically and visibly. It stripped her of adornment, somehow, gave her a ramrod back and granite eyes and dry, gnarled hands like stumps of root ginger.

And yet there was about her stillness something that yielded, that was more than just formidable. The way she swept the hair from his eyes gently, with one crooked finger. The fastidious way she took the top off his boiled egg and ground salt between her thumb and forefinger over the top, and then gave it to him with a smile in her eyes rather then her lips. The way her hand hovered over his head on the pillow when she tucked him in at night. He adored her. And whatever was left in her that was capable of love, loved him back.

"What did you say happened to him?" she asks suddenly.

"Hmm?"

"Your grandfather. Her husband ..."

"He was shot. He was a political prisoner."

Danni folds her arms, like she's building a physical wall between them.

"I see."

"I doubt it."

Danni's eyes narrow like a cat's, the brown of them infused with the orange glow from the light.

"What's that supposed to mean?"

"Danni ..." He shakes his head impatiently.

"What?"

"Every time I try to talk to you about something important ... Why do you do that? It's like you just ... close me down. Or you look at me like that."

"Like what?"

"Like you hate me."

248

She is startled, the lightening fork of surprise striking her face before she earths it.

"Don't be ridiculous," she says, walking to the window and looking out with her back to him.

No matter where she goes she feels his presence, she thinks in despair. She's weary with the effort of resistance. Looking at him, turning from him, ignoring him, confronting him ... it doesn't matter. She leans her head on the glass, looking out into the garden, the overgrown grasses rippling with the winter wind. And all the while he's seeping into her pores; she's breathing him in like some deadly substance. Her back prickles with the sense of him behind her, watching her.

"Tell me," she says turning back to him. "Tell me what you wanted to say."

He struggles to sit up. He looks so thin, thinner even than usual. She can see he feels weak, his limbs unsteady. And then he seems to lose his fight.

"Just read the pages I gave you," he says, his voice defeated. "I can't say it any better than that."

"Maybe I don't want to read it."

He shrugs, closes his eyes.

That was petulant, she thinks, a shiver of regret rippling though her.

She sits down, hesitates.

"What's it about?" she asks diffidently.

He is silent for a minute and when he speaks, he does not open his eyes.

"My grandmother lodged it at her solicitors with her will before she died. She wrote it so that we would understand why my grandfather died ... what had really happened. And I think maybe she wrote it for herself, like she wanted something in black and white that showed he existed, that he mattered ... Oh just read it," he says finally.

The heat from the fire is warm on his closed lids. Then his eyes flicker open suddenly.

"The box," he says, "the gun ..."

She says nothing but gets up and leaves the room. This is her opportunity. Didn't she want a gun? Now one's being handed to her. She has never been more frightened in her life.

She looks at the gun, sleek and black and deadly, and thinks it has its own strange, kind of beauty. A terrifying beauty, seductive in its danger and its power. She puts out a finger and touches it gingerly, like it might live, breathe, move. She holds her breath.

An impulse, a tremor, a shiver; someone walking over her grave. She is out of control, wrapped in fear. She looks at this ... this ... *thing* and she feels terror. She is frightened of what she is capable of. Frightened of what she is *not* capable of. Could she do it? Could she use it? Could she kill?

She puts a hand out to it and lifts it, proves to herself she can touch it. It cannot move without her. It is an instrument of her impulses. Of her will. It is only capable of what she is capable of and she does not yet know what that is. She lays it down.

She closes her eyes, her hand laid flat now on top of the gun. Has she come all this way to fail? Is she too weak, too cowardly, too lacking in resolve ...? Faced with the reality of the gun, the deadly innocuousness of it, she feels uncertainty. *They* didn't feel uncertain, she thinks bitterly. The terrorists. When did their humanity stand in the way of their certainty? She feels a sudden surge of resolve, like an electric current, an impulse, and she reaches out to it, trying mentally to grasp it.

Help me, Marco, she thinks desperately. She needs purpose and meaning and certainty. Her hatred was something solid to hold onto and she is lost without the comfort of it.

It filled her horizon, blotted out the view. Now it is growing thinner, dissolving. It confuses her the new view on the horizon, the colours and the light and the shifting sense of perspective. The world is simpler in black and white.

But the gun is black, she thinks, looking down at it. Black, and darkly beautiful. Capable of whatever she is capable of, a reflection of her soul.

CHAPTER FORTY-TWO

He is uncertain how long he sleeps. Half an hour perhaps. An hour. The sky is turning grey and cloudy outside when he wakes and Danni is standing in front of him in an outdoor jacket. Then he notices the metal box with the gun. She has placed it on the cover next to him.

"We are running out of food. Now you have brought the car back, I'll stock up. Where's the nearest place?"

"Wait until tomorrow. I'll go. We have enough for tonight."

"No."

Her voice is so flat, so definite, he hesitates.

"I need out of here. Alone."

"I'm not sure it's safe ..."

"I really don't care."

He gives her directions and closes his eyes again while she searches for the keys. When he opens them again, she is gone.

She parks and takes the papers out of the envelope, sees the spidery scrawl of a signature next to the typewritten text.

Mary Seonaid O'Connor.

Her eyes scan down the text.

I became a bride as a copper sun set in bands of burnished gold over Kilmainham jail; a widow before it rose again …

She reads with resistance and with trepidation. She reads with empathy and then with fear of her own growing understanding. She reads until the light fades, until the quiet cold creeps furtively round her, until a dead woman comes alive.

And then, finally, she lays the pages down and breathes deeply. Her fingers feel stiff. It is so cold in here. She switches on the engine, puts the heater up to maximum, and looks out at the hillside. Mary Seonaid O'Connor. How real her voice seems to Danni. Perhaps because they have something in common, losing their lovers to the same cause all those generations apart. Almost seventy years between the two men, she thinks, yet they died for a cause that will outlast both of them.

A woman of another generation, yet Danni understands her perfectly. Danni had Marco for longer than ten minutes after they were married, but on the other hand, sometimes that was all it felt like: ten minutes of a lifetime. She hears Mary Seonaid's voice and she recognises it. She has shared those same hopes and disappointments and dreams.

Reading about Michael O'Connor makes her think back to a conversation between Marco and Traynor during one of those Chinese suppers they used to have. The old heroes of the IRA, Traynor had said, were men of principle, revered in their communities. But the new generation of IRA men had taken the struggle into new territories, attacked civilians, children even.

And Marco had replied mildly that in a war zone, frustrations inevitably build up. The nature of a war was bound to change the longer it continued. Traynor still thought the sense of integrity had gone. Listen, Marco had said, through a mouthful of chicken chow mein, if you're in the boxing ring with a guy who continually knees you in the goolies, how long are you going to stick to the Queensbury rules?

Danni had smiled but his death ended her understanding. A few years after Marco died, there was a news item about the death of Gordon Wilson, whose daughter had been killed in the Enniskillen Remembrance day bombing. A Protestant father who lost his daughter but said he forgave her Catholic killers. They replayed the interview on television when he died and Danni had watched and wept for him, for his heart and for his humanity, and then she wept for herself because she could not share them.

The thought of it hardens her, even now. She hates the way she feels and she hates those who make her feel this way. It's as if her intellect and her psyche are separating completely, peeling into different layers inside her. Intellectually, she can understand, of course she can understand, the way this struggle in Ireland has been passed through the generations. She is not the only one to have suffered. But rational understanding does not make it any easier to forgive emotionally.

Perhaps she would have little to say to Mary Seonaid after all. She got to keep her child, didn't she? Danni didn't. And as for Michael, he chose his own path. Marco did not. Every side has its dead, she understands that. But it is her own dead she weeps most for and unless they can be raised from the grave, it is hard to find generosity within herself. Easy to be generous when you have a surplus; hard when you have nothing.

A crown of dark clouds is settling ominously on the hilltop. The light is fading fast; it will be completely dark soon. The engine is ticking over still and the faint sound of water trickles somewhere in the darkness. She should go back now, Danni thinks. But she does not move. The photocopied pages of spidery handwriting are sprawled across the front seat of the car, as much in disarray as her thoughts.

She watches the central white line of the road until it spins into one continuous line in front of her, the miles eaten up by thoughts. Marco. Johnny. She's beginning to have an understanding she doesn't want, an insight she'd rather remain blind to. Since she arrived in Ireland, Marco has never left her. She has felt him in this land and yet somehow he has changed. He is a comforting, background presence rather than the main focus. She thinks of him with a kind of calmness and that frightens her. There comes a point where the only connection left to the dead is the pain of their loss. She doesn't want to lose that. She doesn't want to say goodbye fully. And yet, if she is really honest it sometimes feels like her whole life has been about grief, that the possibility of something else is like winter sunshine on crusted frost. For the while that they both exist, there is nothing more beautiful, but ultimately one will destroy the other. She is not sure which she wants to lose.

Marco. His name has always been a Pavlovian trigger, floods her with gentle warmth. No, he has not gone from here, she thinks, as hills flash by and swollen rivers tumble. If she believed in that kind of thing she might almost think he brought her here, delivered her into new possibilities. And each time she rails at those new possibilities, he turns her gently back to face them. She knows that it is more Angelo who has blocked new life for her in the past. Marco was not her responsibility but Angelo was. And so the loss of Marco is tragedy in her life, whereas the loss of Angelo is tragedy combined with guilt. There was even a phase of her grief where she felt anger at Marco for not saving her boy.

After fifteen years, the pain of Angelo still stabs at unexpected moments. Driving behind a car and seeing a small, single, discarded Wellington boot in the back windscreen, thrown there after a walk on the beach, its partner languishing somewhere on the back seat where it has fallen. It's the careless disregard that hurts, those with a glut of memories who can toss them aside and replace them easily. And then later, there was seeing senior pupils at her local school, the age Angelo would have been then, bags slung over shoulders, walking in shirt sleeves in winter. They were impervious, invincible. Over the years she has grieved not just for what Angelo was, but for what he would have become.

And he, Johnny, is the cause of it, she tells herself. He is to blame. But perhaps he wasn't wholly to blame. Perhaps he was just there, swept up in events.

So why does he create such confusion in her? Something sat between them almost from the start. Even Stella could see that. Is he your man? she had asked. There is a blurring of the boundaries in Danni's head that she doesn't understand. She hates him and that is part of it for sure. But love is passion, and hatred is just a kind of distorted passion. If you asked her the ingredients of love she'd say passion and constancy and she knows the irony in that. That's why love is a knife edge waiting to cut you up, because passion and constancy threaten each other's existence.

It was too soon for either to have faded with Marco. And then there was that incredible gratitude. She never examined how much of her love for Marco was gratitude. The day her mother died, Danni felt completely alone. Then Marco came and stood in the pale lemon hospital corridor with his arms round her, the human traffic continuing to pass them in both directions with curious sidelong glances, and she felt if Marco weren't there she would simply be mowed down with the relentlessness of the world. Trampled. They had stood, like an island in the flow, and Marco had murmured in her ear, "I am here Danni," over and over, and then he had added, "always."

But he hadn't been. How many times she had remembered him whispering, "always". How much of a betrayal the word had seemed after he had gone. Three weeks after he died, when everyone had disappeared and she was left in the empty house alone, she had taken hold of a framed photograph of him and thrown it into a drawer. "Well fuck you then," she'd said, banging the drawer shut so hard the whole cabinet had shuddered. A fortnight later, she had taken it out silently, wiped it with a damp cloth, placed it up beside her bed, and there it had stayed ever since, in the same spot, for eighteen years.

She had, as a young woman, been immensely proud of the way Marco looked. He was substantial, muscular. She pretended to be oblivious to the way other women eyed him, flirted with him, even while she was there. Once, when he was angry with her for something – she cannot even recall what, though she can recall so clearly the aftermath – he had flirted back and she had caught his eye across the room, raising her eyebrows and giving a look of such wry defiance that he had laughed out loud. Disconcerted, his new companion had turned to see what amused him so. Come and meet my wife, he had said, and the woman had shaken Danni's hand with limp enthusiasm and disappeared soon after.

"Let's go home," Marco had whispered and she had known by his tone exactly what he meant.

Marco's appetites were of the earth, somehow. Maybe it was partly because food had played such an important part in his Italian upbringing. Where she reached for a packet of instant, he chopped and whipped and rolled and diced. Hot chocolate made with real liquid Belgian chocolate. Pizza dough that swelled to plumpness under a dusting of flour. At first she had been embarrassed going shopping with him, the way he had sniffed tomatoes before buying them, and handled fruit to test its ripeness, with a display of sensuousness that had seemed so at odds with the Presbyterian indifference of the other shoppers, who took whatever was nearest them as their just desserts. Marco had seemed so vibrantly alive.

And so what is she to make of Johnny, so opposite to Marco with his blue eyed, wolfish sharpness, his angular elegance, his otherworldliness and austerity. The strange, compelling line inside him that divides gentleness and danger, that simultaneously protects and threatens. He is a man to be feared whom she is not frightened of. They fit together, she thinks suddenly, and then immediately denies the thought to herself.

But she has thought it. It is admission. She pulls the car into a deserted layby at the top of a hill, listens to the purr of the engine as she looks down into the valley below, sees the lights from a cluster of houses that cling to the edge of the hillside. As she looks down it feels suddenly precarious and she wonders what it would be like to paraglide from up here, to simply launch herself into space and hear the rush of wind in her ears, the nausea of anxiety in her belly, the excitement of uncertainty in her heart. And for a moment she thinks maybe she's done it already.

CHAPTER FORTY-THREE

Johnny is watching from behind the sun-bleached beige curtain of the sitting room when she arrives back. He does not let it drop; Danni is aware of him watching as she unloads a shopping bag from the car.

"Where were you?" he asks edgily when she opens the door. "I was worried."

He is a terrible colour, she thinks. Grey and glassy eyed.

"No need," she says shortly, and moves to the kitchen to put the food away.

He listens to the sound of tins sliding on shelves and doors banging.

"Where's Stella?" she calls.

"Lying down. Not feeling too good."

She appears at the door, a carton of milk in her hand.

"Physically?"

"More than that, I think."

She turns away to put the milk in the fridge.

"I'd better go and see her."

"No, wait ... I want to talk to you first."

"I don't think I should leave her alone too long ..."

"Just for a minute."

She hesitates.

"Please ... sit down for a minute ... No ... here ... beside me."

She perches uneasily on the edge of the sofa avoiding his gaze. "What?"

"Danni, I think you feel something for me, the same as I do for you, but I'm getting confused. You blow hot and then cold ..."

Oh my God, she thinks.

"Why are you looking like that? I don't understand why you keep seeming to push your own feelings away ..."

She stands up.

"I have no feelings about you whatsoever. I need to go to Stella."

"Danni ... your husband ... is that ...?"

He does not finish the stumbling questions, watches instead the shadow of expressions on her face. Is it anger or sadness that ripples fleetingly across her face? He wants to bring the expression back to examine it, but already it is gone.

"Was he ill?"

She says nothing.

"What happened to him?"

Her heart leaps in her chest. She feels resentful that he won't back off but isn't this exactly what she came for? Is the confrontation finally here?

"Did he have an accident?"

"Yes," she says tersely. "He had an accident."

"What kind of accident?"

"I don't want to talk about it."

"We can't move this on until you do."

"I don't want to move it on."

"I don't believe you."

The colour rise in her cheeks. To feel some kind of chemistry with the man responsible for Marco's death has been hard enough to admit even inside herself. That it should be obvious to him is a humiliation.

"Believe what you like," she says, turning disdainfully from him.

"Tell me how he died Danni," he says, and his voice has softened. "Is that something to do with why you are here?"

This is why she came to Ireland. But the conversation in her head, the one she has rehearsed over and over and which ends with a gun shot – somehow it eludes her in real life. She doesn't know how to make it happen. The words have gone. The certainty has gone.

"He died," she says slowly, "in an IRA bomb."

She almost feels satisfaction watching the shock spread across his face.

"Now I understand."

"Do you?" she says, and there is a warning in her tone.

"I am sorry," he says finally. He is very still, his voice low. "Where?" he asks.

She hesitates, and suddenly she realises she is not yet ready for this, for the final showdown. It has to be in her own time.

"London," she says, and turns abruptly.

"Docklands?"

"Yes."

She walks to the window. She'll never get the truth about Glasgow if he knows of her involvement. But if she looks at him, he will surely know she is lying.

"Why was he in London?"

"He was a journalist."

She lets his voice hit her back. She won't turn to him. Can't turn to him.

"There are things that have happened ..." Johnny says, "that can never be put right. People have died so that things can change. I am sorry your husband was one of them. So sorry."

She knows his voice is willing her to turn to him but she refuses.

"Too many people have died," he continues. "And that's why we can't now resist change. We need the peace process."

"So now we just forget about those who died?

"No we don't forget them. We live for them. We live for ourselves and then we live some more for them. We make it work."

He is surprised by his own words. It is the opposite of what he has done himself. He has constricted his life, narrowed it, lived on the stale oxygen of his own guilt and confusion. And now he looks at her and he wants that to change.

"When things change, the dead get left behind," Danni says.

Her eyes are stinging and she blinks, glad that he can't see her.

"There are dead both sides, Danni. Should I have forgotten my dead? Should I have forgotten Michael O'Connor? Or my brother Pat? Don't you understand? The reason I joined the IRA was because of my loyalty to my dead."

"And you got your way by force."

"Got my way? You think so? My country is partitioned still. That isn't what I fought for any more than it was what Michael O'Connor fought for. But we have reached a point where we can't go on fighting forever. There is a chance for peace that has to be taken." His voice drops. "And maybe in our private lives, people like you and me have to take that chance too."

"Yeah, and people like Pearson?"

He shakes his head.

"Danni," he says softly, "every organisation, every workplace, in the world is made up of the good and the bad, and the principled and the unprincipled, and the downright misguided. Why would the IRA be any different? You think people like Pearson don't seep into everything? Pearson represents nothing other than himself."

She turns from the window.

"I need to know," she says.

"Know what?"

"About the Glasgow bomb."

"Danni …" He shakes his head, burying it into his hand.

"I need to know."

"I understand now why this is important but I can't change it. I can't … I can't make it …"

"I'm not asking you to change it. I'm asking what happened. What you did …"

Johnny sits down, weary suddenly, a little dizzy. His limbs feel weak still.

He has asked himself that question so many times. Was it a combination of circumstances … … a collision of conviction and bravado … a need to prove himself even to people he knew were worthless? Was he ruthless or careless? That bomb … did it encompass everything he wanted to walk towards or everything he wanted to run from? All he knows is that he would not plant it today. Was that a deficiency in him then or now? At what point was there something missing in him?

"You are not going to tell me," she says, into the silence rather than to him.

"What good would it do?"

His eyes drift to a picture on the wall, an old print of a fishing boat in a harbour, painted with the simplicity of a child, the colours stripped of any darker complexity. He has always loved that picture. It is the light; the sun shines with the untroubled brightness of childhood summers, streaming intensely, only illuminating, casting no shadows. Every time he looks at it, he wants to walk into it, into the truth of it.

"You were there."

"I've already told you that."

"Were you alone?"

"I can't tell you."

"Were you alone?" she repeats.

"I can't tell you."

"Can't?"

"Won't. Can't."

"Did you plant it? Or were you just there?"

Her heart is hammering. Just end it, she thinks. Once and for all. Tell her he killed them with his own hands. Free her. She feels a sudden rush of tears behind her eyes, a loss of control more powerful than anger.

Johnny is unaware of it. He leans forward, resting his forearms on his knees, head bowed.

He shakes his head.

"Is that no? Or you're not saying ..."

He shakes his head without looking up.

Not even when the police interrogated him had he felt this way, had so much invested in his own answer.

She gives up suddenly, walking by him to the door with a shake of her head.

"Danni ..."

"I need to go to Stella."

She walks out, refusing to look in him directly in the eye.

CHAPTER FORTY-FOUR

In the days after his recovery, Johnny has taken to spending hours watching from the upstairs window. Pearson must know where they are by now. Why hasn't he come? Is he trying to unnerve him?

There's a padded bench seat that runs underneath the long window in the upstairs hall and offers a clear view right down to the road. He suspects this was why the house was renovated in the first place, that when Mary Seonaid started taking in injured volunteers to nurse, and allowed her land to be used for arms storage, the IRA had provided her with a look out.

His grandmother used to sew up here, in what they called the upstairs gallery. When her eyes began to fail, she said the light was best. The bench seat then was covered in a white cotton fabric with green sprigs all over it. The walls were white and the staircase was painted apple green and it felt light and fresh, like sitting in an orchard. Now the fabric is dirty and in as much as you can see any relief colour in the general grime, the apple has turned into a dull khaki.

Then, he would sit with his feet up at the other end of the bench while she worked. From up here you could see right down the track to the main road. He would watch through the window, gradually realising that the world that seemed so still out there was alive with wildlife, his city eyes gradually picking up the hare that loped amongst the long grasses, or the hawk that swooped from the skies on the nests of mice in the surrounding fields.

"I want you to occupy Stella for a bit," he tells Danni quietly when she comes upstairs.

She looks at him sharply.

"What are you going to do?"

"What I heard from McConnell … I need to pass the name on."

She sits down suddenly on the benchseat.

"To the police?

"It's the only way I can keep all of us safe."

"Who is it?"

"A guy called John James Callaghan, the Director of Public Prosecutions for Northern Ireland …"

"I think I heard his name on the news the night Myra died!"

"Probably. He's a campaigner for zero tolerance in the red light district. But obviously it's better if only you and I know how the police get this information, where it's come from. I don't want Stella to know about any of it."

Danni kicks her shoes off and swings them up on the benchseat, hugging her knees. Just the way he once did, he thinks. All those years ago, before he made any of the choices that have brought him here again.

"We need to get to the police before Pearson gets to us."

"Things have gone quiet now, haven't they? He can't possibly know where we are."

Johnny shakes his head.

"Danni, I don't want to scare you, but this is the most dangerous point of all. I … well, I blew it the other night. I've alienated myself from Pearson. He suspects I know,

266

but he doesn't have a single one of us in his sights to keep tracks on us. Right now he's out there looking for us. And you can be sure he'll find us sooner or later."

"How can he find us?"

"You have no idea how many contacts people like Pearson have. How many contacts being in the Provisionals gives you. He knows the car we're driving, the number plate. That car has been out on the road round here. You think locals won't know there are people in the cottage? And there are mobile phone records – why do you think I didn't phone you those first days when I went back to Belfast?"

They hear Stella's footsteps up the stairs. She stops half way up, looking up through the slats of the staircase to the two of them on the benchseat.

"What are you doing?"

"Just talking," says Danni. "Do you fancy a walk?"

"No!" says Johnny.

Danni and Stella turn to him.

"Sorry," he mutters. "It's not a good idea right now."

He looks up the track. There are headlights right at the end.

"Put the lights out," he says urgently.

"What?" says Stella.

Danni looks at his face and lunges for the upstairs switch. Johnny takes the stairs several at a time and puts out the downstairs lamp, then runs back up.

"On the floor," he says.

"What the hell's going on?" says Stella.

"Please," says Johnny.

Danni sits on the floor with her back to the window seat and Stella slides down beside her. Johnny stands to the side of the window watching the car turn into the track and the headlights suddenly go out. He has difficulty making it out but when his eye picks it out, the car is inching forward and stopping. Inching forward and stopping.

"What's happening?" asks Danni.

"The car headlights have been switched out."

He heads for the staircase.

"Where are you going?" asks Stella, her voice shrill with fright.

Johnny glances at Danni. "There's something downstairs I need to get. I'll be back in a minute."

Danni hears the sound of the cabinet drawer closing downstairs and in a moment he's back, gun in hand. Stella begins to cry softly.

"Oh my God," she says. She looks at Danni. "Are we all going to die?"

Danni takes hold of her hand and they sit on the floor, motionless, waiting, for the black outline of the car to move slowly, inexorably down the track towards them, the rutted pits making it lumber from side to side like a strange, black beast.

CHAPTER FORTY-FIVE

When the shots ring out, they explode into the darkness, shoot like fireworks inside Danni's brain as she lies on the floor next to Stella. Downstairs, the living room windows shatter, and Stella's screams follow, ringing out in the upstairs hall. Danni rolls over clinging to her as the window above the benchseat implodes, glass fragments spraying over their bent heads. That sound is part of her life: shattered glass, breaking lives, the raw, primitive scream of fear and pain.

Still clinging to Stella, Danni glances up to Johnny, sees him flat up against the wall still, silhouetted in the darkness. He is somewhere else, she knows, somewhere inside his own head. Alert. Waiting. He is not focusing on the window, or what's outside, but on here, on the upstairs hall, the gun trained over the stairwell waiting for a figure to appear. But nobody appears.

Danni hears an engine roaring outside, the squeal of tyres. She lifts her head. Johnny is watching the car disappear up the track, lights blazing now, lurching forward at speed.

"Just a warning then," he says thoughtfully. He looks at the two women. "Wait," he says. "in case they've left anybody," and he keeps the gun outstretched in front of him, going downstairs in pitch black to check the unnatural silence that sits, thick and dark, around them.

Stella bolts for the toilet and suddenly Danni's had it, reached the limit. She rolls over and puts her face on the carpet, feels the hard tufts against her skin, and the cold, sharp sliver of glass against her mouth, and she sobs uncontrollably. She does not hear Johnny return up the staircase, only becomes aware of him kneeling beside her, lifting her into him, wrapping long arms around her. And maybe if he had said nothing she would have remained there against his chest, limp as a rag doll, listening to his heartbeat. But she feels his head against hers, hears him whisper, "I'm here Danni. I'm here," and the memory of Marco in the hospital surges back suddenly and she struggles free of him and yells, "Don't say that!"

She heads for the bedroom and slams the door, leaving Johnny behind in the darkness, kneeling in fragments of broken glass.

She hears the phone ring from behind the closed door. The hesitation before he answers.

"Yeah?" Johnny says tersely and then there is a long silence.

"Listen Pearson ..." she hears him say eventually, and she creeps nearer to the door, standing behind it, straining to hear the low tone of his voice. "You don't frighten me. You never have. Stop trying to pull ... my ... fucking ... strings." Behind the door, Danni holds her breath, suddenly chilled by Johnny's tone. She barely recognises the voice as his.

She presses her ear closer to the door as his voice drops. "You will get what's coming to you before I do, Pearson." Silence. Danni hesitates, waiting. Johnny has begun to pace in the hall. She can hear the crunch of broken glass under his shoes.

Tentatively, Danni reaches out a hand to the door handle, pauses, then presses down. The door clicks, creaks as it swings open. Johnny is standing amongst the glass, eyes fixed to the floor. He looks up as she is revealed in the doorway and there's an embarrassed silence between them, a legacy from her earlier display of temper. Danni folds her arms like she's cold.

"I heard …" she says. "What did you mean about Pearson … about getting what's coming to him?"

Johnny tilts his head to one side and looks at her through hardened eyes. "What do you think I meant Danni? That I'd go round there and blast a bullet through his head? Old habits die hard, eh? Is that what you think?"

She shrugs, unable to hold his eye.

"God knows he deserves it. He wouldn't be worth wasting any tears on. But no, that's not what I meant."

He watches as she turns and goes back into the bedroom. She doesn't close the door but perches on the end of the bed. Johnny moves inside the doorway, leaning one hand each side of it.

"What I meant …" he says, then stops and lifts his phone back out of his pocket. "I'll show you what I meant."

He punches in a number, presses 'speaker on', and waits. Danni frowns.

"Hello?"

"Parker?"

"Yeah?"

"Johnny O'Brien."

"Sorry …?"

Johnny walks into the bedroom and closes the door.

"Do you forget everyone you stick inside?"

Oh my God, Danni thinks. He's been in prison. There's

been more than the Glasgow bomb? Johnny ignores her stare.

"Oh, Johnny O'Brien ... Lands Road bomb?" she hears the voice say.

"No ... but that's the one I went down for."

"Is that right Johnny? That's what all you guys say though, sure it is?"

"Some of us mean it."

"Well you're out now aren't you? I heard yous all got out early – you and McCann and Seamus Barclay."

"I'd never met McCann or Barclay in my life before that trial. Did you know that Parker?"

There's silence at the other end. Danni sinks back on the bed, flat on her back, shielding her eyes from the light. Inside. He's been inside. Well what did she expect?

"Anyway," says Johnny, "I'm not really phoning to talk about old times with you. I'm sure that won't surprise you."

"So what can I do for you?"

"I've got some information for you. Remember you wanted me to give you information? Said you'd see what you could do about the sentence?"

"You're about five years too late, are you not, Johnny?"

"I've got information of a different kind for you. About corruption involving one of the most senior figures in the Northern Ireland judiciary."

There's a pause.

"Yeah?" says Parker, but even Danni, who is not part of the conversation, who is lying on the bed motionless, can hear an alertness, awakening interest.

"And I think I can help you with the inquiry into the murder of the prostitute Myra MacIntosh. It's all connected."

"What ...? This person ... this senior figure you mention, murdered Myra MacIntosh?"

"No. No … well, I don't think so. Not directly. I think she was murdered to protect him." Johnny can hear the sound of paper rustling, a page of a notebook being turned. Parker is taking notes.

"You know Sean Pearson?" Johnny asks.

"'Course I know him. We all know him. What I *don't* know is how the bastard gets away with half the stuff he does."

"Well I do. He's got friends in high places."

"Who are we talking about?"

"I'm not telling you over the phone. I want to meet you, get an agreement about protection first."

"You never struck me as someone who watched his back much, Johnny. Quite the opposite."

"There are other people involved now."

"I see."

"This isn't going to be easy for you either," Johnny warns. "Not with the name I'm going to give you."

Parker says nothing.

"Are you prepared for that? You want to meet me?"

"When?"

"Soon as possible."

"Where are you?"

"It doesn't matter where I am. Someone just blasted my windows in with a shotgun so I'm not going to be here for much longer. I'm not sure where I'm headed. But I can meet you in Belfast in the morning. 9.30."

"Where?"

"I'd rather not say right now. I'll phone you at 9 and give you a place. And listen, Parker?"

"Yeah?

"Are you serious about taking this on?"

"If it's true, too right."

"Yeah," Johnny says softly. "I thought you'd be interested.

You might have stuck me inside for something I didn't do but in your own twisted way you were kind of honest. I'll call you." He clicks his phone off.

"You'd better get your things together," he tells Danni, and leaves the room.

Stella is sitting alone on the bench seat outside the room.

"Can I go in?" she asks, like a child seeking permission.

"Yes of course. Sorry, Stella. You okay?"

She smiles at him, a grateful smile.

Downstairs, he sits alone for a moment. He's trying to include Danni in everything. The gun. The police. He's trying to be honest. Except it's not honest, he thinks, this pretence of transparency. He has things to hide. Oh Danni knows all right, about him being a Provisional. Maybe she even knows some of the reasons for it. But she doesn't know the stuff he didn't go to prison for. She doesn't know about Angelo Piacentini.

It was in prison that he first began reading physics. He became fascinated by black holes, the idea of an abyss from which nothing, not even light, escaped. Fascinated by existence and non-existence. The funny thing is that people think that if you've killed somebody you've lost God. When in fact, it was only after he realised that some-body's eyelids had closed for the very last time because of him, Johnny O'Brien, that he found the concept of God which had eluded him most of his life ... well almost believable. Certainly hell became believable. But then he was a Catholic so that explained that. Hell was part of the iconography of his childhood. Perhaps hell was one of those black holes. And perhaps he was going there.

He read physics to understand the universe, and psychology to understand his own mind, and in the end resorted to fiction because he understood neither. The discipline he embraced, the myriad of small, uncomfortable choices, was merely suppressed guilt. Intellectually, guilt didn't exist. When he joined the Provos he believed everything they stood for. Unlike Pearson who joined for something else entirely, because it rose up and met something rotten in him, something that just kept on festering. Johnny believed his country was at war, and while some wars were just, there were still always casualties. Which intellectually was all well and good, but when he closed his eyes at night, it was still the eyes of a child he saw, the dark, brown, haunting eyes of Angelo Piacentini.

CHAPTER FORTY-SIX

Danni does not see his head go down onto the steering wheel. One minute they are waiting at traffic lights on the road into Belfast and the next she hears him mutter, "Oh my God." She thinks less of what has prompted the phrase than how Irish his voice sounds in those three little words. She drags her eyes from the side window of an Italian delicatessen on the street corner, where rich red and gold square boxes of panettone are piled in an artless heap. Johnny's head is forward on the steering wheel, his forehead resting against his crossed arms.

"Shit," she hears him mutter.

"What?" Danni says.

She's trying to pull her thoughts towards him as she drags her eyes from the window display. When she married Marco, his parents gave them a big fat cheque tucked inside a box of panettone. They didn't want to spend the first night of their married life in a hotel. Marco's parents offered them a night in a five star hotel but they went back to Marco's flat instead. The next morning she remembers slipping naked out of bed, putting on Marco's wedding shirt that was lying on the floor, and going into the kitchen. They didn't have proper food in the house but Marco had cut chunks of panettone and put it in the toaster, and she had sat on the wooden kitchen table with her bare feet on one of the chairs, and a bread board on her knee, buttering slices as he handed them to her, watching the butter melt into the yellowy dough, browned with the heat and studded with peel. And she had laughed suddenly and for no reason, and Marco, understanding the impulse, had merely smiled, and then he held out a chunk of panettone, and she had taken a bite from his fingers.

She's looking now at the top of Johnny's head.

"What?" she repeats, almost irritably, unwilling to be drawn back to the present.

Johnny lifts his head.

He nods at the newsagent's in the row of shops across the road.

Danni bends her head to look through his window.

On the billboard: BELFAST PRIEST MURDERED IN CHURCH HOUSE.

He's silent, Johnny, like the world has stopped, like it's frozen, and all the action is inside his head. If he hadn't been careless, if he hadn't allowed himself to be followed, McConnell would have been safe. Another one. Another life to be responsible for. Another death.

"Jim McConnell," he says, his voice low. "I know it."

"It might not ..." she says and her voice trails away into oblivion.

Behind them, a row of cars begins to honk impatiently.

"Johnny," she says.

Honk, honk, honk.

"Johnny ..."

Johnny is visible through the glass of the café window. The window is framed by green leaves that start in a plant pot in the corner behind his chair and creep like ivy across the top of the glass. The leaves have been trained, clipped into position, thinks Danni. Perhaps they are plastic. It is hard to tell behind the double layer of glass. She is parked right outside, just feet away, watching through the car window, through the café window, two panes of glass that separate her. Stella is beside her. Johnny parked the car outside and told them not to move. Stella chews gum and says this is stupid this, sitting here like two stooges in the freezing cold. What's he doing anyway? Who is that guy? Danni shrugs.

She turns the key in the ignition and switches on the heater, then turns to watch Johnny, who is visible in a box, like he is an image trapped in a television without sound. She feels agitated, has a strong sense that talking to the police isn't going to end things. What if they don't believe him? He's a convicted terrorist. Who's going to take his word against someone in the legal profession?

Beside her, Stella pulls the gum absentmindedly from her mouth, wrapping it round her finger then putting it back in her mouth. "Why was Johnny so upset about that priest guy?" she asks, but Danni says nothing.

The gun is in her bag. And yet … she knows her emotions won't steady her arm enough to use it. She swings between … between what? She doesn't want to admit it. Between anger and understanding, attraction and guilt. She stares at the pavement outside the car, unable to lift her eyes, pinning the thought and not allowing it to escape. That's the truth. And up to now, every time that guilt has kicked in, she has tried to think of Marco bending down to Angelo, and the arc of the brown paper bag as it was tossed into the air, and she has hated Johnny all over again. Truly hated him, not least because it has filled a need in her, fitted a pattern that has become embedded in her life and is hard to change.

She has to be careful. She has to work out what she really

feels here. Is the attraction some arbitrary consequence of being thrown together onto the same side against Pearson? A false sense of being part of something together? Johnny, after all, is the only person she's had to turn to. Worse, is it a kind of perverted glamour, the same instinct that makes women – what she always thought of as sick women – write to prisoners on Death Row?

She looks back to the café. The way they are sitting, she has a better view of Parker than Johnny. Parker's face has the soft spread of middle age, but somewhere in the jowls and flab, the boy buried there is still evident. Pink, fresh-faced. There is a boyish untidiness too: an unruliness about the mop of sandy coloured hair, a less than pristine quality to the beige raincoat, and a carelessness about the collar that is half tucked in and half out. He sits round shouldered at the table, hands clasped round the outside of his cup and saucer, shoulders hunched, like his body is keeping in secrets, but there is an alertness about him.

Danni watches their faces trying to guess what is being said. Johnny has handed Parker a piece of paper. It is not Parker's reaction, but the lack of it, that speaks of the importance of the name, his absolute stillness, a rigidity almost. And then Parker sits back in the chair for the first time. Johnny glances out to the car to check on them. She sees the tiger stain flick, his eyes turn on her, rest longer than they need to, and then he looks back to Parker.

"I'm starving," complains Stella.

She is agitated, fidgety, her bare foot shaking up and down inside her stiletto shoes. She's wearing a leather jacket and when she crosses and uncrosses her arms, the leather squeaks. Danni glances at her, then rests her head back on the chair and closes her eyes. Stella sighs.

"For God's sake," she says, the chewing gum stretching like a line of floss from her mouth to her finger.

When Danni opens her eyes Stella's gaze is trained on Johnny in the café window. Like she's naked, that look, Danni thinks, startled. She hadn't realised. Stella looks away.

"You like him?" Stella asks a moment later.

"Eh?" Danni says, buying time, uncertain what else to say.

Stella glances at her. "He likes you."

"I …"

"It doesn't matter," says Stella.

"Of course it matters," says Danni quietly.

"Guys like him never …"

Her expression is one of resignation.

"It doesn't matter …" she says again.

"He's too old for you, Stella."

"I've lived more than my age."

"So has he."

"He's killed someone …" Stella says, looking curiously at Danni. "You know that?"

"I know that."

"He didn't mean to." Stella rummages in her bag for a scrap of paper and puts her chewing gum into it.

"How do you know he didn't mean to?" Danni asks.

"When he was sick. You were asleep in the chair and he kept talking about a boy who died. Then he said something about Pearson making him. I don't know. He was … what do you call it … delrius."

"Delirious," Danni says vaguely. Her insides have turned to ice. A boy who died. So neutral. Her Angelo.

Stella dips her head down to see past Danni through the window. Johnny is pushing his chair back. He and Parker shake hands briefly across the table. Danni sits up, putting her seatbelt on again. Outside, the two men barely acknowledge one another, each going their separate ways.

"Okay?" Danni says as he slides into the seat beside her. Johnny nods.

"Can we get something to eat now?" asks Stella.

"We don't have time to stop," says Johnny. "Maybe you should get some sandwiches in that bakery over there."

"Why don't we have time to stop?" says Stella.

Johnny looks at Danni. "Maybe you should get the sandwiches and I'll explain. With McConnell gone, there's not much need for secrets any more …"

Danni picks up her bag wearily.

"What do you want?"

"Anything."

"Useful," Danni mutters, slamming the door shut.

"What's going on?" Stella asks.

"The police know about Pearson and … and Myra's client. They're about to pull both of them in for questioning."

"You know what you're doing?"

Johnny doesn't answer. He watches Danni inside the shop, picking up sandwiches from a chiller cabinet and examining the labels.

"Why doesn't she go home?" he says thoughtfully, more to himself than Stella.

"Nothing to go home for," says Stella. "Like all three of us."

Johnny glances over his shoulder at her, then turns back.

"It could be different," says Stella.

"Could it?"

He thinks she's talking about Danni. About him and Danni.

"Yes," she says, so softly he catches the suppressed emotion in it and he stiffens suddenly but doesn't turn round. He doesn't know what to say.

Stella bites her lip.

"You fancy her don't you?" she says. "I think you're a bit in love with her."

"Am I?"

Danni is paying now, the assistant stuffing packets of sandwiches into a plastic bag. A shaft of sunlight is catching Danni at the counter, giving a wax polish shine to her hair. He feels a perverted kind of pleasure in the fact that although he hasn't agreed with Stella, he can't deny what she says.

"She's lost a lot ..." Stella says.

"Yes."

"She told you?"

Stella sounds surprised.

"About her husband? Yes. Well, not about him. About the fact she lost him."

"Not just her husband. Her son."

Johnny tenses. He knows the pieces are falling into place, though he has not yet had a chance to stand back and see the full picture.

"Her son?"

"So she *didn't* tell you."

Her eyes have always been so familiar, like eyes that have watched him all his life.

"How old?"

Don't say it, he thinks, but he knows with an absolute certainty that she will.

"Three, I think."

He closes his eyes.

Her name isn't Cameron.

He feels as if he has cracked from top to toe, fault lines shooting throughout his body, and he's simply waiting for the pieces to fall apart.

The car door opens. Danni throws in her bag first then rummages in the plastic carrier for a packet of sandwiches which she throws over the back to Stella.

"Tuna?" she says.

Stella doesn't answer.
Danni looks up at her, then at Johnny, and stills.
"What?" she says.

CHAPTER FORTY-SEVEN

They have a few hours to get their things together, Johnny says. The police will take them to a safe house, in case of repercussions when they lift Pearson. Danni and Stella should stick together to pick up more things from Stella's flat. Johnny will drop them off, then go alone to his flat and come back to meet them both at Stella's.

"Do you think Pearson actually killed Myra himself?" asks Stella through a mouthful of tuna sandwich.

"Coyle will have done the dirty work," says Johnny, starting up the engine. "Pearson directs stuff; he doesn't actually do it himself. He'd have no difficulty extinguishing Myra. Women like her ..." He stops. "Women like Myra always ... Pearson may have made his money out of them but he can't handle them." He glances apologetically in the mirror at Stella.

"Sorry," he says.

Stella shrugs.

"Why?" asks Danni.

"They threaten him. He can't take all that sexual overtness ... It makes him feel ..."

"You mean he's turned on by it and doesn't like being out of control?"

284

"No the opposite. He isn't turned on by it but he's in denial about why not."

"You mean he's gay," says Stella, raising her eyes. "So what?"

"You didn't know his father," says Johnny wryly. "He was a ball-busting maniac and that's part of Pearson's problem. He's a different generation to you, Stella, and the world he operates in ..."

"Wasn't one of the Kray twins gay?" interrupts Danni, turning to Johnny.

"Who are the Kray twins?" asks Stella.

"Oh, old-time London gangsters ... doesn't matter."

Johnny shakes his head. "It's not as simple as being gay. Everything about Pearson is twisted and that includes sex. Deep down it disgusts him. Women disgust him, though he won't admit it. The women who work for him are just a reminder of something he's not part of."

He stops at traffic lights and glances sideways at Danni.

"What about Coyle?" she asks, avoiding his gaze.

"A pretty little plaything for Pearson to have around. But he won't admit it."

"Why did he marry?" asks Stella.

"Cover," says Johnny. "Margaret is ..." he breaks off suddenly, looking down at the dashboard. "Shit."

"What?"

"The radiator light is on. It's okay – it just needs water."

"What's she like?" asks Danni curiously.

"Who?"

"Margaret, Pearson's wife."

"Dumpy. Middle aged. She's been with him since they were 17. They live in a fabulous house and she just stays there. She's a recluse basically, doesn't go out."

"So why make his money out of prostitution?" asks Danni.

"He can do what he likes with them. They're desperate

because they're addicts and they're easy to control because they don't have anyone looking out for them. All they are to Pearson is money-making tramps in cheap clothes and vinyl shoes."

"Cheers," says Stella, a mouthful of tuna falling from her sandwich.

Stella's home is a cramped bedsit, a room in a larger flat occupied by three other women she barely knows, but with whom she shares a kitchen and bathroom. Johnny comes up to check everything is clear before going onto his own place. He goes into the kitchen to fill a bottle with water for the car radiator. Danni sits on the bed while Stella throws open drawers and cupboards.

"Johnny'll be okay on his own," Stella says. "He'd know how to deal with Pearson."

She doesn't sound certain. She wants reassurance.

"Yeah," says Danni.

"He can be scary sometimes, Johnny."

He does not frighten her, Danni realises, lying back on the bed and staring at the ceiling while Stella stuffs things into her bag. Why is that? She trusts him, she thinks, before she can stop the thought.

"Are you scared of him?" she asks Stella curiously.

"Not in a bad way. He's … he's got a kind of wild bit or something … a bit you can't reach … but he's good … like, if he's on your side …"

"Yeah," she says, noncommitally. It's true, she thinks, as Stella keeps talking, fumbling for words to describe Johnny. Danni has become used to Stella's voice prattling in the background, listens only with half an ear sometimes. Then a phrase cuts through her reverie.

"What do you mean, stained by the bomb?" she says sharply, sitting up and interrupting Stella mid flow.

Stella turns from the cupboard, surprised at her tone.

"When he was ill …" she says. "He was trying to brush pink powder off himself, kept saying it was staining him."

"Johnny actually made the bomb?"

"Think so."

"He said so?"

Stella hesitates and comes forward to sit beside her on the bed for a moment.

"I'm sorry Danni. I shouldn't really … it must be hard for you because of … but Johnny … he … he …"

Danni feels like the breath won't come, that her lungs won't fill. She feels sick.

Stella looks at her and feels scared.

"He's finished with that stuff," she says.

Danni doesn't even look at her.

"It was scaring him … you know … when he thought the powder was on him," she finishes lamely.

He wasn't just there, Danni thinks. Wasn't just young and stupid and caught up in something he didn't understand. He ground the explosives with his own hands. Planted the result. She says the words slowly, deliberately, inside her head: Johnny made the bomb that killed Marco and Angelo. The acknowledgement makes her gasp silently. Does it change things? Immediately. The responsibility is no longer shared. It is his.

For a moment the world seems empty, bleaker than ever, because it is filled not just with loss but with disappointment. When hope flickers inside emptiness, and then gets snuffed out … What had she been building inside her head, she wonders, to cause this crushing sense of defeat?

And maybe the anger that comes is conjured up in self-defence, the sorceress's favourite spell, the old familiar cloak of bitterness she has worn so often. She has struggled to find anger, hold it, retain it, while she has been around

Johnny, while they have been thrown together so artificially against Pearson, forcing them onto the same side. But now it flows inside her again without effort, a trickle, a river, a sea until it fills her up, every last part of her, and it washes away every trace of doubt and uncertainty. She knows what she wants to do, and the knowledge brings relief, an end to guilt and to struggle. She is free. Empty and free. "Bastard," she whispers.

She leaves Stella in the room, goes down to the car where Johnny is filling the radiator. She grabs his arm and he turns in surprise, his grey eyes resting on her fingers then flicking up quickly to her face.

"The gun," she says.

He straightens, running his fingers back through his hair, in a way that is now so familiar to her, to catch the straying strands falling on his brow. They are coming to an end now, she knows it. Their forced togetherness, the false sense of being thrown onto the same side, will soon be over. She has to be prepared.

"It's still in the car …" he says, and his eyes don't leave hers.

"I know it's in the car. I want it."

In the silence that follows she feels the erratic thump of her heart in her chest, and her breath quickens. She swallows.

"Get in," Johnny says quietly.

She slips into the back seat, and closes the door. He moves to the other side and gets in, glancing round the back. As his door bangs, the noise of the street is instantly muffled and in here, in their space, the interior of the car feels suspended in another world. Danni stares straight ahead.

"What do you want it for, Danni?" he says, his voice low and tight.

"I think it's best when we're dealing with Parker if you don't have a gun. He's a policeman and he knows your background. If he's suspicious … if you end up being searched … or taken in or …"

She sounds strangely breathy, like her voice is running away without her and she can't quite catch it.

"Right," he says. His eyes roam over the street and he turns and gives a quick glance behind the car.

"And besides," she says with sudden defiance, "I want to be in control."

Her stomach churns as he turns slowly towards her and meets her eyes. But he merely nods.

Danni leans forward to reach under the front seat and tugs the box back from where they put it, lodged under the dip of the seat.

He watches her open her handbag and then she lifts the lid of the box, as if she intends transferring the weapon out of it and into the open bag.

The black gun sits dark and cold against the metal interior of the box on her knee. She hesitates.

"Touch it Danni," he says, quietly. "Hold it. Get to know the feel of it. The weight of it. The power of it. Go on, lift it."

She looks at it still, staring into the box. She hasn't touched it since that first day in Donegal.

"You don't know how to use it," he says, "but I'll show you."

His voice is emotionless. She feels cold, nauseous.

Johnny leans over and picks the gun up, glancing outside the car, keeping it low in his lap.

"It's a Beretta 92," he says, and after that she hears his voice only as a drone in her head, telling her about the mechanics of the weapon. His eyes don't leave her face and his attention is sucking the blood from her, draining it, making her consciousness swim into the distance away from her, and when he reaches out to hand the gun to her, she takes it from him and stares at her own hand as if it belongs to somebody else.

Her hand is trembling now, shaking in a way that feel systemic, as if the shake comes not from her hand but from the core of her. It feels like it will never end. Silence fills up the interior of the car like a poisonous gas.

"You could kill a man with that Danni," he says, his voice low. "It would be quick."

She looks at the gun and she looks at the trigger, the small, silver trigger, and she thinks perhaps she could do it now, at close range, right now when she couldn't miss. Isn't this what she has been waiting for, him and her together, the perfect opportunity? And then she sees Stella, walking from the front door of the flats, looking anxious, wondering what they are doing.

"Stella," she says, and she drops the gun into her bag and stares at him.

Johnny opens his window.

"I thought you were going on to your place," Stella says.

"I am. I'll be back in half an hour."

Danni opens the car door and glances at Johnny. He gazes back with such loaded stillness that she is certain he knows what she was thinking, and she turns away from him, and turns away from what he sees in her eyes, and what she sees in his in return.

CHAPTER FORTY-EIGHT

When he opens the door to his flat it smells stale, cold stale, the floorboards contracting and creaking beneath his feet, the air itself tight and restricted like short breaths forced from ill, restricted lungs. The ceiling is lower than he remembered, like it can't be bothered holding up the walls any more, and he's weary with it already, just walking in here, with the hopelessness of it, the paper lampshade grown brown and grubby with the heat of the bulb above, and the thin carpet that feels like the hard, stiff bristles of an old shaving brush beneath bare feet, and the grim, grey stains round the cheerless gas fire that's trapped like a fuck-ing gashed mouth on the wall. The walls that once held him tight like a womb feel suffocating now, and he wants to leave the front door open, leave it wide open, to let heat and light in, to let the room turn inside out and breathe again with the air of the outside world.

Only a fortnight, Johnny thinks ... Two weeks and a lifetime since he was here. In the bedroom, the bedding piled high still where he struggled to find warmth. In good health it's hard to remember illness, your own weakness. Or maybe that's just because he doesn't like giving into weakness much, never lets himself dwell on it. He picks the duvet up, lets it drop again. He looks round the bare bones of his life and knows he'll never breathe life in this again, never resurrect it. He won't live here again.

He is expecting him already. He knows he will come. Pearson will come.

He'd known that as soon as Parker had called on his way to the flat. The rest were in custody but they couldn't find Pearson. Johnny gave him Stella's address, told him to get a car there immediately. He'd let Parker think he'd be there too but it's better this way. He will be the magnet for Pearson. This way there will be resolution.

In the bedroom, he puts his shoulder to the heavy old mahogany chest of drawers, manoeuvring it slowly, inch by inch, away from the wall and into the centre of the floor. Breathing heavily, he kneels down on the floor and rolls back the carpet, feeling along the edge for the small space at the edge of the wood. In minutes, he has a single floor board up and he slides his hand underneath, reaching for the small ledge. His hand bumps into metal and he stops.

He had hoped never to look at it again. When he'd returned to Ireland, he had promised himself that if trouble sought him out, he would simply leave. People had long memories. The possibility of trouble was always there, especially with Pearson's careless talk. The guns were the insurance policy he hoped never to have to claim. One in Donegal, of course, but one under the floorboards of his Belfast flat. And if things had gone right, he would have left it here when he moved on, buried under the floorboards where nobody knew it existed. Tenants would have come and gone above it, slippered feet and bare feet, children's running feet, and the secret of another life, another existence, would have died with him.

He fingers the trigger. He wishes … but there is no point in wishes. His life has not been like other people's.

Guns, prison … Principle or folly? A few weeks ago, he'd have killed Pearson rather than let him across the door. This world in here, for a time it was different. He wouldn't have allowed Pearson to contaminate it. But this place, it's empty now, finished, there's nothing to contaminate. Spent like an empty cartridge. He looks round the bedroom and snaps the light off. He will sit down and wait until Pearson arrives.

In the front room he looks through the window then crosses to a battered second-hand cabinet in the corner and opens a drawer. He lifts out a packet of cigarettes, then opens a pull-down door and takes out a bottle of whisky and two glasses, tucking the bottle under his arm and carrying the glasses between two fingers. The cigarettes are an old habit. He gave up in prison and hasn't smoked since. It started out as a test of discipline to have an opened packet, though to tell the truth he hadn't remembered in a long while that they were there.

Music. He rifles through some CDs, smiles wanly at the irony of his choice. Jim Morrison. Plucked guitar notes growing, reaching out of silence, like a living thing, like a plant reaching towards the light.

Exotic. Eastern. The rattle of a tambourine. He loves Jim Morrison. "This is the end," he hums low, "beautiful friend. The end." But for whom, he thinks?

He turns the music up. He takes his overcoat from the cupboard in the hall. Drums beating like the pulse in his temples. Rolling like waves of his own blood. He always feels music inside him, like it's growing from the inside out.

He puts his coat on and lights the fire, turns the chair towards the door. He strikes a match and lights the cigarette, drawing on it, pulling the smoke deep inside himself. It's the last cigarette he'll ever smoke. He blows out the match, puts one hand in his pocket for warmth and tilts his head, blowing smoke upwards, narrowing his eyes against the fug, letting it settle round him, letting the smoke and the music curl round him, inhabit him.

CHAPTER FORTY-NINE

She doesn't believe it. Not any of it. Stella looks at her sharply then continues packing.

"What?" Stella says.

Danni doesn't reply.

"Danni?"

"Johnny texted. Parker called. They moved on all of them but ..."

"They've got Pearson?" Stella says so eagerly that Danni realises fully how frightened she is of him.

Danni shakes her head.

"Everybody *but* him. They got Coyle but not Pearson. They can't find him."

"Shit."

"The police car's on its way here. Johnny says it will reach us before he does. He'll come later to the safe house."

Stella starts throwing things into a case.

"Fuck it, Danni, I want out of here. I hope they get here soon."

"I'm going over there," Danni says suddenly.

Stella freezes. "Over where?"

"Johnny's flat."

"No way. Johnny will be on his way over and you could

get stuck between here and there. The police will be here any minute. Just do what he says."

"I want out of here before they get here," says Danni. "There's something going on over there. He's waiting for Pearson."

"Danni you can't …"

"I'm going."

"Shit Danni …" says Stella, throwing her hands in the air. "You can't go over there on your own."

Danni picks up her bag, feels the heavy thump of it against her leg, knows the gun nestles inside. It's time.

"See you later, Stella." Stella kicks the suitcase on the floor savagely with the toe of her scuffed white stilettos. Mad bloody cow. She grabs her handbag and runs out into the stairwell after Danni, banging the door behind her. Danni is already at the bottom of the steps.

"Oi!" Stella shouts.

She grabs the handrail, tries to run down the stairs as fast as her tight skirt will allow, legs flailing out to the side, heels clip clopping on the stone stairs.

CHAPTER FIFTY

In the fug of smoke, it is Danni's face he sees. That look when she demanded the gun from him. It haunts him. In that moment, she wanted him dead. He knows it. He closes his eyes momentarily as it to shut the expression out but it looms clearer than ever in his imagination. Clear-eyed. He did not see her confusion, only her coldness.

She is brave enough, his instincts tell him that much. She could do it. With the right heat ... the right moment ... the swell of desperation. He nods to himself silently as the music fills him. You get to recognise that capacity. That night all those years ago, when Devine asked what road he wanted closed, where his body should be dumped, Johnny came close to dying. He knew it, saw it, felt it, like he does now. A wrong word, a wrong move ...

He knows something else too. He will kill himself before he allows her to kill him. She is focused entirely on the action, and not the aftermath, and he knows what that does to you. You have to wash the blood off fast or it stains you forever. She has no idea what it is like, the black hole that opens up, the search for soul, the terror of immortality. The questions, drumming incessantly in your brain. He will not allow her to find out. He will kill himself before he allows her to kill him.

He fingers the trigger of his gun reluctantly, trains it on the open door as if Pearson is here already. Then he hesitates. Perhaps … perhaps the answer is simply to let Pearson shoot him. End everything. Become her altar. How else can it end now? He can't go back.

He lowers the gun, the music enveloping him still. *Beautiful friend, the end.* Johnny pulls another chair over beside him, places the gun where he can see it. He will not touch it. Let Pearson pull the trigger first.

CHAPTER FIFTY-ONE

The taxi smells of artificial air freshener with an underlying note of staleness. Like someone has been sick in here, Danni thinks, wrinkling her nose. The hire car is still outside Stella's flat, where she's left it, frightened it would identify them. If Pearson showed up, he would see it outside and assume they were there, which might delay him for a bit. But she doesn't think Pearson will go there. He'll be drawn to Johnny. Like she is.

"Can you go any faster?" she says. The taxi driver says nothing but she feels the surge as he puts his foot down. The car slows as he rounds the corner, slap bang into a long queue of traffic behind a jack-knifed lorry.

"No," she wails.

"It's okay Danni," Stella says quietly, reaching out a hand to her arm.

Up ahead, a car driver blasts its horn and a chorus of toots begins. The taxi driver jumps out, peers into the darkness.

"We'll be here a while," he announces, as he slams the door shut again.

The heavily perfumed atmosphere of air freshener is making Danni feel sick. She opens the window a crack.

Johnny made the bomb that killed Marco and Angelo.

Over and over inside her head. It makes her hold her breath.

Outside, a few cars inch forward. "Make it move!" Danni explodes, leaning forward. "Go up on the pavement and round! Go!"

Stella's hand reaches out and slips through her arm, her thumb drawing small, quiet, soothing, circles on Danni's arm. The driver's eyes flick up to his mirror and meet Danni's, and then he glances away again, too unwilling, too embarrassed, to meet her distress head on.

CHAPTER FIFTY-TWO

He is here. Pearson is here. He didn't hear him because of the music but he can feel him without opening his eyes.

"Careless of you Johnny, leaving your door open." Pearson says.

"I was expecting you," Johnny says.

He sees immediately Pearson resents that. He does not like to feel he can be predicted. He is too smart, too cunning.

"You're taking a chance," Johnny adds. "I knew you'd take a chance." He see the gun, hanging at Pearson's side like an extension of his arm.

"Those who take chances win. Y'know?"

Pearson preens himself, seeming to grow an inch in his navy pinstripe suit.

"Closing your eyes, Johnny. Caught without your gun. You're going soft." Pearson takes off his jacket, transferring the gun from one hand to the other, and throws the jacket on the back of the chair. He loosens the tie round his lilac shirt with one hand, his gold rings flashing in the overhead light, the gun still in his other hand, flat against his thigh.

"The police will be here soon."

"Yeah? But I got here first, didn't I Johnny? I can have you blasted to kingdom come before they arrive."

Johnny smiles, picking up his cigarette that has been resting on an ashtray. He offers the packet to Pearson who shakes his head.

"No, you don't any more, do you?"

He relights his own, watching Pearson above the flame as he strikes a match and lifts it to the cigarette in his mouth, cupping his hand protectively round it.

"Blasting to kingdom come isn't your style, though, is it? Too quick. You need play time. Cat and mouse. How fast was it with Myra?"

"How would I know Johnny?"

"The police will know soon enough."

"There will be nothing on Myra that links her to me." He smiles. "What do you think I keep Coyle for?"

Johnny look at the curve of his belly beneath the lilac shirt, the slight paunch, the soft flabbiness of indiscipline. That's always been the trouble with Pearson. Johnny breaths out a soft mist of smoke. Smart enough. But not so smart he doesn't need other people to know it.

"How do you feel afterwards?" He's genuinely curious. Do other people feel like him? "To be responsible for a person's death ..." Johnny continues.

"Your hands are dirty, same as mine, Johnny."

"That always made you feel better, didn't it?"

"You're too emotional. It's business. You kill or you get killed. It's not complicated. Why would I feel anything? You know what Myra was. She was a whore."

"You always had trouble with women."

"And you always had trouble with your big mouth, Johnny. Maybe you should just shut the fuck up."

"Can you kill us all? Myra. Jim McConnell. Stella. Me."

"You missed one."

"What?"

"You missed one. The Scottish dame. What's her name?"

302

"Danni."

"Danni, yeah."

He hates hearing her name on his lips. Curious. Just the sound from those thin lips makes him want to break Pearson's neck. There is something in Johnny's manner that Pearson picks up on. Animal instinct. Pearson folds his arms and perches on the edge of the sofa opposite Johnny and leans forward, the blue river veins visible in his neck.

"You know what I think Johnny?" His voice is dangerously civil. "I think you're a bit sweet on this Danni. I knew she was your type. Lively. And you know how it is when you get involved like that. You develop weak spots. Like Roisin."

He can feel it like a rush of wind in his ears, the rustling of leaves, an old familiar anger, dark inside him, deep inside him. A physical force, wooshing into his lungs with the nicotine, making his heart beat faster, giving a second's blackout, a brief power cut, inside his head. Steady. Steady.

"You can't get rid of us all, Pearson."

"Why not?"

"You'll go down anyway."

"Yeah but I'll take you with me."

They are silent now, him and Pearson. Too much to say and not enough. The landscape of all those years stretching between them. And maybe there's a sliver of regret that things have to be this way, that things couldn't be different. Because there's something, Johnny knows, that binds the two of them, even if it's just childhood when differences between you don't matter as much. It doesn't matter that you're different and incompatible and maybe even hostile because you're bound by something bigger, bound by being kids in a world that you are only just beginning to understand.

Back then, character was only a tendency, an instinct.

It wasn't rigid; it morphed, took shape, changed shape. But that's before the choices were made. That's when life stretched ahead, possibilities glittering like lakes on the horizon. And after the choices were made, tendencies and instincts solidified into hardened traits. The glittering lakes were dull and barren now, dry bedded, lined with cracked mud and silt. And now, things can only be the way they have to be, with regret but without choice.

CHAPTER FIFTY-THREE

Johnny pours two glasses of whisky, Pearson watching silently.

"They're looking for you, Pearson."

"I know."

"Are you going to kill me or what?" asks Johnny, sliding one across the small table beside him.

"I need to get out of here," Pearson says. It's cold in the flat but there are beads of sweat on his thin, upper lip. When he moves, Johnny notices the darker lilac of damp patches under the arms of his shirt.

"I'm not going down," Pearson says, lifting the glass and taking a gulp. "I'm not going inside. I'll shoot you and I'll shoot me before I do that ..." His voice drops. "We were a good team, Johnny."

He looks into Pearson's eyes and is shocked. What is that flickering there like a light bulb, making and breaking connection repeatedly? Something from childhood. An appeal. He saw that look once, such a long time ago. With Pearson's auld man.

"A good team?" he says.

"We could move off, start up again," Pearson says. "Business opportunities everywhere Johnny."

Jesus, he's mad. That's why he's come here … Johnny says nothing and Pearson understands that silence, the rebuke of it, and the light goes out as if it had never been on.

"You never saw things very clearly," Pearson says.

"We were never a team."

"We could have been."

"You've always worked for yourself. That's why I went down."

Pearson shrugs.

"They knew about a job."

"So you swapped my freedom for yours?"

"That's business, Johnny."

Business.

"Remember Jimmy Gillespie?" Johnny says suddenly.

"No. Who's he?"

Johnny rolls his eyes.

"He was a cleaner at an RUC station. You wanted me to shoot him."

"Oh him … yeah."

"Fuck, Pearson, you don't even remember him properly do you? You wanted to shoot him! You said he was a traitor. But all the time you were squealing to the Brits yourself."

"Oh don't talk shit! I let them think I was working for them. I had a foot in both camps and we needed that. It was useful. I manipulated them. You went down for the Lands Road bomb but you'd have got a lot longer if you'd gone down for Glasgow."

Johnny shakes his head. Always an explanation. Always a self-justification. The trouble with Pearson was, he always ended up believing his own fantasies.

Johnny hadn't wanted to be part of the whole nutting squad thing; it never appealed to him to be part of "internal discipline". But the night they went to Gillespie's house, Pearson had made sure he got pulled in from above. He

306

knew how was it going to look if he didn't go. An order was an order. There had been three of them, him and a guy called McGill that he'd never met before, led by Pearson. They had knocked on Gillespie's door, armed with guns, ready to force entry when it opened.

Pearson wouldn't tell them what Gillespie had done but Johnny couldn't believe his eyes when he saw him. An old guy in carpet slippers. His wife had answered the door, screaming like a child when she saw masked men on her doorstep. Gillespie had rushed out instinctively when he heard her, then froze in the hall, unsure which way to turn. Johnny had looked at the old guy with the grey stubble and cardigan and wondered what the hell was going on.

"Inside," Pearson ordered Gillespie's wife, pushing her in and slamming the front door behind him. But she remained rooted to the spot in the hall.

"In there," he screamed, nodding at the sitting room. She moved fast then, collapsing onto the sofa beside her daughter and her seven-year-old grandson, who cowered, howling, beside his mother.

"It's okay," Johnny said to Gillespie's wife and daughter, as calmly as he could. We just want a chat. Nobody's going to get hurt. He kept Gillespie out in the hall and closed the door.

"What is this?" he said to Pearson.

"Shoot," Pearson ordered. "Back of the leg."

Gillespie's eyes were darting everywhere, Johnny noticed, trying to look for an escape. Just as he had himself all those years ago in the warehouse.

"Pearson, what the fuck's going on?" he hissed.

"You don't need to know that. *Follow orders.*"

"Please," said Gillespie, grabbing hold of Johnny's arm, "it's only a few hours cleaning a week. It's the only job round here. I won't go back. I swear I won't go back."

"Shut the fuck up!" shouted Pearson, lashing out with his closed fist. Gillespie fell back against the door with a thump.

"Grampa! Grampa!" The screams rose hysterically from behind the door, followed by the child's fists battering against the wood before being dragged away.

"Get on with it!" Pearson yelled at Johnny.

"Come on, come on!" Jim had been muttering through the whole exchange. He looked hyped up, Johnny thought. Trigger happy.

"We need to get out of here! I'll do it!" McGill shouted now.

Will you fuck, Johnny thought, throwing open the sitting room door and pushing Gillespie through. A shot rang out, followed by screaming.

"Out," Johnny yelled at the others, and they ran through the front door and into the car.

"Why did you push him into the room?" demanded Pearson belligerently, removing his balaclava as they drove off. "You got him?"

"You know me, Pearson" said Johnny dryly. "Not much of a shot. Think I might have got the floor in all the confusion."

Pearson had been furious. He could easily have put the bullet in Gillespie himself but he had wanted Johnny to do it.

"You were useless that night with Gillespie," Pearson says now, gulping back his whisky. "You always bottled it. You always let us down."

"Let you down!"

"We could have been a good team."

"He was an old guy, with no job, trying to make a couple of pounds as a cleaner. Was he really worth our attention because he happened to be cleaning an RUC station?"

"You know your problem, Johnny? You always try to take the moral high ground."

"Yeah, I'm a convicted bomber with a prison record. Most people's idea of the moral high ground right enough," says Johnny, stabbing his cigarette out. He shakes his head at Pearson. "It's certainly not something anybody could accuse you of."

"And you know the beauty of that, Johnny boy?

Johnny sees Pearson lift his gun. His own sits on the chair in front of him still but he simply sits back calmly, does not move for it.

"What?"

"I never miss. I never hit the floor when I mean to hit a man."

CHAPTER FIFTY-FOUR

The gun is in her handbag, nestling against her purse, a pink lipstick, and a handbag mirror in the shape of a shell.

He is *her* quarry. If anyone kills Johnny, she does, not Pearson. She won't have that taken from her.

"Stay in the taxi and go home, Stella," she says, getting out of the cab.

Stella scrambles out, refusing even to answer her.

"Take your shoes off then," Danni says as she pays the driver.

"What?"

"Do it!" says Danni quietly. "You can be heard a mile off."

The taxi driver stares out of the window at her and then takes off, shaking his head.

Stella leans on Danni's shoulder and Danni whips the stilettos from her, running to the entrance of Johnny's block with them. Stella hobbles in stocking soles after her, reacting silently to the pain of pebbles beneath her toes.

"Danni, Pearson's probably not even going to be here," she whispers. "I think you're overreacting."

"We'll see."

She takes a deep breath, leaning on the wall at the bottom of the stairs. They move silently to the first half landing and Danni stops, her stomach lurching. She grabs the banister and turns to Stella.

"The–door–is–open," she mouths silently.

Stella's eyes flick up the stairwell. She sees movement from Danni, and looks back, to see her take Johnny's gun from her bag. Stella stills. Her eyes darken, reasoning, assessing, her brain making the myriad of split second calculations that it can under pressure. She points at the gun.

"Let–me–see–that," she mouths at Danni.

She's unzipping her skirt, silently stepping out of it, then pointing at the gun like she has spotted something wrong with it. Danni looks in bafflement. What the hell is she doing? Stella nods her head reassuringly while holding out her hand.

"I'll–give–it–back," she mouths in reply.

Danni looks up the stairwell frantically, then feels Stella's tap on her arm. She watches as Stella carefully, carefully takes the gun, still pointing at something Danni cannot see. Danni looks uncomprehendingly at her.

"What?" she mouths, and even though it's silent, Stella senses the desperate urgency. Stella feels remarkably calm. If anyone's going to do any shooting here it will be her, because her life's tainted already. And anyway, Myra was hers, or as close to hers as she gets. Once she has the gun, Stella flees silently. Up the stairs, away from Danni, two steps at a time, legs free now from the restriction of the skirt that sat tight round her hips. And Danni can do nothing but follow, her entire body screaming with silent ferocity.

CHAPTER FIFTY-FIVE

Johnny notices how steady Pearson's hand is as he lifts the gun. No tremor, no fear, no regret. You can't learn empathy as an adult.

Turmoil inside his head. Fragments of energy, shooting stars of thought, exploding, dying, disparate and connected … the last place you inhabit, inside and out … this sad, barren place. He wonders what part of this last exploding energy contains him, his essential self. What will depart last?

Grey metal of a handgun rising, rising, and he's thinking about this place, not that it is no place to die but that it wasn't any place to live. That he'd sucked the colour out of his own existence. It was what he'd figured he'd deserved, and maybe he wasn't far wrong. His gun is still on the chair. He could reach for it. All those years ago, in the warehouse, when he was nineteen and he thought he was going to die, he would have taken any chance. But he is not nineteen. He looks up, sees Pearson's hand steadying, a deliberate aim, a focus …

The shot comes. He hears it magnified inside his head, sees blood and is bewildered. A thud. Blood, trickling, a black powder rash from the bullet sprayed in a sick, peppered tattoo over the side of the head. Screams he cannot recognise or make sense of, high pitched, hysterical. Another shot, desperate fire, filling the room, filling his head. He should be dead now. Is he dead? Is there some confusion that the blood is over there and he is here? His mind dull, saturated with sensation, drowning in it. Senses fighting and tumbling. A rainbow of lilac and red. Lilac shirt, red blood.

Danni slumped against a wall, her fingers gripping the side of the door like she'll fall of the edge of the world if she doesn't hang on. Stella, white and trembling, shaking and shaking till the gun drops from her fingers. He sees them both but cannot process them, looks down at himself, and realises all blood is external to him. And Pearson lying, eyes open, seeping lilac into blood and blood into lilac.

Stella is skirtless still, vulnerable, a broad ladder in her tights climbing up her thigh. Danni sees the white skin in the gaps of the tan ladder, realises with an adrenaline shot of fear that blood is dripping from an unknown sky, big rain drop splodges of red splashing down onto the white landscape of Stella's skin, rolling onto the tan tights. Where's it coming from?

Pearson is dead, eyes staring. But he had fired back as he fell. Stella is swaying, eyes fixed and glassy, a chalky whiteness rising through her face, the gun falling from her hand to the floor. Her eyes desperately seek out Danni and Danni lunges forward to her, sensing the imminent fall. But Johnny is there already, arms circling Stella, catching her, cushioning her. She's grabbing hold of him like he offers her salvation.

Then Danni spots her salvation. Johnny's gun is sitting on the chair still where he left it.

* * *

They had spent the whole evening with Stella at the hospital and they had both known, as they sat silently either side of the bed, that though Stella would make it, the ordeal was not finished. The gun was in Danni's bag and the knowledge of that was like an extra presence in the room.

There was a police guard on the door of the private room but he was there for Stella's protection. When Parker arrived, Danni had watched his every move silently, eyes following him, as he spoke to Johnny.

"You're not going back to the flat for the night?" he'd said, merely shrugging when Johnny insisted he was. Forensics had finished with the place. They weren't going to hang around for long when the corpse was Pearson. Stella prosecuted? Highly unlikely.

He would put a policeman on the outside door of the flats, Parker had said. Just in case they needed him. Neither replied. Parker had glanced between the two, as if aware of unspoken tension. He would need to talk to them in the morning, he said abruptly. Don't go anywhere.

CHAPTER FIFTY-SIX

That opening note! Like a muted gun shot, Johnny thinks. The music is thumping loud in his chest like a tribal drum and he looks at her and thinks that however it began, this is where it ends. He sees the anger that makes her hand tremble with the effort of containing it, and he tries to shrink inside himself, make himself small and neutral and passive. He barely recognises her; whatever emotion she feels right now is beyond anything he has seen in her before. She has a gun. The bullets are the least of it.

"Don't move," she says, articulating the words precisely, voice tight as a drum. The gun is pointing at him, exactly as he has prepared for … and yet part of him is still surprised. The way a person's death can surprise you, even when they are terminally ill. The music beats round round him, beats inside him. He feels the tension of it building into a wall, brick by brick. Like the tension between them.

Her eyes look sensitive, as if the light hurts them, the unnatural brightness of fever or exhaustion. He knows how vulnerable that mixture of emotional and physical tiredness makes you, the way it places you on the edge of a trap that can spring at any moment.

She can do this, he thinks calmly. Her loyalty is ferocious enough. He thinks wistfully of what it would take to earn that loyalty. He glances up at the clock above her. 1 a.m. The second hand ticks steadily around the clock face as they sit without speaking.

The words of the song snake into his consciousness. "Do you plan to let me go, for the guy you loved before?" Danni's eyes blink.

"Are you capable of murder, Johnny?" she says, and the contemptuous way she uses his name pierces him.

"We're all capable of murder."

"You should be scared then," she says.

"I'm not scared."

"Could you do it? Could you pull the trigger?"

He doesn't answer

"Yeah, well we know the answer to that already," she says, and her eyes don't lift from his face.

"You don't …" he begins and stops. "You don't know what you are capable of until you are truly desperate."

Her voice, when it comes, is barely audible. "I know everything there is to know about desperation."

He nods calmly and the gesture seem to inflame her.

"Not frightened, Johnny? Why aren't you scared? You think I won't do it?" She supports her right arm with the left and raises the gun slowly.

His mouth dries.

"The only thing I think, Danni, is that you could and you might."

"So why no fear?"

"I'm not scared of dying." As long as it's oblivion, he adds silently. But he's frightened of living, of going back to the way things were before she came.

If he had said she couldn't do it, she thinks calmly, if he said she wasn't capable, she'd have squeezed the trigger there and then. The certainty makes a surge of heat sweep through her body, a prickle of sweat break out on her back. She is not sure if the surge is fear or triumph.

She feels powerful. It is not altogether unpleasant, though the irony does not escape her. Is this how they feel? The balaclava men? In control.

"Tell me something," she says suddenly, "you IRA people, you're all religious folk aren't you?"

His eyes are pinned to her fingers. If it goes off, he thinks, she will kill herself too. He is sure of it. He senses her recklessness. She is not afraid of dying either.

"Do you believe in God?" she says.

"Do you?"

"No."

She shakes her head dismissively. Where's God been in her life, she thinks impatiently. She watches as Johnny lowers himself slowly into a chair.

"But that's irrelevant. You," she says. "You lot. You're the believers. With your bombs and your bullets. I don't get it. When you go up to your … to your fucking heaven …" Her voice has a tremor.

Johnny rests his head against the back of his chair. He closes his eyes, imagines spinning in space and time, falling headlong into a black hole. A speck in the universe, drifting like the stray black embers from a fire. Trapped consciousness engulfed by space. By nothing.

"What do you say?" she says. "Are you scared of meeting Him?"

He open his eyes and she's standing still. Arms by her side, gun pointing at his face now.

"Or is it okay, because God's on your side? Is he a Tim? Is he a Republican, Johnny? Did he whisper in your ear to save his holy emerald isle from the Prods?"

He says nothing.

"So do you believe in him?" she persists. "You still haven't said. Don't tell me you don't know?"

"Sit down," he says.

"I'd rather stand."

Thump, thump, thump. The handle of a broom on the ceiling below. He feels the vibration ripple through the floor. The music's not that loud but it is so late. He waits but does not move. He sees her tense, watches her eyes dart from the floor to him. "Turn it down," she says, glancing up at the clock. 1.30 a.m.

It occurs to him that perhaps this is the moment, that she wants him to turn his back on her. He does not flinch. She must come to this her own way. As he turns, he remembers the feeling of blood trickling unexpectedly down his hand in the nightclub, and wonders if pain from a bullet is instant or delayed. Not that he is frightened of pain. Not pain she has inflicted. In a strange kind of way he almost relishes the idea of embracing it, surrendering to it. It would be a release, like cutting open his own veins and watching the poison drain with his blood. Part of him understands self-harm. Sacrifice.

But the shot does not come. He sits down, the music playing softly in the background.

"I don't know about God," Johnny says quietly. Words, he thinks ... how can he find words? But they're all he has. "But I believe ... I believe in soul. I believe in something inside that's bigger than the rest of you. Something that reaches for more, for something beyond yourself. Something that strives to be better than you are. An instinct that's more generous, more loving, more ... just *more* ... than you know yourself to be."

Her eyes flicker uncertainly.

"What if there isn't more? What if there's only meanness and hatred and murderous ... murderous ..." She cannot continue.

Sadness twists inside him watching something inside her that he knows he helped create.

"Is there a person alive who's beyond redemption, Danni? Pearson maybe? A person who's completely evil? Maybe. Maybe there is. I don't know. But you know what? I wouldn't like to be the judge of it."

"I would," she says. "Judge and jury."

She sits down on the armchair suddenly, as if her legs are giving way beneath her. He watches her, then leans forward towards her, his body alert.

"There was a woman," he says.

He's looking at her as if his life depends on her understanding, and maybe it does, but she's not looking back at him.

"A French woman ... during the war. One day Nazi soldiers came to her apartment block and they seized her Jewish neighbours. They were being taken away to Auschwitz. And the French woman ran next door while the soldiers were there and grabbed hold of her neighbour's child and pretended to scold her, saying, what are you doing in here? She hauled her out of the apartment and took her next door to her own home. She kept her, looked after her."

Danni raises her eyes to him.

"That was soul," he says.

"Why are you telling me that?"

"It's a true story, Danni."

"Why are you telling me?"

"What made her do it? What courage, what ... heart ... propelled her into that room to take that risk? I don't know. But what I do know is that it would be awful if the hate of those soldiers was seen as stronger than her love."

"Hatred always wins," she says. "Where it co-exists."

"No," he says. "No."

She shrugs.

Johnny takes a deep breath. His heart starts to pound. It is time.

"He was your son, wasn't he?"

She looks up at him, shocked.

"Who was my son?" she whispers.

He knew all along? The secret she held with such bitterness? With such hatred.

He swallows.

"Angelo."

The name floats from his lips, hangs in the air like an object, drifts downwards like a feather in a breeze. Such an alien sound, he thinks. The unspoken name articulated after so long. The name that he has heard over and over and over again in his head but has never uttered. Angelo. Angelo Piacentini.

CHAPTER FIFTY-SEVEN

The name disappears into the depths of her eyes. This is what the shifting shape of hatred looks like: dark and fragmented, a firebed that grows and builds, becomes red with heat, until flames of anger lick into being around the glowing coals. The heat is in her eyes and the darkness is dancing and suddenly as a flame leaps tall and savage, she thinks this is it. She can use the gun for Angelo.

Then all of a sudden … there … there he is … his face … the milky white skin … she can conjure him finally, eyes glowing, the light filtering through the translucent hazel of his eyes. Limbs plump with the remnants of babyhood still, but growing steadily, sturdily, towards the transition into boyhood. He's looking at her, not just with love but with trust, with that unquestioning acceptance, a fixed belief, that what she says is simply the way things are, because she is his mother. Her view of the world is his view, and she will not taint his innocence. Despair sweeps through her. Whoever she does this for, it cannot be Angelo.

Danni takes the gun and curls up on the chair, placing it next to her stomach where she can reach it quickly, drawing her knees up round it. Christ, he thinks, imagining it exploding in her gut, and he closes his eyes momentarily. Jesus Christ if you are there at all, help me.

The black clock hand moves with staccato rhythm towards the hour. 2 a.m. The future depends on her making her own decision. He tries to remove any emotion from his expression. But inside, he is not neutral. Inside he pleads with her, for her. Hold my heart in your hand. Feel the pulse of it quivering against your cupped palm. The rhythm of my life beats against your skin. My blood, warm and sticky, seeps lightly into your fingers like a bruise. I stain you. You contain me. His anguish rises silently to meet hers, an arc that forms across the space between them, like the rain-washed arc of a rainbow.

Her gaze pins him. Shoot me, he says with his eyes. Shoot me if you must. If you can. Hold my heart in your hand. Hold it … hold it …

His gaze sweeps over her small, brittle frame, compact and curled in the body of the chair. He has always thought she looks younger than her years but she suddenly looks a little older than before. Those shadows under her lashes, black and grey like a smudged winter dawn. And still he feels the pull of tenderness inside him, the catch of desire in his throat as his glance traces the snow white range of her cheekbones, blanched now of all colour, her pupils floating like blue tinged icebergs in the lakes of her eyes.

"Yes," she whispers, as if he has only just asked the question. "He was my son. My lovely boy."

Retribution, he thinks. Atonement. Penance. Hell is not a black hole, a void; it is watching her pain.

"Once," she says, and it occurs to him that she is not particularly speaking to him though there is no one else in the room, "once … after he died … maybe two months after he had gone, I heard him cry in the night." She shifts her head on the sofa, nudging a cushion away from her. The

322

gun nestles against her stomach. "I went to his room and I lifted him from his bed and took him down to the kitchen. I gave him a glass of milk. And then we climbed the stairs again together. We played the counting game. One step … two steps … I heard his voice. I felt his fingers in my hand. Then I took him back to bed to tuck him up and I realised … I realised … he wasn't there."

"Danni …"

He is leaning his elbows on his knees, his head in his hands.

"He wasn't there," she repeats. "But he felt so real."

He pushes his hair back, leaves his fingers knotted into it, gripping tight.

"What did you do?"

"I howled," she says.

His eyes close.

"I came to Ireland to find you," she says.

"Yes."

"And Pearson put me in touch with you for his own reasons."

"Pearson always had his own reasons."

"Stella said Pearson betrayed you … that day … the day Angelo died. Marco."

He shakes his head. "It's not my excuse."

"When I came, I wanted to kill you."

"I know."

"Part of me still wants to kill you."

Her fingers reach out instinctively to the gun, flutter over it.

"Let me take the gun," he says.

"No."

She lifts her head slightly from the sofa.

"How did you know?" she asks. "At what point did you know about Angelo?"

"Not till the other day. Something Stella said. When she

said you lost your son … but on some level I think I knew before that."

The light is fading. She is becoming an outline in the darkness. He stands up.

"Where are you going?"

She sits up further, hands reaching for the gun.

"Just to switch the light on."

Her eyes blink against the light when he flicks the switch. She puts her forearm over her eyes, hears the drag of the curtains as he draws them closed.

"The first time I saw you," he says, "it was like I knew you. Like I'd always known you."

I felt that, she thinks.

"Your eyes were so familiar."

Angelo's eyes. He has carried those eyes for so many years inside his head. Could he live with them, he wonders. Then he thinks he cannot live without them.

The black hand on the clock doesn't pause for thought. It moves relentlessly and he wonders how much time is left. She is so still, curled in that chair, it is almost as though she sleeps. 2.15. Perhaps she does.

Marco? He is no longer behind glass. His hand is raised and she raises hers to meet it, palms touching. He smiles at her.

"Please move the gun from your stomach."

She looks up, confused. Johnny.

"Please," Johnny says.

She lifts the gun automatically, then hesitates. He holds out his hand but she shakes her head and lays it on the arm beside her. She is not ready to give it to him. Things will be on her terms.

She sits up, swinging her legs back round to the floor. She feels utterly drained. Everything inside her is battling, turning in on itself against her. She cannot understand why hatred never worked. She never wanted to be burdened with understanding.

The truth, she thinks – and there is no time now for anything else – is that she is drawn to him. There are threads that she cannot untangle, that are so intricately knotted that she cannot find their source, their ending, their pathway. Maybe in some strange way they are linked by pain; he is the only possible link left to Marco and Angelo. And she is the link to his conscience.

She is drawn to his darkness, his complications, his simultaneous capacity for danger and tenderness. She is drawn to his neurosis, to the hole inside him that will always disable him. He will always be damaged, as she will; their damage unites them. And if she is truly honest – she is drawn to the enormous possibilities of him. What did he say soul was? The capacity for something beyond yourself. Well then, he has soul.

She is drawn to his blue, tiger stained eyes.

It will never be perfect, she thinks, but the thought does not dismay her. Life isn't perfect. Imperfection has ways to grow. Maybe the beauty of life is what you can reach for, strive for; learning to touch what is just beyond your finger tips. A sense of peace floods her. Marco.

Johnny is watching her.

He is almost like a sculpture, she thinks, or a line drawing. If she closed her eyes and drew her fingers over a row of faces like a blind woman, she could pick his out. She knows the angles of him intimately: his nose, his cheekbones, his shoulders. She has never allowed herself to drift into the fantasy of him. At times, she has hated him. But she knows she wants him. What she doesn't know quite yet, is whether she can live with that truth.

He is standing up, walking towards her. She watches, motionless.

"Time to choose," he says, standing in front of her.

Life or death. Damnation or redemption. There is no way out of here separately. No way back to old lives for either of them. They have sniffed something live again, something that has been so long in coming.

She feels the metal of the gun in her hand. A bullet through him. A bullet through her. Or they walk out together.

She stands up from the sofa and faces him.

He is right next to her. She can feel the heat of him. The sweet, musky heat of him.

Johnny watches as she lifts the gun. He does not flinch. She raises it to his temple; he feels the metal cool and light against his skin. A small shiver.

"Are you finally scared, Johnny?"

"I have never been more scared."

"But not of death?"

"No."

"Me neither."

His eyes don't leave hers.

She presses the gun harder.

"Bang, bang," she says.

And then she lowers it.

"I said love wins." His voice shakes slightly.

"And desire," she says.

She does not have the strength to turn down what he offers. She is not finished with life.

He holds out his hand, and she hands the gun to him. Then he reaches out and runs one single finger gently down her cheek, over her lips, falling off the edge of her chin and down her neck. She catches his hand and holds it because she wants to, and for the second time in her life, she steps into a future that she could never have dreamed of.

READING GROUP GUIDE

for

Kiss the Bullet

including an interview
with the author

and

suggested topics for
discussion

A – Interview with Catherine Deveney

1) What were the inspirations for *Kiss the Bullet*?

There were two inspirations – almost disparate trains of thought that suddenly fused together. Sometimes writing fiction can seems like a kind of alchemy, a process in which the base ingredients transform into something else entirely.

The first was reading a news story about a woman who was going to marry the man who had killed her brother. It really got me thinking about how powerful chemistry can be, and how it can overrule so many other instincts. It also got me thinking about the limits of love. Would it have made a difference if an elderly parent had been killed? Or perhaps a partner? What about a child? When it comes to falling in love, what is unforgivable?

The second inspiration was visiting Kilmainham jail in Dublin, a powerful museum which tells the story of the early rebels of the 1916 Easter rising. There are many stories held within the walls of Kilmainham, but one in particular touched me. There is a tiny whitewashed chapel in the jail, and it was here that Joseph Plunkett, a poet and journalist, and one of the leaders of the rising, married his fiancée Grace Gifford. They were given just minutes together and hours later, Plunkett was executed. I sat in the chapel and tried to imagine them standing before that altar, knowing what lay ahead of them.

The story of *Kiss the Bullet* is not the story of Joseph Plunkett and Grace Gifford, but this bleak, true event triggered my imagination and sparked the novelist's usual train of thought: what if this happened ... and what if that happened ... Terrorism seemed to provide an interesting backdrop for my story about the limits of love. If Danni's husband and child had been killed by, say, a drunk driver, she would have only weakness – or perhaps addiction – to forgive. But how would it change things if the killer had taken your loved one deliberately, for a cause? Is that possible to forgive? Perhaps not if the killer feels no remorse. But what if he, too were tortured by events?

We have seen, with Brighton bomber Patrick Magee for example, that friendships are possible between bombers and the families of their victims. Johnny argues that love is stronger than hate and that can only be true if love has redemptive qualities. It was that possibility I wanted to explore in this novel.

2) Your day job is interviewing people for *Scotland on Sunday*. How do you reconcile your fiction and your journalism – and do they help or hinder one another?

Journalism has been my apprenticeship for fiction writing, and yet the demands of each are very different and can seem conflicting. Generally, everything has to be as concise as possible in journalism and, contrary to some popular misconceptions, you have to work with fact and can't make up the material! It does sharpen your approach to language, though, making you more conscious of what is redundant and the job each word is doing for you.

Fiction is almost the opposite: ideas need to be given space to grow and develop and you have to colour in every part of the picture rather than giving a quick, impressionistic sketch. I love the liberation that fiction brings, the freedom it gives you to make things up and lose yourself inside a story that you have created.

I don't think I would have become a novelist if I hadn't been a journalist first. I have been exposed to so many different people and situations that I simply wouldn't have encountered if I had stayed in my original job as an English teacher. I don't think I would have had the depth of experience, the understanding of how people think and feel and behave and react in different situations, if I hadn't been a journalist. I have interviewed families who have lost a loved one to murder, but I have also interviewed a murderer, and that gives you an insight it's hard to get anywhere else. A lot of my interviews now are with celebrities, but often I prefer interviewing ordinary people with extraordinary stories. You learn so much about human nature.

There is one particular lesson that journalism teaches you that can be very useful for a novelist. Truth is not a fixed point. Before I did the job, I was probably quite black and white in my approach. I thought truth was something you uncovered. Then I realised that two people can tell you two conflicting things about a situation and both can be telling the truth as they see it. Understanding different perspectives, and the complexity of truth, is a good start for a fiction writer.

3) You explore extreme emotional themes in your fiction. Why do they fascinate you?

As a journalist, I have been very privileged to talk to many people who have found themselves in extreme situations.

I say 'privileged' because it is often when people face terrible challenges that you see the most inspiring things the human spirit is capable of. I have interviewed people who have experienced terrible events. People whose family members have died through accident, illness, addiction or suicide. People who have been beaten or raped or abused or tortured or violated in the worst ways imaginable. In all of these situations, you turn up nervously, half expecting them to be broken. They so very rarely are. In my work, I have said that it often feels as if something redemptive nestles at the heart of tragedy, like a jewel half buried in mud. Those who dig for it find something that at the height of their despair, they never expected to find. They often become bigger, kinder, more empathetic, more generous. I once asked a woman who had lost everyone close to her, how her experiences had influenced her as a person. She said, "If these things hadn't happened, I wouldn't have been as nice a person."

It's also true that I have occasionally seen people broken by tragedy, and their bitterness can be a very sad and uncomfortable thing to be around. In *Kiss The Bullet*, Danni is almost at that stage – but not quite – and when life holds out an unexpected opportunity to her, she is forced to examine what she really wants to be. If she wants that opportunity, she has to reach almost beyond herself to achieve it. Danni thinks she is emotionally dead, but she's not.

Obviously, extreme situations provide great drama for fiction. But it is also in those situations that you really get insight into what you are capable of, and what your life is really about. That's what fascinates me. The veneer is stripped back and only the naked truth is left.

4) People talk about time healing grief. but in your novels there is a sense that the sadness doesn't disappear – it just goes somewhere else. Do you agree?

Grief and loss are so much a part of life that I find it hard to imagine writing any story that doesn't contain them in some form. It wouldn't seem realistic to me. In my first novel, *Ties That Bind*, loss changes everything – temporarily – for several of the characters. In *Kiss the Bullet*, Danni nearly loses a sense of who she really is because of it. Time doesn't take the grief away but it teaches you how to live with it. It gets absorbed into who you are, becomes a layer that you wear like an invisible skin.

In many ways, we don't want to let go of grief because it's our last connection to people we have loved and lost. If they have gone, and the pain has gone, what's left to prove they existed, that they mattered? The tricky bit is to keep that live connection without letting it destroy you.

Grief is one of the most formative experiences in life and I think it can be very closely connected to creativity. All that emotion seeks a release. I sometimes think of grief as a furnace. You get blasted by intense heat for a time and in that extreme temperature you become molten, malleable, ready to be shaped into something else. Afterwards, when you have cooled down, you can find yourself in an unfamiliar new shape, the old you fossilised inside. My stories deal with that process.

Sometimes, that new shape can be more rounded. I wrote my first fiction after my own father died. I found pain sharpened my perceptions and I simply saw the world differently. Sometimes, I think of fiction almost as my dad's parting gift.

5) In the midst of tragedy, you often include a very simple moment of kindness or empathy. Do you believe that the goodness of humanity prevails?

It's all too easy to get dispirited about the terrible things human beings are capable of, and to believe that there's more bad than good in us. But I do think that the heights of people's capacity for love and generosity can be every bit as extraordinary as the depths of their capacity for evil. In *Kiss the Bullet*, Johnny tries to point that out to Danni, telling her about a French woman who risked her own life to save a Jewish child from Nazi soldiers. Was the French woman's love less potent that the Nazis' hatred?

As an interviewer, I find myself drawn to people's weaknesses more than their strengths. Perhaps that's because I think that it's in our weaknesses that we are at our most human. Supreme confidence in people can be formidable. It can even be amusing. But I rarely find it appealing.

I've come to believe that what matters in life are those moments where you achieve real empathy, and real honesty or connection with another person. A moment where your guard can come down in some way. I try to capture some of those moments in my fiction.

6) Both your novels have Irish themes or settings. Where does your interest in Ireland come from?

When I was growing up in Glasgow, Ireland was a frightening place. I only saw it on the news when bombs went off. I certainly didn't want to go there.

Brought up a Catholic in a city where religious tribalism was part of the landscape, Ireland just flicked my 'off' switch. I had enough of that at home and didn't want to engage with it. But many years later, I would travel there for work, interviewing both Martin McGuinness and Ian Paisley Junior. At the time, I described it as being like looking at one of those pictures that contain two images, and which one you see depends on which angle you look from and what's inside your own head.

I also married a man with strong Irish connections and went to Donegal for the first time. I was smitten, and I also grew to love Dublin. My switch definitely flicked to 'on', my curiosity piqued by this beautiful country where the people were warm, engaging and humorous yet had been embroiled in so much violence and turbulence. It was hard to understand how all the pieces fitted together.

Ironically, my grandfather was Irish but sadly he died before my father was born. My father therefore knew nothing of his Irish roots and when he investigated his family tree, looked only at his mother's Scottish ancestry. Recently my brother has investigated our Irish family, but when we were growing up the only thing we knew was that my grandfather had worked as a Red Indian in Hengler's circus, which seemed a very romantic tale to us! I am Scottish through and through, but now when I land in Ireland, there is a little part of me that feels like I'm going home.

7) Have you been too sympathetic to the IRA in this book?

I don't think so. Personally, I have no sympathy with violence that targets innocent people for a political cause. But I have tried to show the conditions in which violence flourishes, and the reasons why conflicts intensify. I also try to show the opportunism that goes alongside that, and how politics can be an excuse for criminality. But you have to separate those things out. Pearson is a damaged man, but he's damaged by personal circumstances, not the political conflict. He's a thug and a criminal and he enjoys violence for its own sake. But Johnny isn't a bad man. He's highly principled and takes a particular – if misguided – route because he can't see any other way open to him. Crucially, he believes he's at war and he behaves as people do when they are at war. That is his truth.

I wanted to show how the experiences of one generation drip into another to fuel conflict, and how over time, the nature of that conflict can shift and change and refocus. It seems to me that the lessons we should have learned from Ireland have been quickly forgotten when it comes to the current terrorism threat. In 2002, Cherie Blair whipped up a storm of controversy when she said young Palestinian suicide bombers committed atrocities because they felt they had "no hope" but to blow themselves up. The outrage her comments provoked was very disturbing to me. This wasn't a defence of suicide bombers. It was an attempt to understand the conditions in which they flourished. How do you stop something if you don't understand why it happens? Without understanding, you have nothing.

8) What effect would you like your books to have on readers?

The thing I would most like to do is touch readers emotionally in some way, and make them empathise with the characters and their different dilemmas. I'd like them to recognise some kind of truth in the story, perhaps something that makes them look at life slightly differently. People are rarely black and white and I like stories that play a bit with your emotional responses, making you respond favourably to someone at one point, but question them at another. The language is important to me and like any writer, I'd like readers to enjoy the language and think the story well-written. But I am not just aiming for a clinical stylistic perfection. I'm aiming for the active involvement of a reader's heart.

B – Questions and topics for discussion

1) Both Johnny and Pearson are – or have been – terrorists. What are the differences and similarities between them? How do they compare, from a moral point of view?

2) How does Danni's motivation change throughout the novel? To what extent is she aware of her own feelings?

3) The story is written mostly in the present tense. Do you think this works? What effect does it have?

4) *Kiss the Bullet* has been described as a 'thriller' and even as 'crime fiction'. Are these accurate labels? How would you categorise its genre? Are such categories helpful?

5) Deveney's characters undergo extreme emotional experiences – bereavement, guilt, violence. Does she succeed in writing convincingly about these experiences?

6) What do you think *Kiss the Bullet* says about the effect of loss and grief on people's lives?

7) At its core, *Kiss the Bullet* is a love story, albeit a rather unusual one. Did you 'believe' in this element of the novel? Why (not)?

ACKNOWLEDGEMENTS

With thanks to friends who read and advised on early drafts. Love to Eileen, Brian and Anton for unwavering support.